THE GOVIL

And The Protector

ISBN-13: 978-1-7343981-2-0

The characters in this book are entirely fictional. Any resemblance to actual persons living or dead is entirely coincidental.

Edited by Sandy House.
Front cover image by Jennifer B. Litherland.

This book is dedicated to my children, Noah and Avery.

CONTENTS

Chapter 1: The Unsolterra Protectors

Far away in the dark of a moonless, summer night was a gargoyle-like creature carrying a large boulder. This large boulder was unique and glowing a light purple. It approached a group of robed people standing together in the middle of a field of pumpkin vines. The boulder had on it a special symbol that glowed a little brighter than the rest of the rock.

"What is it?" Tristan, a cartographer, asked Chief Hiksum.

"That is a flindishk, a master of portals. He is here to connect our two worlds together," Chief Hiksum replied. He looked over to a couple others and asked, "Are you ready, Sam and Chris?"

Sam, a pregnant woman, looked at Chris and replied back to the chief, "As leader of the Unsolterra Protectors, this very group here tonight with the mission of rescuing as many humans as we can from the devastating tragedy of the Bridge of Kardun, my husband Chris and I are as ready as we will ever be. Yes, tonight is an exciting night full of wonder and hope!"

She held Chris's hand as she watched the flindishk approach from the mountains. It wasn't hard to see because of the glow of the boulder, but they were in a very lowly populated area in the pumpkin patch, behind 14 Pumpernickel Drive outside of Stonevue. There was little chance anyone would see the glowing boulder and the flindishk carrying it was as black as the night.

"The Bridge of Kardun was meant for treacherous reasons. We must not make any mistakes in how we attempt to rescue our fellow humans on Lunia. It has been nearly a century since its collapse, so the humans on Lunia have found a home there and may not receive our efforts well. To them, we may be removing them from their homes rather than saving them. If any of them so choose to stay, we must honor that." Sam looked over to Tristan and motioned for him to write.

Tristan quickly pulled out a leather-bound book and began writing in it. He had already drawn a map of the pumpkin patch and just needed to add the boulder once it arrived. He had heard of so many things about Lunia and was eager to see it in person. He was also skilled at making maps. Tristan was writing a book of the events along with things he had heard about. He was in the process of creating a large map to be on display in the town library.

Sam and Chris had already been to Lunia by way of a portal made by a flindishk. The portal was quickly destroyed once the elder flindishk learned of its existence, because it was too risky to leave open. They explained to Sam and Chris the previous existence of a similar type of magic called the Bridge of Kardun that had been created nearly a hundred years earlier. The flindishk elders then explained how tragedy befell humans with that magic and that its ultimate demise was a blessing.

As he waited for the flindishk to arrive, Tristan reviewed his most recent notes regarding the Bridge of Kardun. It was said to have been a colorful tunnel through space that ferried vampires from Lunia to Earth, where they gathered humans against their will in large masses from towns all over the countryside. In many instances, entire towns were rid of people overnight. Tristan had been unable to write down how many people died or what exactly happened to them once they made it to Lunia, as that would be information obtainable only from the vampires. No one was willing to talk with them. They had been able to determine, though, that at some point the vampires discarded the humans like trash for reasons unknown. Those humans managed to survive and prosper. Rescuing the humans on Lunia was the Unsolterra Protector's main mission.

"What do we plan on doing once we have the other humans back here on Earth?" Tristan asked with a pen in hand.

"We will most certainly have the portal destroyed to prevent anything coming back through that shouldn't," Sam replied coolly.

"As we have experienced in the past, there are things on Lunia that would desire things on Earth," Chris replied as well. "Maybe humans, maybe resources, but there will always be something desired by those who want more."

"It is almost here," one of the other members of the group stated.

Within a few moments the quick moving flindishk arrived and carefully set down the boulder. He had been carrying it with a set of thin chains that glowed yellow and green. As he set it on the ground, he let go of the chains and they dropped to the ground. He then sat atop the boulder and it glowed an even brighter purple.

"Is this a good spot for you?" the flindishk asked Sam.

"It will most certainly work, Haliokog. Thank you so much for what you are doing for us." Sam approached the still glowing boulder as she spoke, "I do not know how we can ever repay you as we are magicless humans."

"It is not the intent of the flindishk elders to be repaid for our efforts. We seek only to assist in any way we can to right the wrong humans have suffered," Haliokog replied.

Sam was now caressing the smooth boulder. It felt warm on her hands and she teared up as she imagined going back to Lunia for the last time. The flindishk had agreed to help under the condition that the portal must be destroyed, and no further contact made once the last of the humans had made it through.

Tristan walked back some to get a full view of where the boulder was placed and began to draw on his map.

The chains that held the boulder during flight fizzled away and disappeared. Haliokog hopped off and landed on the ground behind the chief. The others from the group followed Haliokog as he walked toward the humble house that the chief lived in.

Not all the members of the Unsolterra Protectors had been to Lunia, and seeing Haliokog was their first magical creature encounter. As he walked, he towered over all of them at around seven feet tall. Even though it was exceptionally dark outside, the others could make out the large talons for his feet and his extremely large bat-like wings. Chris led the group, even though he had been to Lunia before, because he was always in awe of the fact that something like the flindishk even existed.

Chris asked Haliokog, "Could you explain in better detail to our friends here why it would be a bad idea to keep the portal open?"

Haliokog replied back softly, "There are forces on Lunia that would ravage the non-magical Earth you call home. We have a very powerful enemy growing in our midst on Lunia called the Reign of Karakaziem. They would certainly find something about Earth to exploit. Nothing would get in the way of their destructive and evil powers. Opening the portal now is already risky, but we must try and set things as right as we can. This portal is temporary and is set to be destroyed as soon as possible."

"How are you so sure that this temporary portal will not be used for nefarious purposes?" Chief Hiksum asked.

"As we speak, the other side of this portal is being transported directly to the human city on Lunia, called Earth. There, it will be guarded by my fellow flindishk to ensure it is not destroyed. If there is any sign of danger, we have been directed to destroy it at once."

Haliokog stopped in his steps.

The group had arrived at a point not far from the backside of the house. There were several large logs scattered around an old firepit. Haliokog sat down on one of the logs and the firepit burst into flames. The members of the group had only heard of the magical things the beings from Lunia could do. It was surprising to see even the smallest type of magic as the fire lit up the night in front of them.

Up in the field was Sam still touching the boulder. It was still warm from the day's sun. She thought about all the people she could help and hoped they would want to be helped. It was hard for her as she visited Lunia to not have magical abilities, and she could only think of how difficult it must be to live there without any magic. She touched her pregnant belly and thought of the life she was bringing into this world. Since she learned of Lunia, she had not been able to stop thinking about helping those people. If she and Chris had simply ignored what they had learned, there would be no real way to explain that to her child. She knew she had to act.

"I love you so much my little blessing," she whispered to her belly. "I can't wait to meet you."

...

It was nearing the end of the day on Lunia. The night was quickly descending on the land and a single flindishk was carrying a large boulder down from the mountains. The boulder was glowing purple just like its counterpart on Earth. She carried the portal boulder in the same manner as Haliokog had with his portal, with an enchanted, thin chain that surrounded the rock. The mission was clear: get to the human city of Earth as fast as possible.

At her fast pace, she would be there in a couple days. The mission had been entrusted to her and she wasn't going to let her elders down. She flew fast and with intent. The mission was a secret mission, known only to the elders and a few other flindishk.

"You've got this, Lanakog!" she whispered to herself as she flew. "You aren't going to let them down."

Below her were the last of the rocks on the mountainside quickly passing by. She was headed towards a grand field of tall, colorful grasses that expanded in every direction as far as she could see. She knew at her speed, though, that she would be over a forest soon. Her path was not a direct path. This way no one other than her would know it. The way was documented only in her head and she had planned it well in advance without advising anyone else, even the elders. She planned to zig-zag through the lands between the mountains and the city of Earth. Flying like this would be harder than if she flew directly, but secrecy and unpredictability was a must on this mission.

She knew the dark of night would give her some cover soon. Her altitude was high up so as not to be too obvious, but the thinner air made it difficult for her to breathe. As darkness came over the lands, she descended some in order to breathe more freely. As she descended, she began to hum and sing to herself. She was rather pleased with the speed at which she was going. She was chosen in part due to her ability to fly faster than a typical flindishk. Another reason she was chosen was that she had been able to befriend the elders of the human city years prior. She prided herself in her ability to make friends with many different magical and nonmagical beings. Humans were definitely nonmagical, and she felt bad for them being stuck in the wrong place against their will.

"Your friends are finally going to get to go home!" she said to herself, smiling. "I'm so dang excited to see the looks on their faces when I finally deliver this to them."

After a few hours of flying in the dark, Lanakog began to see trees in the distance. She knew she was still on the right path and the sight of the trees reassured her of this. Within a few moments, she was over a dense forest and everything was pitch black. It was a moonless night on Lunia, which was the reason this night had been chosen.

Lanakog looked down at the glowing portal, "If only you didn't have to glow when you're around one of us!" She was slightly annoyed but used to portals glowing around her and other flindishk.

She looked down at the ground beneath her as she flew and watched the landscape fly by. She noticed a sudden, solid dark patch on the ground and realized it was a small lake. She smiled as the air streamed by her face and through her wings. Then, she looked back in front of her and saw a small amount of light deep in the forest.

"Who would be out in Wellwood Forest at this time of night?" she asked herself out loud. "It's probably that pesky Frinkul fella. Better fly higher."

She began to ascend higher into the sky, thinking nothing of it.

Suddenly, a large spear flew past her at an amazing speed. The sound of it made her flinch, and she slowed down for just a moment as she tried to comprehend what had just happened.

"I'm way too high up for anyone to shoot at me!" she exclaimed. "What was that?"

Then, another spear followed by a flash of light. The

accompanying flash of light lit up the projectile and that was when she noticed it wasn't a spear at all, but a very large arrow. Another arrow shot at her as she continued to climb.

"You've got this, Lanakog! You've got this!" she reassured herself. "There's no way they know what I have; I didn't tell a soul which way I was going."

She knew the light emitting from the portal boulder was giving away her position in the sky. She was an easy target until she could get high enough to escape their arrows. It was already surprising to see the speed and height the arrows were climbing to.

Another arrow and flash of light came at her. They were headed directly for her. She attempted to maneuver out of the way, but the boulder made that difficult to do. The arrow struck her in the right wing and went straight through. She suddenly felt a searing pain and began to drop out of the sky. Fighting the pain, she tried even harder to climb. As she regained her bearings, she began to fly upward once again.

Another arrow found her! This time though there was no flash of light, so she didn't see it coming. It hit her directly in the chest. She let out a loud gasp for air as she suddenly fell from the sky. She looked around frantically, hoping to find a lake to crash into - there were no lakes. The lights in the forest were far away now, but she knew she would not be able to complete her mission. The ground grew beneath her at a quick pace. She fluttered her wings in a desperate attempt to stay in the air. Her eyes grew heavy and her wings became limp. She held on as tight as she could to the boulder that was her mission, as her last breath escaped her body.

She fell straight out of the sky and into a clearing in the woods. When the portal hit the ground, her body landed on top of it. The chains fizzled away and disappeared. A small trinket fell out of her pocket and skipped down the side of the boulder until it landed softly in the grass below. The portal slowly stopped glowing and began to look like a big rock just situated in the forest.

Lanakog's blood ran down the side of the boulder, causing it to light up bright purple. After a few moments, a sudden burst of energy blew out from all sides of the portal and into the surrounding forest. The trees swayed with the intense pressure while leaves and branches fell to the ground. Then, the boulder's light went completely out.

...

Sam was still touching the portal on Earth when a sudden burst of energy emitted from it, knocking her down. Chris ran up the field and helped her get back up. The sudden force of the blast had caught her off guard.

"What was that?" Chris asked her.

"I ... I don't know," Sam responded, still trying to comprehend what had just happened. "I was just touching it when it blew out a shockwave of some sort."

Haliokog was already by their side as well, having flown up to where they were at. The others were running through the pumpkin patch to meet up with them.

"What did she do?" Chris asked Haliokog. "I thought only a flindishk could open it."

"It is not open. I do believe something outside of our plans has happened on Lunia," he said somberly. "I don't think the portal made it to the city of Earth yet. Something powerful has happened here. I must return to Lunia to investigate."

"We will go with you!" Sam spouted out as soon as Haliokog finished his sentence. "There's no way we're going to let this fail. We're too close to completing our mission."

"Honey," Chris looked at Sam, still holding her, "don't you think it would be better to let Haliokog check things out first? I really don't think you're in any condition to put yourself in unnecessary danger."

"Look!" Tristan was pointing at Sam's belly.

For a few moments, a purple haze swirled around her midsection.

It was the same color as the light from the portal boulder when Haliokog was carrying it and the shockwave that blew out from its sides just moments before. Sam quickly tried brushing it away, but it seemed to be stuck to her as it moved back and forth over her belly.

"What's happening?" Sam asked.

"I do not know," Haliokog said as he hovered one of his hands in front of her midsection. "I don't think you have anything to worry about. It is just a remnant of a magical shockwave."

After a few more seconds, the purple haze disappeared. It looked like it absorbed into her. She felt her belly with her hands, and it felt warmer than usual, but she felt fine.

"Will my baby be okay?" she asked Haliokog. "Shouldn't I see a healer just in case?"

Haliokog nodded his head in agreement, "I have not seen anything like the events that happened here tonight. It is not unwise to seek assurance from a healer. I must also speak to my elders and let them know what has transpired here."

He walked over to the portal, bent over and slowly swiped his hand across a small symbol at its base. The boulder cracked open and a loud rushing noise could be heard. The inside of the boulder shone a bright whitish blue. Haliokog reached for Sam and grabbed her hand. Chris followed behind her.

"We'll be back as soon as we can!" Chris shouted over the rushing noise of the open portal.

Within seconds, the three of them disappeared into the rock and as suddenly as it opened, it closed back up and all the light faded away. The night's darkness took over as the rest of the group stood there in awe.

"Should I put that in the book?" Tristan asked Chief Hiksum.

After a brief pause, Chief Hiksum replied, "I don't think it would be wise to indicate anywhere in any mechanism that there is a portal here. Just mark it on your map, but merely show it as a unique boulder. I trust you can find a way to do that."

He started walking back to the fire and the others followed; they all remained quiet. The night had already been a big night, but now it seemed like everything was going wrong.

"What if it was discovered on Lunia?" Tristan asked. "What if Sam and the other two get caught in a trap and something tries coming through? You heard the ... the, uh ... Haliokog. He spoke as if there were evil forces that might try coming through."

"We cannot worry ourselves over something we know nothing about. All we'll end up doing is panicking," Chief Hiksum replied back. "Let's continue to do our part and be ready for their return."

...

Haliokog was the first to exit the portal on the Lunia side, followed by Sam and then Chris. It was the middle of a dark night much like the one on Earth. As he began to look around, Haliokog quickly noticed Lanakog's body. So did the others.

Pointing to the large arrow protruding from her chest, Haliokog stated, "She appears to have been shot down. Something or someone will be here any minute once they have found out where she dropped. We must leave this place at once."

"What about the portal?" Sam asked. "We can't just leave it here."

"I'm afraid that if I fly with it now, we will likely meet the same fate as Lanakog," Haliokog said. "We will have to come back with reinforcements. The portal is safe for now. No one other than the elders can open this portal."

"But ..." Chris interjected.

A loud rustling noise could be heard coming down a nearby path.

"We must go now!" Haliokog quickly jumped into the air and dropped a net for Sam and Chris to get into. He then grabbed the netting and took off into the dark of night.

Shortly after the trio departed, an ape-like creature carrying a large bow and quiver of arrows appeared. He grunted as he inspected the rock. He took his bow and nudged Lanakog's body. It rocked a little and the ape-creature looked satisfied.

Just moments later, a wooden carriage came crashing through the trail in the forest. It was adorned with torches that brightly lit up the night all around the carriage. The door of the dilapidated carriage flung open and a small, frail old man stumbled out. He had pointed ears and oversized eyes. He looked around and saw his companion looking at a big rock in the clearing.

In a scratchy voice, the old man yelled to his companion, "What are you looking at? Why are you messing with that stupid rock?"

The ape-creature pointed at Lanakog's body and grunted out, "Frinkul, look!"

Frinkul nearly ran to the boulder and began looking it over. He smiled as he looked at Lanakog. Then, he looked over the boulder intensely. He noticed a small trinket on the ground and picked it up.

"What is it?" the ape-creature grunted out again.

"Something special, I presume," Frinkul said angrily. "Why would a flindishk be flying over Wellwood Forest in the middle of the night? Why alone? What is she hiding?"

Frinkul stashed the trinket into his satchel and looked at the boulder again. He put his hand on it and felt its warmth. As far as he could tell, there was nothing special about it, other than the fact that the flindishk was carrying it somewhere in the middle of the night.

"No flindishk ferries such an item without intent," Frinkul said aloud. "No doubt, she was helping those pesky Govilians build something silly. Come, Asagu, we must not delay any longer. I have some wonderful Prunklesnider brewing, and I don't want to waste any more time looking at this dumb rock. Grab her, she'll make some wonderous meals!"

With that, Asagu, the ape-creature, grabbed Lanakog from off the top of the boulder and flung her heavy body over his shoulders. Although he was big himself, her large build caused him to stumble a little in his walk to the carriage where he threw Lanakog's body on top of it.

The two very noisily set off in their carriage into the night, with Asagu riding on the front. Silence quickly fell upon the clearing in the forest and the darkness once again filled the air. All that remained was the boulder, the trees and the stars. Not even Haliokog nor the others would find their way back that night. In fact, it would be some time before the boulder garnered attention once again.

Chapter 2: Fire and Lightning

Jack woke to the smell of Geller's traditional bread. He sat up and looked at the covered window. Light shone through the cracks of the coverings, and it felt like a warm sunny morning. But Jack knew the light outside the window was a false promise of sunlight. In fact, there were no suns coming up on the horizon. He stood up and walked over to the window.

After moving the curtain out of the way, Jack saw what he had grown accustomed to seeing recently. Looking out the window, he saw light emanating from glowing orbs that floated inside of glass boxes, sitting atop lampposts scattered throughout the streets. He looked up toward the dark sky and could make out swaying, lit up roots of trees from above ground. Some of the roots were extensive and looked like upside-down trees. It was a familiar site to him as he had been there before.

The cavern under Gargantulua was massive. It was so large, the entire city of Gargantulua moved into it every winter. Even with all the lampposts, torches and firepits, it still felt dark to Jack. He watched as the streets woke up to their daily routines. Mostly, though, Jack only ever saw military related traffic. It was because there was a blacksmith not far outside his window. He could hear the clanking of the smith's hammer against an anvil. The soft thudding sound of carts rolling over the mossy cobblestone was about the only other thing he could hear.

Jack got dressed for the day and headed to the main room of his new home. There, he was greeted by the familiar fireplace burning brightly and Geller's wonderful bread. He realized immediately that he was not the first to wake up.

"There you are!" Anna snapped as he walked in. "You shouldn't sleep so much, it's not good for you."

"Leave him alone," Fink shouted out from the kitchen. "He sleeps as much as he needs."

"That's not how it works," Anna retorted.

Jack rubbed his eyes and said, "Good morning to you all as well."

Anna replied, "Fine. Good morning. It might as well be afternoon, though."

"I can't tell ya what time 'o day it is!" Gink exclaimed. "You would think that Gubuyis fella would do something about the darkness out there."

"He's got bigger and better things to do than make your day sunnier," Anna stated. "On that note, Jack, Gubuyis has called on us to meet him at the Panthyun this morning."

Jack ate some prepared bread and mumbled a response back with his mouth full of food, "What does he want?"

"I heard he found sumthin' that you might recognize," Fink said. "Mysterious one, that Gubuyis is."

Having already gotten ready, Jack felt no sense of urgency to get out the door. He sat down in a chair at the table and looked around at the house's main room. It looked just like the one from above ground. The fireplace and the kitchen were in the same place. He would have sworn that the house was simply picked up and moved down here in the cavern. There was a small bookshelf to the right of the fireplace where he could read books on any subject he could think of. The chair he was sitting in was made of a heavy, dark wood and it reminded him of the doors of the library in Stonevue.

"We really should be going, Jack. Don't make yourself too comfortable," Anna said while grabbing her coat.

Although they were out of the winter weather from above ground, they were still in a dark cavern in the middle of winter. It was rather cold outside. It was a bearable cold, but the darkness made it feel worse. Jack longed to see daylight again. He wanted to feel the warmth of the sun on his skin. The gloominess of shadowy streets under a perpetual night sky made him feel sad in a way.

"Okay," Anna finished putting on her coat. "Let's go."

As the two walked down the streets toward the underground version of the Panthyun, Jack observed his surroundings. Anna was talking about how Geller wanted them to meet him, but he wasn't paying much attention to her. His thoughts were trained on what he saw as they walked. Even though the house was not that far from the Panthyun, he still had plenty of opportunity to see the life of the streets.

He watched his feet at first as they stepped on a mossy walkway. The cobblestone was damp, and the moss was wet. It made a slight squishing sound as they walked on it. He noticed slight streams of blue glowing water that trickled between some of the cobblestones. This reminded him of the blue path they followed not long before as they headed to Wyvergia. His attention was grabbed by a cart being pulled across their path as they came to an intersection. It was full of fruits and vegetables of all kinds that Jack was unfamiliar with.

A light rain started. Jack looked up without surprise since it happened frequently down in the cavern. The massive roots of the trees were dripping water. It was just another way Jack felt miserable at times. He yearned for sunlight again

"Are you even listening to me?" Anna sounded annoyed.

"Sorry. I was just thinking about how nice it will be to be above ground again and out of this forsaken cavern," Jack said gloomily.

Trying to reassure him, Anna responded empathetically, "I know it's miserable down here, but it's so much better than being stuck in the freezing cold. I hear the snow is at least twenty feet deep up there right now."

"I just miss home is all," Jack responded.

They had arrived at their destination in front of the Panthyun steps. There waiting for them was Gubuyis, dressed in his usual robes and looking more upbeat than Jack felt.

"Ah, there you two are," Gubuyis greeted them. "We must make a visit to the royal blacksmith at once. We have found something that maybe you could help shed some light on, my good Jack."

Jack looked surprised. He couldn't think of anything that he could help with. Gubuyis had already begun walking up the grand staircase and was headed for the entrance to the Panthyun. Jack and Anna followed suit and climbed the stairs, too.

"Forgive me, sir, but I don't think there is much I can help you with I don't think." Jack was a little concerned that he might be expected to provide help with something he had no idea about. "May I ask what it is you need from me?"

Gubuyis stopped and smiled back up at Jack, "I'm hoping you'll recognize it when you see it. It has to do with something one of our cave scouts recovered."

The three entered the Panthyun and Gubuyis walked to a small statue of a flindishk holding two swords crossed in front of her.

"We'd like to see the blacksmith, please," Gubuyis spoke pleasantly to the statue.

Without hesitation, the statue sheathed her swords, turned around into the wall and disappeared. Then, a set of doors opened in the hall next to the three of them. They all passed through and ventured down a long set of winding hallways and staircases, until they found the royal blacksmith's entrance.

As they entered, the blacksmith saw them, and he approached Jack specifically. He held in his hand a severely damaged piece of metal, charred and bent up. Jack hoped this was not a new type of shield for him as it definitely looked damaged.

"Good day, Mr. Sussel!" Gubuyis greeted the blacksmith. "I see you have the shield out already."

"Yes, yes! Good day to you as well, sir." The blacksmith didn't seem too concerned with Gubuyis as he walked straight up to Jack.

"What is that?" Anna asked, pointing at the burned shield.

"That is what I'd like you to help me identify, Jack" Gubuyis said coolly. "As I mentioned before, one of our cave scouts retrieved this battered shield far into the cavern. I have a feeling you might be able to help us identify it."

Jack looked confused.

"I can't say that I do," he said. "What makes you think that I might know what it is?"

The blacksmith held the shield up more and turned it around for Jack to see the whole thing. It was quite large for him to hold and he was visibly struggling to keep it upright. Despite it being severely burned and slightly melted around the edges, it was surprisingly shiny in various areas. Suddenly, Jack realized what he was looking at. He had seen it before as he fell from high up in the cavern when there was a storm. It was the piece of metal that he used to shield himself from the oncoming fire of the dragons.

At this realization, Jack nearly shouted out, "Of course! I think I recognize that as the piece of metal that saved me when I was being attacked in the cavern before."

"Are you sure, Jack?" Anna asked. "Couldn't that have been any piece of metal? And why does it even matter anyway? It's not like it means anything, right?"

Gubuyis motioned for Mr. Sussel, the blacksmith, to set the shield down. Mr. Sussel looked relieved and quickly trotted off to a counter and leaned the shield against it. He was panting from having to hold its awkward size for his small body.

"I think you are right, dear sir." Gubuyis spoke to Jack. "And to answer your questions, Anna, we have scoured the cavern looking for any remnants of the storm as we looked for clues to who may have been helping Jack. We are certain, especially now, that someone was indeed helping him."

"Did you find someone?" Jack asked.

Gubuyis looked a little disappointed in himself and answered, "We have not yet ascertained the whereabouts of this individual or perhaps even a group of individuals. But this shield indicates someone large was helping. We are considering the fact that it could have been a cave dweller of sorts. We haven't found any signs of life out there, not of the type that could have helped you, that is."

"So, you're sure somebody has been helping to protect Jack for some unknown reason, but you don't have any idea who it is?" Anna asked.

"Or what it is?" Gubuyis added to her question. "There are still questions to be answered but finding this shield does give us some clues."

"Eh-hem," Mr. Sussel interjected quietly.

"Ah yes," Gubuyis sounded off. "We have other matters to deal with today."

Quickly following Gubuyis's words, Mr. Sussel nearly ran over to a large book sitting open on his counter. He checked the page it was on before picking it up and bringing it over to Gubuyis.

"Mr. Sussel here has informed me that he has been researching how you can wield two separate weapons' magical abilities at a time."

Guybuyis looked over the pages in front of him and mumbled as if he was reading aloud to himself. Jack and Anna were both intrigued and leaned in. Jack tried to read the book in Gubuyis's hands, but it was both upside-down and in a different language. He looked at Anna who had just failed to read it as well and he shrugged.

"Well now, this is interesting indeed!" Gubuyis spoke in a little bit of excitement. "I do believe I have heard of this before."

"Heard of what?" Anna quickly asked. "Jack can't do magic, can he?"

"That remains to be seen, I would think," Gubuyis looked at Jack inquisitively. "But I am not saying that he is able to. I have not seen any proof otherwise, however," he walked over to the counter and set the book back down, "there is a known instance where a being can wield the magical properties of multiple weapons at a time."

Jack felt confused all over again, "I don't understand. Is it something I do that makes me be able to do it? Is it really that big of a deal?"

The blacksmith laughed but quickly stopped.

"Dear Captain, I am so sorry for my outburst," Mr. Sussel said embarrassed.

Gubuyis walked back over to Jack and Anna, who for whatever reason had not left the area directly in front of the doorway. He grabbed Anna's hand and led her over to the counter in front of the damaged, cave dweller's shield.

"It has been seen where individuals from one race can wield multiple weapons at a time." Gubuyis motioned for Jack to come over to the counter as he continued to explain. "The race is well known to us, as you may have seen their statues all throughout the Panthyun. They are called the flindishk. It has been seen from time to time where one of their kind could wield multiple weapons' magic. It's not too common, but in their circles, it is not unfamiliar either. It is considered a special magical ability."

"I don't see where this is going," Jack said with confusion in his voice.

Gubuyis laughed a little, and stated, "I do not know what the connection is, my dear sir. But this gives us perhaps another clue to finding out the reason you are here. Have no doubt, Jack, you are here for a reason. All things happen for a reason. Is there a connection between you and the flindishk? That remains to be unknown at this point."

They walked throughout the royal blacksmith's shop as Gubuyis spoke.

"If there is a connection, though, between you and the flindishk," Gubuyis continued, "we may never learn what that is."

"Why is that?" Anna asked.

Gubuyis spoke lightly, "The race of the flindishk has been massacred by the Reign of Karakaziem in the last few years. It was a prime objective of theirs to rid Lunia of them. You see, they have very special abilities that ..."

Something behind them on a rack clinked. It startled both Jack and Anna but didn't seem to faze Gubuyis at all. He simply looked at the rack and smiled.

"Well now, it appears you have been selected for another weapon, good sir." Gubuyis was smiling.

Jack turned around to look at a trembling dagger not much different in size than his original dagger. It was reddish in color and its blade had a slight waviness to it. Jack went to pick it up when he was suddenly interrupted.

"Remember," Mr. Sussel started saying, "once you choose that dagger you will not be able to use your ... wait. Maybe we shall see." The blacksmith looked excited and eager to see Jack choose the weapon. "I can't make any promises, Captain, but maybe you can use both the weapons?"

Mr. Sussel found it hard to contain his excitement at the prospect that Jack might be able to wield two weapons at a time. This was something that would be very out of the ordinary for him, and he was very eager to see it happen. He rushed over to the trio and watched intensely as Jack slowly moved to pick it up.

Jack's hand grabbed the hilt and it instantly stopped trembling. His hand slipped over its handle with ease, like it was made for him specifically. He remembered how his first weapon reshaped to fit his hand and this one must have done the same, he figured. It glowed red for a moment as he picked it up.

"Very good, sir!" Mr. Sussel was still eagerly watching Jack's every movement. "You will find that this weapon will give your enemy a bit of a burn. It is imbued with fire and requires a higher skill level to wield. It has chosen you for this reason. Your battle experience has given you the ability to wield this dagger."

"Neat!" Anna exclaimed. "What does he do with his current dagger?"

"Yeah," Jack said. "What DO I do with my 'lightning' dagger?"

"Normally, sir, I would offer to dispose of it if you so choose to," Mr. Sussel spoke excitedly and slightly fast, "or you could keep it as a souvenir of past battles. But, perhaps, in your case you could use both weapons."

Jack was studying the wavy blade and its mesmerizing reddish color. It felt light but sturdy in his hands. He was listening to Mr. Sussel speak and figured he could try holding both daggers at once. So, he pulled his other dagger from its sheathe and held it out side by side with the new dagger.

"Those are quite nice, dear sir," Gubuyis responded as Jack looked the two daggers over. "Now, try and run the blades together, but softly please."

As Jack began to cross the two blades together, Mr. Sussel ducked behind a nearby rack. Gubuyis stepped back calmly. Seeing their reactions to Jack's movements, Anna also decided to back up a couple paces. Jack slowly ran the two blades together and small streaks of fire and lightning sparkled out at their contact points. He jumped back a bit at the sight of the daggers' reactions to each other. His sudden recoil caused him to press the blades together harder. This caused a single shot of fire and lighting to shoot across the room and into a rack of armor. The wooden rack instantly exploded into thousands of splinters and its contents crashed to the floor.

"Woo hoo hoo!!!" Mr. Sussel emerged from his hiding spot behind a rack. "This is certainly a wonderous day, Captain! You can wield two weapons at once!"

"This is indeed great news, Mr. Sussel," Gubuyis spoke, "but we must still ascertain the meaning behind this. We may be on the right path of knowledge with the flindishk idea. We just have to know where to look to learn more and I think that may be a good starting point."

Jack smiled as he clumsily stood back up straight having been caught off guard by the sudden stream of fire and lightning in front of him.

"My apologies about your armor rack, sir," Jack said to Mr. Sussel. "I don't think it can be fixed."

"Ha ha good sir!" Mr. Sussel spoke in excitement still. "You have given me quite the show to the likes of which I do not ever recall seeing in my shop before. Never you mind the rack, I have plenty of those. You need some training, though. That will get you more skilled at wielding the two together."

"I believe our General Geller would be more than pleased to get you some training," Gubuyis stated. "We mustn't forget about the shield, though."

Gubuyis walked back over to the shield, which stood slightly taller than him. He tapped a knuckle against it, and it gave a small, tinny ringing sound in return. It was certainly in bad shape, not like one someone would still use in battle. The edges were partially melted in areas and it was dented heavily in various spots. It looked like there used to be a design imprinted on it, but Jack couldn't make it out in the mix of char and wear.

"We are running low on scouts, as many are assisting us in determining the whereabouts of Shamakul," Gubuyis was still studying the shield as he spoke. "He is a very powerful wizard and is a part of the Reign. He may have been behind the attacks in the cavern previously, but that is still just a theory."

"I thought Ghowla was behind the attacks in the cavern," Anna replied without hesitation.

Gubuyis wiped one of his hands against his outer robe as he tried ridding it of some char that he got on him. He looked at both Anna and Jack, nodding in agreement with Anna.

"It is very possible that Ghowla was behind those attacks, but the magic used was more apt to be that used by Shamakul," Gubuyis said. "In time, we will certainly ascertain the chain of events that occurred and in what order and orchestrated by whom. For now, though, you should be getting to the barracks training yard and become more accustomed to your new weapon, my dear Captain Jack."

"What about me?" Anna asked. "Do I just keep my dagger?"

Mr. Sussel spoke up, "I did not see any weapons choose you this day, little madam. I do believe another time, perhaps."

Jack was still holding his two daggers in his hands, having forgotten about them for a few moments. At Anna's questions, Mr. Sussel walked over to Jack and handed him a sheath appropriate for his new dagger. Jack then sheathed the two daggers. He felt bad for Anna not getting anything special, but he also felt like maybe she was luckier than him. No one was trying to kill her like they were him.

"You two enjoy your training now," Gubuyis stated.

At that remark, Gubuyis turned and walked out of the room, leaving Jack and Anna with Mr. Sussel. The blacksmith was still smiling with a sense of jittery happiness because of what he had just witnessed moments before. Jack felt a sense of nervousness as he thought of how to use such weapons. He hoped Geller could effectively train him, but he also hoped he would never have to use them again.

Chapter 3: Training

As Jack and Anna left the Panthyun, they were greeted once again by the darkness of the cavern. It was no longer raining, but the ground was cold and wet. The air was cold enough to easily see their breaths. Jack hesitated for a moment at the top of the grand staircase as he took in the sight of the underground city all around him. It was impressive to him that a whole city would just simply move to such a location because of the weather outside. He hadn't actually seen what it looked like outside since they came down here at the end of Fall, but he figured it must be bad if magical beings needed to avoid it.

"Hello up there!" Geller shouted out from the bottom of the staircase.

Jack and Anna proceeded to walk down the steps and meet up with Geller. He looked upbeat and was smiling at Jack. It was quite obvious Geller was curious as to what new weapon Jack got. Then, his smile faded some as he noticed two sheaths on Jack's belt, one on each side of his hips.

Pointing at Jack's new dagger, Geller asked, "What've you got there? Are you keeping your old one for a keepsake?"

Before Jack could respond, Anna answered for him, "He got a second dagger, and he can use both of them together! It was awesome and scary at the same time!"

Jack smiled. His smile felt forced, though. He wasn't sure how excited he really should be. This just meant he might be expected to fight more often, and he would really rather not fight at all.

"Well, that's something I would never have expected, but somehow doesn't seem to surprise me either," Geller was full of smiles again. "You needed training already, Jack, but now you're definitely going to need some assistance in learning how to wield two weapons properly. Here, have some of this. You're going to need it for your training."

Geller pulled some of his special bread out of his pocket and handed it to both Jack and Anna. He ate a small bit for himself as well. Then, he began walking.

"Gubuyis said you were going to train us how to use our weapons," Jack stated as they walked around the large Panthyun building. "Do you think I can learn to fight with at least one dagger?"

"You have two daggers, sir. You will learn how to use both of them separately and together. It is in your best interest to do so," Geller snacked on a little more bread as he spoke.

"What about me?" Anna asked. "My dagger isn't even enchanted and I'm not that good with it. I don't see how you can train me."

Geller stopped and turned to the pair of them, "Don't you worry, neither one of you. I have trained many soldiers in my time and there have been much worse trainees." He began walking again, "Trust me, you'll both be just fine."

Jack laughed inside as he heard Geller's words. The fact that Geller mentioned there were worse cases meant that he was also considered bad at wielding his dagger. He watched the Panthyun for a few moments as they walked by. It was massive and stood out grand above all else in the city. From its top, one could see out farther than the city walls. Jack couldn't help thinking though, how much more massive it was on the inside than the outside. He knew it had to be some kind of magic.

Eventually, the three of them ended up behind the Panthyun where another large building stood. It was made of a white stone similar to that of the Panthyun. There were hundreds of small windows in it from top to bottom. They almost looked like canon openings rather than windows for looking out. The front of the building faced away from the back of the Panthyun and there were several dozen Valindi in its courtyard.

The closer they got, the louder it got. The Valindi weren't peacefully sitting around in the courtyard but were instead fighting dummies and practicing spells against them. There were clinks and clanks of swords and shields, and there were booms and bangs from spell misfires. The air was filled with a light smoke.

"Here we are," Geller stopped at the front gates of the courtyard. "Have you both eaten? Good. This is the barracks. We will practice here until you are both familiar with your weapons. You must become acquainted with them in such a way that you find ease and comfort in using them."

"I refuse to fight like that!" Anna pointed to a couple of Valindi that were fighting hand-to-hand combat style. "Tell me I don't have to do that?"

Geller laughed, "Only if you want to, Anna. Only if you want to. I am here to teach you weapons training. If you so desire to learn hand-to-hand combat training, then I will get you to the right individual."

"There you all are," Selini said as she approached the group. "How was the meeting with my father?"

"Well," Jack knew she would be excited about the news of two weapons, so he started with that, "I have selected a new dagger." He pointed to his hips.

Selini's eyes lit up, "Why are you carrying two of them?"

Jack could hardly contain his smile. Somehow, he felt special for being able to use two different daggers at the same time. He wasn't so sure he cared to, but it was gratifying to have others be so impressed by his hidden ability.

"He can wield both of them together," Anna spoke for Jack.

"You don't say!" Selini seemed impressed. "What does the new one do?"

"It's, er, a fire dagger of sorts. I didn't really see it work alone, though." Jack said as he thought of how the new dagger might work when used by itself.

"You already combined them?!" Geller asked eagerly. "In the

Panthyun? I bet you made a mess of things really quick."

"He wrecked Mr. Sussel's shop for sure," Anna laughed.

"So, what did it look like when you combined the two together?" Selini asked inquisitively.

Jack hesitated for a moment as he tried to think about what it looked like. He realized he didn't see all of it because it had caught him off guard, and he might have been closing his eyes. One thing was for certain, though, he made a mess of things when he did it and wasn't prepared to show them out in the courtyard.

"It was bright and pretty powerful," Jack answered, "but I don't really recall what it looked like."

"Not to worry, my good Captain," Geller spoke up. "We will have plenty of opportunity to test it again."

"Did my father have some news for you?" Selini asked. "I thought I heard that he may have found something in the cave that you would recognize."

"It was a badly burned shield, larger than Gubuyis himself," Anna stated. "Jack recognized it as the shield he used to protect himself against the dragons in the cavern when they attacked in the storm on our way to Wyvergia."

"Really? You must tell me, does he know who it belongs to?" Selini asked quietly.

Jack responded this time, "He wasn't sure who it might belong to, but he said it possibly belongs to some kind of cave dweller."

"Interesting," Selini said with a serious look on her face. "Who might be living in the cavern that would also be trying to help Jack?" She pondered aloud.

"He said we're too low on scouts to have anyone really try to find the cave dweller," Anna commented.

"Well, that most certainly won't do!" Selini had a sudden look of determination on her face. "I will search for this individual myself if I have to. I want to know what his or her intentions are. Was this 'cave dweller' really helping or are there different plans in mind?"

Without even saying goodbye, she turned and quickly walked away with determination in her steps. A part of Jack hoped that she wouldn't find the cave dweller. He could not think of any reason someone would want to help him that didn't know him, and the others kept making it sound like something nefarious was at play.

"Thunk"

Jack was startled by a sound from right behind him that caught him off guard. It seemed that Geller had taken his own dagger and lobbed it at the closest dummy. It hit the center of a bullseye painted lightly on the center of the dummy's chest. Within seconds, the dummy's body turned green and wilted in front of their eyes like a rapidly dying plant.

"Shall we?" Geller looked pleased with himself. "We need to get you two some training."

The three of them found a set of dummies to begin practicing on. The dummies looked like they were made of potato bags stuffed with straw, but Jack knew there had to be more to them than that. As he looked around, he saw dummies fighting back against their practicing assailants. Each dummy was mounted on a wooden pole that went straight through its center from bottom to top. There were legs, arms, a body and a head, but no face.

"We'll start by throwing the daggers, which can be really useful if you want to keep the fight away from your body," Geller said matter-of-factly. "Before I begin your training, I would like to see you both practice throwing so I can see your skillsets. We shall start with you, Anna."

Anna stepped forward and pulled out her dagger. She didn't look very confident, but Jack didn't feel like he'd be confident either. He couldn't quite tell but it looked like her hands were shaking a little.

"Where should I aim?" Anna asked Geller. "My dummy doesn't have a target on it."

"Think of where you intend to hit the dummy first and the target will appear in that spot. Then, aim and throw your dagger at it," Geller explained, "Don't just throw it, aim. Think about it. Then, throw."

Jack watched as Anna thought about where to throw the dagger. Then, a painted-on target appeared on its chest. He thought that was a safe choice because there was more chance that she would hit it on the larger surface. She took a moment and Geller watched intensely. Without taking too long, she held her dagger above her shoulder beside her head. It shined brightly in the dim light. She held it there for a moment more and then threw it at the dummy in front of her. It landed just barely within the target. The dummy slumped over as if to die.

"Why didn't it turn green?" Jack asked. "Do they react differently to different people?"

"They will react the way they need to react," Geller stated. "Mine turned green because my dagger is poisonous. Her dummy died because she hit the target and it was in a deadly spot. When we get more advanced, the dummies will fight back if you don't kill them first. We're going to take it easy today, though."

Jack felt nervous. He had no desire to fight against a magically enchanted dummy that was probably better at fighting than he was. He took a deep breath in and gave a little sigh.

"You're next, good sir," Geller instructed Jack.

Jack stepped in front of his dummy. Quickly, Geller motioned for Jack to step back some. He did, but Geller continued to motion for more. Eventually, after about six feet of distance, Geller seemed happy with the distance between the dummy and Jack.

"Do I throw both of them?" Jack looked over to Geller.

"Choose one," Geller replied.

A little eager to use his new dagger, Jack pulled out the fire imbued dagger and thought of where he wanted to hit his dummy. After a second of thinking, a target appeared on the face of the dummy. Jack wanted to impress Geller by doing better than Anna. He pulled back his dagger and threw it at the dummy. It flew past its head and smashed against the wall behind it.

"Hmmm," Geller sounded out loud. "Try your other dagger."

Jack quickly unsheathed his other dagger. He felt embarrassed by his miss. This time he envisioned the target on the chest of the dummy. He knew he could hit that at least. He pulled back his dagger and threw it as hard as he could straight at the dummy's chest. It flew past it as well and smashed into the wall.

"Well, now," Geller stepped forward as Jack and Anna retrieved their daggers. "We shall try a run at melee."

"Try what?" Anna asked, confused.

"We will attack the dummies up close, without throwing the daggers," Geller said.

Geller then walked up to his dummy, which stood as high as a human. Without hesitation, he pulled out his dagger and began to jump around in an organized fashion and slice and stab at the dummy very quickly. The dummy looked like it was bleeding before it turned green and went limp as if it had died.

He turned and looked at Jack and Anna, "Let's have you two give it a try."

Jack stood there with his mouth open. He knew there was no way he could do what he just saw Geller achieve. Having built some confidence with throwing, Anna stepped forward towards her dummy and pulled her dagger out. Jack wasn't too familiar with hand-to-hand combat, but he felt the way Anna was holding her dagger was not right.

"I think you're holding it wrong," Jack said hesitantly for fear of sounding like he knew what he was talking about.

Anna looked back at him, "I think you're throwing it wrong."

Jack felt foolish for even saying anything.

"Remember, we're trying to see where your skills may lie, so don't overthink it," Geller chimed in. "Also, be aware that your dummy will try to defend itself. Since we are practicing at a very easy level, it will only use defensive maneuvers to protect itself."

"Why didn't yours do that?" Jack asked half complaining.

Geller laughed and said, "Mine did not have a fighting chance to even attempt to defend itself. My hope is to one day get you to that level of skill, where your opponent doesn't stand a chance against you."

Anna had stopped in her steps. She didn't look as confident hearing Geller's words. She shook her head, though, and proceeded forward. She held the dagger in front of her with both hands like one might hold a large stick. As she got close to the dummy, it twitched and swiveled a little. She inched forward and pushed her dagger into the abdomen of the dummy. It quickly blocked her lunge with its arms and knocked the dagger out of her hands. She picked it up, her face turning red from embarrassment. She then tried another go at it, but the dummy defended itself and knocked the dagger from her hands again.

"Maybe we should try you on a bow and arrow, my friend," Geller spoke up. "I will certainly try and train you in melee, but I think your strong suit may very well be projectiles."

Jack knew it was now his turn to attempt fighting the dummy up close. He felt more confident, though. He had fought previously with his dagger and felt he did alright with it. As he stepped forward, his dummy stood up straight and swiveled a little to face him head on. Jack pulled out his shocking dagger because he had fought with it before and felt more comfortable with it. He sliced at it but was blocked quickly.

"Again!" Geller commanded.

So, Jack stepped forward again and sliced at the dummy. This time he concentrated harder on where to land his hit. A small target appeared just as he began to swipe his blade across its arm. As he hit the dummy's arm, a small shock spread across the dummy. He succeeded in his attempt to cut off one of its arms so that it would be less able to defend itself.

"Good! Good! Again," Geller commanded.

This time Jack took out his other dagger. He aimed for the other arm and within seconds sliced it off near the shoulder. Even though Jack knew the dummy was just enchanted to fight back, he disliked the fake blood that spurted out of its missing arms.

"Now finish it," Geller said calmly.

Just as Jack was about to take aim at the torso of the dummy, it grew back both of its arms plus two more. They were moving rapidly in front of it. Jack hesitated.

"You can do it, Jack," Geller encouraged him.

"This is just pretend," Jack whispered to himself.

He moved in on the dummy once more and envisioned a target on its midsection. Then, he lunged forward. The dummy's arms blocked him entirely and they kept swinging back and forth as they waited for him to attack once again.

"Use them together, Jack!" Anna exclaimed.

Jack remembered how he had put the daggers together in the royal blacksmith's shop. He lifted both daggers and crossed them together while thinking of what he wanted to have happen. Suddenly, a powerful stream of lightning and fire spewed into the dummy's body. It caught fire while an electrical shock covered its entire body. After a couple seconds, the dummy went limp.

"Well, well, well!" Geller looked impressed. "That is a skill that will definitely come in handy. We just need to refine it some."

Jack looked around and saw that branches of magic hit various spots around the courtyard, leaving other dummies charred. Several Valindi could be seen putting out small fires around the area, too.

"You mean I can control how it happens?" Jack asked Geller.

"With some teaching and skill refinement," Geller replied back, "we can get you to a master level, I'm sure of it! You've got some skill at melee, but you need to be trained on both offensive and defensive maneuvers. Eventually, we'll have the dummies attacking you."

"I think I'll stick with the bow and arrow," Anna stated.

"It is imperative that for your own safety, you also learn how to defend and attack," Geller said sternly. "I hope you never have to use these skills, but you will be better off with them. How about we call it a day? We'll have plenty of time to train."

As they all walked back to the house, Jack could not stop thinking of how awesome his new dagger was when combined with his old one. He felt bad for Anna, though. She was unable to wield a magical weapon. He thought maybe she might find an enchanted bow that worked for her.

Geller and Anna talked mostly about strategy and which weapons might work best for Anna. She was still trying to settle down from seeing Jack's daggers explode everything around them. Geller also seemed excited at the turn of events he had just witnessed.

Jack's heart was still beating fast. He kept reminding himself of what he just accomplished. Now he wanted to be back at the barracks training. It was a much better experience than he had anticipated. He smiled. Maybe things would start looking up for him after all, he thought.

Chapter 4: Shamakul Approaches

A couple weeks had passed, and Geller continued to instruct Jack and Anna in their weapons and combat training. Instead of daggers, Anna had switched to archery. Her skill in using a bow and arrow was rough at first, but she quickly gained experience during her training. She still had to learn how to fight with a dagger in case she ever had to fight in close combat. Although she was not that good with it, she had definitely improved over the course of two weeks.

Jack improved in both throwing and fighting with his daggers. He was far from a master level of fighting, but he had certainly shown that he had promise. There was significant improvement in his ability to control the reaction of the daggers when combined. No longer was he dealing damage to an entire area. Now, he was able to nearly control the stream of magical damage with effort.

At the house, Jack missed talking with Selini in the mornings. She had left on a mission to find the cave dweller two weeks prior. There had been no word from her, but Geller assured both Jack and Anna that Selini was sure to be doing well. He told them that she was very skilled and would have no problems keeping herself safe. Jack took Geller's word for it, but he could tell Anna was still concerned for her.

It was late in the morning and both Jack and Anna were nearing the end of the day's training. Jack had just finished throwing his fire dagger at a dummy and it hit just outside of its target but had at least hit it. The dummy turned red and a small fire started at the puncture site. It did not die, however, and it pulled the dagger out of its abdomen and dropped it.

"One day," Geller said as he approached Jack, "the dummy will throw the dagger back at you if you don't kill it first. You've got to hit your target right where you mean to."

"Thunk"

Anna had just shot an arrow at her dummy from thirty feet away. The arrow just barely made it inside her target and the dummy went limp. She pulled back another arrow and shot it at the dummy next to hers. It landed in a similar fashion, just barely within the target. It was obvious to Jack that she was getting more accustomed to using the bow.

"Very good, Anna!" Geller congratulated her. "Keep that bow up, and don't let loose with a bad posture. You'll never hit it perfectly until you work on a natural stance."

Jack retrieved his fire dagger and pulled out his shocking dagger. He quickly took ten paces back from his dummy and combined the two daggers together. In a sudden fury of heat and electricity, a stream of magical damage exuded from his weapons and blasted his dummy until it blew up. Several small streams of damage still broke off from the main stream and hit the wall behind it, causing a small amount of damage to the rocks that made it up.

"Show off," Anna looked annoyed.

Jack smiled, "I'm getting better at that!"

"Yes, you are, sir." Geller said. "But you must work on your combat skills as well. What will you do if your enemy is immune to both fire and lightning damage? It is better to have multiple sets of skills for ever changing situations."

As Geller finished speaking, another Valindi came into the courtyard and headed straight to Geller.

"General, sir, you have been summoned to the Govilian Council Room." He spoke directly to Geller as if the other two were not present. "The matter is urgent."

With that, the individual left the courtyard as if on a mission.

"Well," Geller turned to them, "I guess this is where we call it a day. It appears I have some business to attend to. I trust you'll have no issue getting back home without me."

Geller quickly left. Jack sheathed his daggers and Anna retrieved her arrows. The two looked at each other and shrugged.

"What do you suppose that's about?" Anna asked. "Do you think Selini is back?"

"I dunno," Jack shrugged it off as typical Valindi business. "Do you want to head over to Bolar's?"

He had a sudden craving for Prunklesnider and hoped that even though Anna hated it, they could still go somewhere other than the quiet house. It had been several weeks since he was last at Bolar's. The atmosphere there made him feel at ease somewhat. He felt he could just let the noise of the room drown out his own thoughts sometimes. Now, he definitely wanted to go and decided to himself that if Anna didn't want to go, he would walk her home and then head over to Bolar's tavern.

"Um, sure. I guess we could go there," Anna said hesitantly. "I just wish they had something I liked."

Jack didn't care if they had something there for her or not. All that mattered to him was that she had agreed to go. Before she could change her mind, he quickly set off and headed out of the barracks courtyard. As Anna caught up, Jack offered to carry her bow for her. This way, he figured, she would be more likely to stick with him than to decide to break away and head home. He could use her company since he didn't want to sit there by himself.

As they opened the door to Bolar's, they were greeted by the heavy smell of fire and cooking meat of some sort. There were several dozen Valindi and various other magical beings throughout the tavern. Someone was playing a strange instrument in a corner near the kitchen and next to a staircase that went up to the second floor. Jack figured the second floor must be where Bolar lived because no one ever went up the stairs. The air was filled with the dull roar of laughing, talking, and some yelling.

It turned out, the yelling was coming from the bar. Jack and Anna hadn't even fully entered the main room when they recognized the yelling voices. It was Gink and Fink explaining some elaborate story about a potion gone wrong in the past.

"And then his toes shrunk up 'n disappeared!" Fink had just finished yelling out when he caught a glimpse of Jack and Anna coming in. "Excuse me," Fink said to his listeners as he got up from the bar and, carrying Gink, quickly hobbled over toward the two of them.

"Alo!" Fink yelled out to the two of them as they approached.

It was certainly loud in the room, but Gink and Fink's need to yell was unnecessary. Jack watched as Fink made his way over to them. He smirked as Fink ducked out of the way of a large individual's sword's hilt sticking out behind his back. Although Fink ducked because he saw it coming, Gink was facing the other way and not paying attention. His head thunked against the sword's hilt. It was comical to watch.

"Ey! Watch it!" Gink yelled back to Fink.

Anna looked embarrassed to know the two of them as she watched them approach.

"Quick," she motioned to Jack, "let's find a seat. Preferably where there are only two chairs."

Jack looked around for a table for four. He saw one against the wall not far from where Gink and Fink were originally sitting. He pointed to it.

"I think that should do," he was already walking toward the table.

Anna quickly looked around for a different spot, but Jack was already making his way to the table he pointed out.

"I don't think you looked for a two-person table at all," she muttered as they walked.

Fink changed course and began following the two of them through the labyrinth of chairs and tables.

Once they all sat down and got situated, Gink climbed off of his spot on Fink's back, and plopped into the seat next to him. The two of them looked at Jack and Anna as if they had something to say. Jack couldn't think of what it could be, though, since they had just seen them in the house that morning. He wasn't sure he wanted to hear another potions story, but maybe it would be better than sitting in silence back at the house.

"Oh, stop it!" Anna snapped at the two of them and their ridiculous looks. "You obviously have something to say, so say it already."

"Miss, you really don't like mystery, do ya?" Gink asked, smiling big.

Fink decided to fill them in on what all the fuss was about, "We 'eard Shamakul is heading this way."

"Shamakul?" Jack asked. "Isn't that who Gubuyis said their scouts were looking for a couple weeks ago?" He was looking at Anna as he spoke.

She thought for a moment and then asked, "Isn't it too cold or whatever outside for someone to be heading here right now?"

"Ahh," Gink answered back, "but 'e can control weather, he can. I wouldn't put it past 'im to have a weather enchantment in play."

"Yes," Fink continued for him, "he can make some of them there tornadoes. And some fiercely massive storms."

"Jack, maybe that's why Gubuyis thought he might be behind the attacks in the cavern before," Anna said. "What if this Shamakul character made the storms?"

"Well, it would be beyond me why he would want to attack me," Jack stated. "What did I ever do to him?"

"He is under the control of the witch wizard, Karakaziem, 'e is," Gink said. "If the Reign wants ya dead, they'll use whatever resources they can ta make that happen."

"He's the same wizard that destroyed the flindishk," Fink said somberly and more quietly now. "E'ery single one o' them."

Jack looked at Anna. They had heard about the flindishk from Gubuyis as well. He had mentioned that the Reign was behind the reason they were all gone. This saddened Jack some as he thought of how Gubuyis was certain there was a connection between the flindishk and Jack's weapon wielding abilities. There would be no answer to that, it seemed.

Jack was suddenly startled by several loud bangs at the end of the table. He looked up and saw it was Bolar bringing over drinks for them. He hadn't ordered anything, but he knew Bolar had just brought him some of his favorite Prunklesnider.

"Ay! That looks like water!" Gink exclaimed in disgust as his cup was passed to him.

"Mine as well!" Fink said as he got his cup.

"That's all ya need. The two 'o ya might try an' concoct somethin' funny with those potions o' yers if ya 'ave anything else to drink," Bolar smiled as he answered their dissatisfaction.

"Hey, lil' miss and sir," Bolar said to Jack and Anna. "Good ta see ya again. I couldn't help but overhear with me big ears that someone mentioned Shamakul."

"Yes," Jack spoke up, "it sounds like he's heading this way."

"Ooohhhh," Bolar looked worried, "dat wouldn't be any good now. That's da wizard dat massacred all 'o them flindishk on one very dreadful night."

"What happened?" Anna asked. "Why would he do that?"

"He destroyed their entire city in just one night in a sneak attack, he did." Gink looked sad as he spoke.

"The flindishk can fly and use portals, so a sneak attack wuz de only way he could o' had his victory," Bolar said as he leaned in over the end of the table.

"I heard he used tornadoes and storms to keep them from flying away," Fink belted out. "That 'an lightning, lot o' lightning."

"If they can make portals, why didn't they just leave?" Jack asked.

"Ahhh, dat's the kicker," Bolar replied. "How come they didn't just up an' leave? With dat many deaths, you haf ta think there must've been sumthin' else goin' on."

"He used some kind of protection spell, I tell ya!" Gink slammed his cup against the table. "Ain't no one been believin' me, but that's the only way."

"What do you mean?" Anna asked back.

"What we know is," Fink replied, "that when we use a protection potion, a portal cannot be opened into or out of it. So, we think that Shamakul used some kind of city-wide protection spell an' prevented any of them from getting out o' there."

"Although de attack wuz a surprise," Bolar said, "it wuz no surprise that they were attacked, ya see."

"Yeah, they had been targeting flindishk for years," Fink continued, "killing dem off one by one."

"That's horrible!" Anna said in disgust. "Why would they do that?"

"The flindishk were feared by the Reign because o' their magical abilities. An' any remaining flindishk have been hunted down and killed," Fink said. "It is thought that all the flindishk have been wiped from the face of Lunia."

They all sat in silence for a brief moment. Bolar looked like he might begin crying and Gink and Fink just stared at their waters. Jack looked around the tavern hoping to see something he could change the subject with, but he found he was rather curious about what had happened to the flindishk. Ever since Gubuyis mentioned them before and the possible connection they might have to Jack, he felt like he needed to know more.

"What are their magical abilities?" Anna asked softly, noticing that the others were saddened by the subject.

"Well," Fink answered after another brief moment, "they can make portals for one."

"Portals like ye have ne'er seen dat is," Bolar added. "They can make dem portals as small or as large as ye might need."

"And they can carry hundreds o' times their own weight in flight," Gink said. "I mean it was somthin' magnificent to see a flindishk flying around with a small building in his talons."

"Why would the Reign be afraid of that," Anna was as inquisitive as Jack, and she was beating him to the questions.

"I ain't too sure 'bout why they'd be afraid 'o them lifting heavy things," Bolar answered back.

"But the portals were definitely a threat," Geller said as he walked up to the table.

Geller had just walked in and had overheard a portion of what Bolar was saying. He pointed to Jack's Prunklesnider and motioned to Bolar that he would like one as well. At that, Bolar quickly left the table to retrieve another drink.

"What did you have to go to the Govilian Council Room for?" Anna asked him as he pulled a chair up to the end of the table. "Did they find Selini?"

"I'm afraid not, Anna, I'm afraid not." Geller sat down. "However, I have learned that Shamakul has amassed his army and is heading this way now. Shamakul is the wizard behind the demise of the flindishk."

"So we were just being told," Jack replied back. "We were wondering why they were so feared by the Reign."

Bolar returned to the table and brought with him a cup of Prunklesnider for Geller. He didn't stick around, though, as his tavern was pretty busy, and he needed to tend to his other tables.

"Imagine, if you will," Geller spoke after taking a small swig of his drink, "that you have a race of beings that have proven time and again that they will not fight with you in your efforts to control the world. Then, imagine that those same magical beings can make portals large enough to ferry entire armies across the globe if they so desired."

"They could have been used to bring the armies to Ezjuin," Anna said out loud as she thought about how they could have used a portal in their last battle.

"You're thinking too small," Geller replied. "What if we could summon numerous portals both big and small into the heart of the enemy's lair? Think of how devastating that would be to them. Or create a portal right under Karakaziem herself and transport her straight to a holding cell where she could no longer spread her disease of evil."

"Why didn't the Govilian Council help the flindishk?" Jack asked. "Were they like the Frost Birds, not allegiant to any side."

"Ay!" Gink sounded miserable as if he had just heard bad news.

"They were our allies," Geller replied. "For many more years than I can think of they were our allies. This is why the Reign of Karakaziem felt they had to do something to extinguish them. Their mission was one of stealth and secrecy. We would have helped if we could have, but no one knew it was going to happen. As a matter of fact, they are revered in our great city. You have seen statues of them throughout the city, especially in the Panthyun."

"I wish I coulda been here to see it happen." Fink started to explain. "When they helped you build the Panthyun, all those portals in one spot is enough to make my head swirl."

"I could only dream o' making that many portals at once," Gink said.

"That's right!" Anna sat up quickly. "You two can make portals with your potions! Why didn't they come for you?"

Gink and Fink laughed a little.

"We can make a portal potion or two, but nothing as grand as what a flindishk could simply snap into being," Fink explained. "First, our portals are only as big as the potion that makes them. There ain't no way we could make portals large enough to be a threat. Second, it takes ingredients, lots o' ingredients to even make a portal potion, so you's gotta use them wisely."

"Their portals aren't really considered a big threat. They could be used to sneak a few fighters behind enemy lines," Geller said. "But nothing big enough for us to strategically use. Plus, what Fink forgot to mention, is that their potion driven portals are close ranged, meaning they can't be used over very long distances like those of the flindishk."

"I guess I should mention," Fink interjected, "the portals we make are only one way. So, it'd take two o' them to do a round trip."

"They told you Shamakul can control the weather?" Geller asked Jack.

"Yes," he replied, "they mentioned that. Do you really think Shamakul had anything to do with the attacks in the cavern?"

Jack recalled the fights with the dragons. Both times the cavern filled with storms that were confusingly strong. It didn't seem like someone with that kind of power could be beat.

"That remains to be seen, of course," Geller said. "But I would not be surprised. That wizard has a way of just shooting storms wherever he finds something he doesn't like. What he doesn't like about you, Jack, would be interesting to find out."

Anna quickly spouted out, "That'd be nice, right? Knowing what he hates you for."

Jack nearly rolled his eyes.

"I would like it more if he just didn't care about me at all," he said with a bit of frustration in his voice.

"Well, he is heading our way," Geller chimed in. "That is

something our scouts have been able to ascertain. It will be about two months before they get here, so we've got a lot to do in a very short period of time."

"Two months?" Jack asked concerned. "That's still in wintertime. How will we fight them?"

"That is correct," Geller affirmed. "It will be at the end of winter, but in winter, nonetheless. How we fight them will be up to the Govilian Council to determine."

"How is he getting here?" Anna asked. "Isn't it too cold to travel in the winter?"

"Ay! Treacherous it is," Gink chimed in. "Dozens o' feet o' snow there is."

Geller spoke, "Shamakul is closer than you might think he would be for being two months out. But you are both correct. There is too much snow and he has to move an entire army through the cold. Our scouts are working on learning how this is possible."

"If there's any place I'd like to be," Fink said somberly, "it is here in this great city of Gargantulua. No other place seems right in times such as these."

Geller stood up and finished his drink. He put his chair back from where he found it and stood at the end of the table, preparing to leave.

"I have got to find Selini," he said. "She must know as soon as possible. We have too much to do."

He turned and left the tavern.

Chapter 5: Cave Dweller

It was halfway through the day a few days later. Jack and Anna were just returning home from practicing at the barracks without Geller's instruction. As they entered the main room, they saw Selini and Geller talking at the table. Although Jack felt a sense of relief that she was now there safe and sound, he didn't get emotional like Anna did. She ran over to Selini the second she realized that she was there.

"You're okay!" Anna said with tears in her eyes. "Where have you been?"

Selini stopped chatting with Geller and walked over to meet Anna and Jack. She hugged Anna and thanked her for her kind thoughts. Then, she turned to Jack and shook his hand with a big smile on her face.

"I found him!" she said with delight in her voice. "I found the cave dweller!"

"Um, that's great, I think," Jack responded back.

He wasn't too sure if he wanted the cave dweller to have been found. Everyone seemed worried that whomever it was may have been helping for nefarious reasons. Finding the individual just meant more questions had to be answered.

"It is definitely great," Geller spoke up from across the room. "Now we can all relax because nothing bad will ever happen again."

"Oh hush!" Selini snapped back. Then, she spoke to Jack. "His name is Valkog and he is a flindishk."

"How do you know he is who we're looking for?" Anna asked. "I mean, couldn't there be another cave dweller out there? Wait?! Did you say he's a flindishk?"

Selini smiled and nodded. She headed back over to the table and took a seat. There was a small plate of food in front of her. It appeared that they had just interrupted her eating a meal when they came in. Jack and Anna followed her. Jack's eyes were open wide now at the mention of Valkog being a flindishk. He didn't know why, but his heart was pounding in his chest at the mention of this news. He remembered how Geller had said they were revered in Gargantulua. He figured this must mean Valkog was certainly good. But he wanted to make sure.

"Yeah," he repeated Anna's questions, "how do we know he's the one we've been looking for?"

"Well, there aren't too many cave dwellers to pick from," Selini said matter-of-factly, "so the choices are pretty dang slim. I only found him in the entire time I was out there. Plus, he said he was the one who helped you."

She leaned in and ate another bite of her food as if she hadn't just told them a big piece of news. Anna's mouth dropped open at Selini's words. Geller jumped up and down with joy and clapped his small hands together.

"Okay," Jack responded back, "that's certainly an easy way to answer that question. But I thought the flindishk were all killed."

"He has survived by remaining hidden in the cavern for many years," Selini explained. "Life must have been really dull living down there all alone in the darkness."

"I only just barely met him when I found Selini," Geller interjected. "But I'm willing to say almost entirely because he is flindishk that he has good intentions."

Jack felt a sense of relief from Geller's conclusion. His heart was still beating hard, though. He was becoming more excited than nervous. There was more food at the table than what Geller and Selini looked like they were going to eat, so Jack decided to join them for a bit of a meal. Sitting down at the table, he grabbed a small plate of what looked like peppered, scrambled eggs. A smile began to creep across his face as the relief of the situation came over him. He tried to hide it, but it was hard not smiling about such good news.

"Just because he's a flindishk?" Anna asked sternly. "You don't even know him. How can you make that assumption?"

Jack's smile began to disappear as reality set back in. The fact was, Geller and Selini had only just met him. They didn't know much about him.

Geller smiled and replied, "To understand why I might come to such a conclusion, it is important to know the relationship between the Valindi and the flindishk." He pulled out a chair and sat as he spoke. "You see, there has been a strong alliance between the two nations for more than a thousand years. It is more than just an alliance where we respect each other's rights and traditions. We are friends in the strongest of ways. Although we have our own traditions, many of our traditions are shared. We celebrate many of the same holidays and accomplishments."

"Yes," Selini continued for him, "and one such celebration is that of the construction of the Panthyun. It was built primarily with the help of the flindishk over many centuries. At first, it was merely a meeting hall for several nations to congregate and work out their differences together. Over time, though, our alliances grew, and the meeting hall was too small. Then, we needed to add new rooms for various reasons. Eventually, the Panthyun grew to the size it is now. It will perhaps never be larger without the flindishk."

"Why couldn't you build more on to it if you needed to?" Jack asked.

"The Panthyun outgrew its physical size hundreds of years ago," Geller stated. "It has more hallways alone than space in the physical building itself. I'm sure you noticed the Govilian Council Room is quite large and if you think about it, probably takes up the entirety of the building's space."

"I don't think I understand what you're saying," Jack looked confused.

"Me neither," Anna added.

"The flindishk are very skilled with the use of portals," Selini explained. "It was them who brought the stones to build the Panthyun from far away. They can carry tremendous amounts of their own weight, so they carried many large stones over great distances."

"Why didn't they just use their portals?" Anna quickly asked. "Why would they carry them if they can make portals?"

"The reason we cannot add to the Panthyun ourselves anymore," Selini explained more, "is that in order to make an addition, we must do so through the use of portals within her walls. The flindishk helped us add on by creating permanently enchanted portal stones that would bring individuals to the rooms of the Panthyun. To permanently enchant a portal stone, it requires the heightened skill level of a handful of flindishk elders."

Geller spoke up and added, "And, flindishk elders rarely left the confines of their city. So, they would enchant the portal stones there. To answer your question, Anna, it is not possible to carry a portal through a portal without making a big mess of things. So, they would enchant portal stones in their city of Flindishia and then carry them a great distance to get them here to help complete the construction."

"There are a great number of portals that exist within the walls of the Panthyun," Selini explained. "We use animated statues of the flindishk to grant access to those portals. In fact, pretty much every room you have been to in the Panthyun has been through the use of a portal of some sort. Especially so for the Govilian Council Room."

"I don't recall seeing a portal or going through one," Jack said. "It looked like I was just walking straight into the room."

Selini continued, "It is normal to not notice the portal, as that's one of their designs. When you walk into the Govilian Council Room, you are walking into a room where the location of it is undisclosed and unknown to others. This secrecy keeps its effectiveness at being a safe place to gather."

"What if the Panthyun was destroyed while the Govilian Alliance was meeting in there?" Anna asked.

Selini thought for a moment before answering, "I guess I'm not too sure. Maybe the portals would be collapsed and everyone in whatever rooms they were in would be left out in the middle of nowhere."

"It is important to know," Geller added, "that the Panthyun has never even been attacked before. She is well guarded and highly respected."

"So, there are portals for each of the flindishk statues?" Jack asked, as his curiosity on the subject grew.

"Geller and I are not too sure about that," Selini responded. "Over the years we have seen portals from flindishk statues that we thought were just for decoration, but there are many we have never seen used."

"It is possible that some statues were put in place as placeholders for future portals, but our father hasn't confirmed that for us," Geller said cheerfully. "I even think there are some books in the library that are portals."

"Books that are portals?" Anna asked in return. "To where?"

"Not sure," Geller responded. "Only our father might know that."

"So where is Valkog now?" Jack asked.

"He is speaking with my father," Selini replied. "As you might imagine, there is quite a lot to learn from him."

"I stand by my conclusion," Geller interjected. "I believe he was acting for good, not bad. If he is anything like his brethren, we are in good hands and have found a powerful ally. I just don't know why he helped in secrecy, though. Did he realize Gibble was an impostor? Was there some reason for him to mistrust us?"

"Father will get to the bottom of it," Selini said. "There must have been a good reason. I mean, his entire race has been annihilated and he may have been trying to be secret to protect himself."

They all sat in silence as Geller and Selini contemplated reasons why Valkog remained secret. Anna had taken to finding a seat at the table and was dishing herself some of the peppered eggs. Jack had been so intently listening to the conversation, he hadn't even taken a bite of his food yet. He took a bite and was impressed by the amount of flavor in the dish. Normally he'd be more surprised, but he knew it had to have been prepared by Geller and his dishes were always impressive.

Jack watched the fire for a bit. He thought of being back home again sitting next to the fire in his own fireplace. He longed to be working in the pumpkin patch over the constant worry that someone or something was always trying to kill him. Although he could read books here, he missed the library where he could relax and get lost in stories. Then, he realized that Anna must definitely be missing the library and her mom. He felt bad for her, since it wasn't her fault at all that she was on Lunia.

He gave a small smile as he remembered her pestering him about touching the map in the Stonevue library. The map was intriguing to him. It seemed to have had some elements of Lunia built into it. Then, there was the book that he started reading. Suddenly he remembered having seen the flindishk referenced in it.

"I think I recall having seen a reference to the flindishk in a book I read in the library of my hometown," Jack said, interrupting the silence.

"Really?" Selini looked curious.

"Yeah, the Avnoli Map book, right?" Anna asked Jack as she began to recall it, too.

"Yes, I'm sure of it." Jack was remembering the book as he spoke. "At first, I thought it was just a book of mythical creatures. I remember the page well because I've seen it here. It was a picture of an arbolio. I recall it having emphasized roots and had wondered why that was, until I saw one here of course."

"I don't remember well enough, Jack," Anna began asking him a question, "but, was there any mention of the flindishk?"

"Um," he responded as he thought, "it didn't say flindishk, but if I remember right, it was beginning to explain them. It said they could carry hundreds of times their weight." Jack hesitated for a moment as his heart sank, "It also said they 'repel' humans."

"What do you think that means?" Anna asked Geller and Selini.

Geller spoke first, "Humans and flindishk don't really get along too well for some reason."

"For some reason?" Selini asked sarcastically. "For many years, the humans would use their interactions with the flindishk to try and enslave them to do their heavy lifting and work. It's not like the flindishk hated the humans, but they actively tried to avoid interactions with them after a while. It seemed backwards. The non-magical humans trying to work the magical flindishk. They were lucky the flindishk didn't turn around and enslave them themselves."

"I'm very interested in how elements of Lunia were in a book on Earth," Geller leaned in towards Jack.

"Maybe it was from a time when the Bridge of Kardun was open," Selini suggested. "It is possible that some humans were able to return, maybe."

"I'm not too sure of that," Anna spoke up. "The book was written maybe ten or fifteen years ago. It wasn't that old."

"Do you think," Geller was looking at Selini now, "the flindishk had found another way to planet Earth and had crossed over there? Or somehow the humans found a way to Lunia?"

"One thing is for certain," Selini stated, "there is a portal between the worlds. That is how Jack and Anna are here today. If it was indeed the flindishk who made that portal, it would be very interesting to learn why. But that may never be learned now."

"Jack?" Geller looked as if he was solving something. "You said you came through a large boulder, didn't you?"

Jack nodded.

"Selini, it is not uncommon for the flindishk to make portals from enchanted mountain rocks," Geller stated. "I wouldn't be surprised if they were behind the creation of that portal."

"How would Jack have been able to open the portal, though?" Selini responded back. "A flindishk portal can only be opened by a flindishk."

Excited about the possibility of an answer, Anna quickly interjected, "What about the portals in the Panthyun? They can be opened by others who aren't flindishk."

She was obviously excited. Jack sat up a little to hear the response. There had to have been some reason he was able to open the portal from the other side and maybe he could do it again from this side.

"Those portals have been set to be opened by flindishk and those of rightful blood. They have been enchanted specifically so," Selini replied.

Jack sat straight up now.

"Wait a minute!" He exclaimed. "If it can only be opened by a flindishk, maybe Valkog can get us home."

He was unable to contain his smile as his eyes lit up with excitement at this new conclusion. Even if Jack could not open the portal from this side, it seemed like there might be another way. Valkog was a flindishk and if the portal was in fact made by the flindishk, he would be able to open it for Jack and Anna.

"There has to be a connection," Anna said, agreeing with Jack and Geller. "They build portals out of rocks from mountains. The boulder in Stonevue was obviously out of place, like it didn't belong there. And it was a large boulder. There is no way a bunch of people would have moved it all the way from the mountains just to sit it in the middle of a pumpkin patch. That just doesn't make any sense. But maybe a flindishk carried it there. I don't know why there specifically, but it would have been much easier for a flindishk to carry it there than a bunch of people."

"I won't deny that there seems to be some kind of connection," Selini stated. "But, why in the middle of a field and why help the humans at all? I'm not saying humans aren't worth helping, but the flindishk and humans weren't really on speaking terms as far as I knew."

"Well, one thing is for sure," Jack stated, "I'm definitely going to ask if Valkog can open it. We have to at least try."

"Maybe he could just make a portal for us if that doesn't work," Anna said. "If they've done it once, they can do it again, right?"

"I don't think it works that easily," Geller responded. "Making portals is what they're skilled at but making a portal across a vast amount of space to a whole other world is something quite powerful, indeed."

"What he's trying to say," Selini said, "is that one flindishk is not likely going to be able to open that kind of portal. It would require too much skill and mana for a single flindishk to summon."

"Yes, it is more likely that the flindishk elders would have been involved in its creation," Geller added. "Which would itself be interesting to know why they would have kept such an event a secret from the Govilian Council."

There was a little bit of disappointment in Jack's face as he heard Geller explain that his only way home was still just a hope. Hearing that Valkog would not be able to summon a portal to get them home was an issue. However, there was still some promise in the fact that he was a flindishk that was willing to help Jack in the past and might be willing to help open the portal sitting in Wellwood Forest. Although he was a little disappointed, he felt some comfort in knowing that Valkog might be able to open the portal for them.

"But he could still open the portal in Wellwood Forest, right?" Jack asked.

"Maybe," Selini answered back. "It really depends on the enchantments on the portal. I would hope for the sake of Lunia that only a very select few could open the portal in Wellwood Forest."

"A portal that powerful needs to be protected from both sides," Geller said. "It's a wonder as to why they put it in the middle of the forest, too. Something must have gone wrong is all I can think. Which is even more reason that I say there should be protections on it so that not anyone can open the portal."

"If it's so dangerous, how come it hasn't been moved?" Anna asked.

"Only a flindishk can move a portal," Selini replied. "Since it wasn't heavily guarded by the Reign, it is very possible that Frinkul didn't know what it was. We have plans to begin guarding it in the spring, by building around it. It will be quite the task."

"Now with Valkog," Geller said, "maybe we can have him transport it to a more secure location."

Selini nodded in agreement. Then, there was a knock from down the hallway.

The main door could be heard opening and someone talking. Then, the door shut and the four of them could hear the light footsteps of Gryan, the watcher of the house. He came into the main room and addressed the group.

"Master Gubuyis has requested your presence in his library," Gryan stated in his low, rough voice.

Without saying anything else, Gryan left the room.

"I'm sure you two are eager to meet Valkog," Selini said as she stood up from her chair. "We shouldn't linger."

Chapter 6: Meeting Valkog

As Jack, Anna, Selini and Geller all walked to the Panthyun, they were greeted by the familiar sight of Fink carrying Gink down the street away from Bolar's tavern. Fink appeared to be in good spirits as the two of them sang some ridiculous song of a past potions story. Jack found that for the most part, the songs Gink and Fink sang were made up, usually on the spot. It was incredible to him how the two always seemed to know what words to sing together.

"Oh great!" Selini stopped in the road. She only seemed to tolerate their presence, but Jack knew deep down she liked the duo. "You two. Don't you have some ingredients to steal from somewhere?"

"Nope!" Gink replied back, "We're all done pilfering for the day."

Jack laughed, but he had to wonder if that was actually true. The two had been known to "borrow" ingredients from others when they had a potion they wanted to make.

Selini rolled her eyes at them and began walking again. Fink followed the group.

"So, where are we headed?" Gink asked. "Somewhere important, I hope. I could really go for a change o' pace."

"We're headed to the Panthyun," Anna replied. "Selini found the cave dweller and he's a flindishk! He's the one who helped Jack in the cavern when we were attacked."

"You don't say," Fink responded. "A flindishk, eh? There's a particular ingredient we could benefit from if he has it."

"Always with you two," Selini spouted out. "It's always gotta be about what new ingredient you can get your hands on. It was the first thing you thought of. You didn't even care that he may quite possibly be the last of his kind."

Gink gleefully chimed in, "We care! Without him, we would have to find the ingredient ourselves. But, with even just one flindishk, we can possibly get what we're lookin' for."

Selini shook her head in disgust at their lack of regard for the situation. Jack watched ahead as the sight of the Panthyun grew ever larger above the buildings on their approach. He realized he was still wearing his armor and daggers from their morning training routine. It hadn't occurred to him to take them off, but he wasn't out of place. Both Selini and Geller were carrying their weapons and Anna had not had a chance to rid herself of her armor or bow either.

It only took about ten minutes before they arrived at the grand staircase of the Panthyun. Although Jack was eager to meet Valkog and see what a flindishk looked like up close, no one else in the group seemed to have the desire to walk faster. This slightly frustrated Jack as they walked; he felt they were all walking slowly on purpose. He knew that wasn't the case, but he felt that way, nonetheless.

They all entered the Panthyun and began walking down a long hallway that felt longer than possible, for the size of the building. Eventually, though, they came to a dead end where a small flindishk statue sat on the wall reading a book. Geller approached it and tapped the book with his finger.

"We're here to see my father," Geller spoke to the statue.

At that, the statue stood up in his nook and turned around into the wall, disappearing before their eyes. Within a few seconds a bunch of loud clinks and clanks came from inside the wall. A doorway began to appear as the stones themselves moved out of the way, forming a small passageway between them and another hall. Jack remembered the conversation about how the Panthyun was full of portals, and he wondered if this doorway was a portal itself.

After the door appeared, Geller stepped through. He was immediately followed by the rest of the group. The passageway was rather large and dimly lit by the occasional torch on the walls. After a few moments of walking through the curved hallway, the group came upon a large, heavy wooden door. Geller walked up to it and knocked before he opened the door.

Inside the library, Jack saw the familiar floating globe that hovered above a desk that sat slightly off center in the tall room. The room was dimly lit much like the passageway, but it was much warmer than outside. It was cozy to Jack as the air felt thick on his skin.

"That's awesome," Anna said, looking at the globe.

It was slowly turning and was covered in snow and ice in many places. It even looked like there might be clouds floating above its surface, but it was hard to make out in the dim light. Jack looked up and felt a sense of awe as the bookshelves climbed higher than he could see. Even in the dim light, Jack could tell the ceiling wasn't anywhere near where he expected it to be.

Then, something else caught his eyes. It was Gubuyis sitting in his chair at the desk. He was finishing up writing something in a book. That's when Jack recalled why they were there to begin with. He looked at the chair across from Gubuyis. Sure enough, there was someone large sitting in it. Jack moved closer to get a better look.

Jack's eyes opened wide as he took in the sight of a flindishk. It was Valkog and he looked like he could stand nearly seven feet high. He saw Valkog's talons resting on the floor. They looked like they could hold two or three large pumpkins each. Noticing that he was being observed, Valkog stood up.

"Jack," he spoke with a smooth, deep voice. "Pleased to meet you."

Jack stood there not knowing what to say. He was shocked at this new magical creature he was seeing. Valkog stood in front of him with his massive wings at rest that looked like they were folded several times to fit behind his back. At the end of each of his wings was a claw-like hand. His face had a small snout that had several pointy teeth sticking out. His snout was smaller than it seemed like it should be. From the top of his head were two tall, pointy ears. There were some patches of brown fur around his chin and ears, but he was mostly just bare skin.

Realizing that he had not responded, Jack finally replied, "Um, pleased to meet you, Valkog?"

"It is I, Valkog," he replied.

Valkog lifted out his wings slightly and slowly spun around for Jack to see him. Jack noticed that the clothes he was wearing were in disrepair. He was wearing tattered, light brown pants that only went halfway down his legs. It appeared that the shirt he was wearing was once white, but it no longer maintained the color. It was full of holes and stains of various kinds. The shirt looked more like a vest that slipped over his head and was held together on the sides by buttons or snaps of some kind. Some of those were missing. It was easier to make out the details of Valkog as he stood in the light, turning around. Jack felt bad for observing him so closely, but he also felt like he should be allowed to. He felt a small bit of connection to him but wasn't sure why.

Valkog stopped turning and smiled at Jack. Jack smiled back. As Valkog sat down, Jack noticed his skin color was a mixture of blacks and browns all over his body. It reminded him of a stone slab he once saw at the stone cutter's shop in Stonevue that was called marble. After Valkog sat down, Gubuyis stood up.

"Welcome all of you," Gubuyis greeted the group. Motioning toward Valkog, he said, "As you are all already aware, this is Valkog. He is our cave dweller that has been helping Jack through some tough times."

Interrupting Gubuyis, Jack looked at Valkog, "I would like to thank you for all of your help. I cannot pay you anything, though, as I am not from around here and do not have anything in my possession to offer you."

"I will fight for you to the end, Sir Jack," Valkog responded.

Before Jack could respond, Gubuyis continued his speech.

"I think you'll find that Valkog here is not seeking payment, good Jack. He has been helping you since you first arrived here on Lunia," Gubuyis said.

"Forgive me sir, but does he know where I'm from?" Jack asked.

Gubuyis nodded, "He is well aware of where you are from and may even know more about you than we have learned."

"How is that possible?" Anna asked.

"Can you get us home?" Jack quickly inquired.

"To get to the end, we should first start at the beginning of your presence here on Lunia," Gubuyis began explaining. "Valkog here was close behind you when you were attacked by Frinkul and Asagu, his companion. He was present after you had destroyed Frinkul's cabin in the woods. In fact, after Geller had fought Asagu, Valkog here had just arrived. He took the quiver and several items from Asagu's belt."

"Why would you do that?' Selini asked.

Valkog simply shrugged and responded, "I knew the quiver was enchanted to have unlimited arrows. I didn't want that falling into the wrong hands."

"Yeah," Fink chimed in, "some youngling could have been walking by and come across them and, you know, made a real mess of things."

Jack couldn't tell if Fink was being funny or sarcastic, but he was very eager to hear more about how Valkog had been involved in any fashion.

"Why have you been hiding in the cavern?" Jack asked.

Gubuyis looked at Valkog and smiled, "Well now, it seems I have lost them. Are you prepared, Valkog?'

In his deep, smooth voice, Valkog calmly replied, "I can certainly try and answer any of your questions. To answer your questions thus far, I have been hiding in the cavern for roughly eight and a half years. I have been hunted and am still wanted for dead by the Reign and I was not certain of how I could make myself visible without compromising my duty to protect you, Jack."

Eight and a half years sounded familiar to Jack. He thought about it hard and thought that sounded like when the witch wizard Karakaziem disappeared. That didn't seem like a big deal, though. What was a bigger deal to Jack was that Valkog had just said it was his duty to protect him.

"What do you mean, it's your duty to protect me?" Jack asked.

"Jack, I am your protector," Valkog stated. "And, I haven't seen you since you were just a small child. I knew your parents and swore to them that I would watch over you if ever you returned to Lunia."

"What?!" Anna sounded surprised.

Jack's head was filling with questions quickly. He wanted to know more about his parents, but he wanted to know how or why he was on Lunia before. He also wanted to know why his parents thought he needed protection.

"Let's not get lost in those details, though," Valkog stated. "I believe we have plenty of time to work through those. I think it is important to know that I have been helping you and watching over you from afar. But I will no longer be outside of your reach; I am dedicated to assisting you in close contact."

"So, you were hiding because of the Reign?" Jack asked as a follow up to his original question.

He figured he would have plenty of time to get down to all his questions.

"I was unsure of who to trust over these last few years. Everyone I ever knew had been killed," he said somberly. "There had to have been spies and I just didn't know who I could trust anymore."

"Why appear now, then?" Anna asked.

"I saw how your new friends fought for you and worked as hard as they could to keep you protected. Eventually, I figured they had to be trustworthy and able to keep you a secret, as you have been well protected by them," Valkog replied as if Jack had asked the question.

"Was that you that killed the dragons in the cavern with the light that rained down?" Geller asked.

Valkog nodded, "Indeed, it was. I used a very powerful spell to conjure tens of thousands of small portals that fell out of the sky. As they fell, they transported small bits of the dragons elsewhere, which ended up destroying them."

"What about the shield?" Jack asked. "We found a large shield that I used to protect myself from the dragons in the storm."

"That was indeed my shield, my friend," Valkog replied. "It would have been impossible for me to fly in that kind of storm, so I sent you my shield. I could not fight that many dragons. In fact, I can hardly fight a single dragon without the use of magic. And, by the time you had come back through the cavern and found yourself in that storm, my powers were already getting low. I have not been able to replenish my mana in years, and I haven't had to use much magic these last few years either. With your sudden appearance and the first attack of the dragons, I used way too much of my remaining mana. The shield and a levitation spell were about all I could muster during the storm."

"Why didn't you help during the battle at Ezjuin?" Jack asked. "If you're supposed to protect me, why weren't you there?"

Valkog looked embarrassed, "I was afraid I had lost you in the storm. Everything was so confusing; I couldn't see what happened to you. I searched for weeks before finally coming to the conclusion that you were found by your friends. I had hoped with all hope that you had not been eaten by the dragons. It wasn't until Selini here came searching for me that I learned you were doing well."

"How is it that you think you saw me as a baby?" Jack asked.

"Ah," Valkog responded, "I do not know what you are aware of. Have you heard of the Unsolterra Protectors?"

Jack shook his head and looked over to Anna who also shook her head.

"I can't say that I have?" Jack replied. Then he asked, "Is that a

Govilian Council thing?"

Valkog gave a small laugh at Jack's question and said, "The Unsolterra Protectors are a group of humans on Earth that sought to return the humans on Lunia back to their real home. They knew that humans held no magical powers on Lunia and therefore led a difficult life living off lands that were many times taken from them by magical beings."

"How does that involve Jack?" Selini asked.

"The Unsolterra Protectors were led by Jack's mother, Sam," Valkog replied. "The flindishk elders and a group of flindishk underlings, including myself, were involved in the creation, protection and transportation of the portal between worlds. The portal was protected with enchantments and spells that would only allow flindishk and humans through. The elders were very afraid of what could happen if the Reign was able to use it. It would be bad for both worlds. There are vast amounts of resources on Earth that are unprotected by magical beings. They would decimate humanity just to get what they wanted and then, when they were done with Earth, they would leave it in ruins. We have seen that here on Lunia. The Reign has stripped various regions of Lunia of her resources by taking what they wanted, and then leaving the ground tremendously marred."

"It is true," Gink spoke with a somber tone, "we have seen places where the Reign has destroyed the land as they tore away the resources it once had."

Jack had rarely ever heard anyone speak of his mother with such familiarity. It had been years since he last heard her name used. He knew her name was Sam, but it still sounded foreign to him as Valkog spoke her name. A small bit of pride filled him as Valkog spoke of how his own mother was the leader of the group that was trying to rescue the humans on Lunia.

Valkog continued, "Eventually, the elders were becoming increasingly suspicious of everyone. There were spies in the ranks. The mission was already highly secret, but they were getting fearful that it would soon be found out. They were going to add several more safeguards to the portal, last I knew, in order to only allow a select few flindishk to pass through. It wasn't too long after that the surprise attack happened on Flindishia."

There was a brief moment of silence. Valkog sniffed a little. Jack could tell he was holding back tears. It must have been hard to have watched everything he knew be destroyed, Jack thought to himself. He wondered if Valkog had lost anyone that he loved but refrained from asking. He didn't want to make the conversation painful for Valkog anymore than it already was.

Valkog spoke again, "I do not think the portal was ever completed in full. It ended up in Wellwood Forest as we all learned recently. From my conversations with your mother and father, Jack, it sounded as if Lanakog was shot down. Lanakog was the one designated to carry it in secret across the regions to the city of Earth here on Lunia. Her path was a secret from all, including me."

"Lanakog?" Anna asked slowly. "Was she related to you?"

"I would call her my sister," Valkog explained, "but, you would refer to us as simply members of the same clan."

Anna spoke sympathetically, "I'm so sorry to hear that, Valkog."

"I have had many years to grieve," Valkog responded. "My losses have been great, and they have also been painful. Everyone I ever knew, including my family, has been killed by the Reign of Karakaziem. If I am to die as well, I would very much like to die fighting rather than in hiding."

Geller interjected, "We would be honored to fight by your side, Valkog. The flindishk have always been good to us throughout time. You have probably heard, Shamakul is heading this way as we speak. If you so choose, there will be ample opportunity to show him that he has not fully succeeded in his mission to rid Lunia of the flindishk."

"How did you ever meet my parents?" Jack asked.

There was so much Jack wanted to know. He was feeling more at ease with Valkog now that he had openly explained so much. With every answer, though, it seemed like there were more questions.

"Your parents were both very instrumental in creating an alliance between humans and the flindishk," Valkog explained. "The two races were not really at odds, but there was little that joined them together before Sam and Chris appeared."

"How did they appear?" Anna asked. "How did they get to Lunia in the first place?"

Before Valkog could answer, there was a sudden interruption from a small flindishk statue that had been sitting on a nearby bookshelf.

In a screechy voice, it said, "Forgive me sir Gubuyis, but you are needed in front of the Panthyun."

"Ahh," Gubuyis stood up from his chair, "I have been expecting to hear from one of our scouts. I believe there will be more time to speak with Valkog as the days progress. Let us take our leave for the moment, though."

Gubuyis walked toward the door and opened it, motioning for the others to follow.

"There is someone here I think you would all like to see," he said.

Jack felt like he still had so many questions, but he knew it was going to take time to get them answered. Reluctantly, he followed as the others began to leave. As he left the room, Gubuyis tapped his staff against the ground lightly and all the torches dimmed to a small glow that barely lit the library. The one light that shone brightly was the still spinning globe.

Chapter 7: Mini Portals and Mana

Outside of the Panthyun, the group was met by Vlagar. He sat awkwardly as his body rested in both the street and on part of the grand staircase. Although the city in the cavern was grand like that of its above ground counterpart, things were a bit more cramped.

Having not seen Vlagar for some time, Jack and Anna quickly made their way to meet him. He was quite the sight. His scales shined brightly in the dark, but dimly lit cavern. They were a bluish grey, with streaks of silver throughout and blue edges. Jack was rather pleased to see him.

"Vlagar!" Anna exclaimed as they approached him. "How have you been?"

"In his rough, deep voice", Vlagar responded, "I am well! It is very nice to see you all once again. I have been working so hard to gather some information for Gubuyis here. And it is important that I speak to all of you."

Vlagar's eyes fixed on Valkog for a moment. Jack could tell Vlagar was surprised to see a flindishk alive, but he did not say anything about it.

"It's good to see you again, Vlagar," Jack said pleasantly.

Gubuyis and the others were still several steps behind the two of them. Jack had not really seen Vlagar since the battle at Ezjuin a few months prior. He figured there were many reasons Vlagar did not come to visit often, one being that the streets of the Gargantulua underground were quite a bit smaller than the streets above ground. He also figured Vlagar and the other Frost Birds were rebuilding their home since it had been devastated by Ghowla's actions. It hadn't occurred to him that the Govilian Council had employed him to do scout work. As he thought about it though, it did make sense to him. The Frost Birds could easily scout out in the freezing cold weather that everyone else was trying to avoid. He remembered that he had been told Frost Birds were one of the few races that could stand the cold of winter.

"What news do you bring us?" Gubuyis asked as he finally met up with Jack and Anna a few steps up from where Vlagar's body rested.

Vlagar spoke with intent as he leaned in toward the group so that he could speak more softly, "I have seen Shamakul and his forces."

"Where are they now?" Gubuyis asked.

"They are moving at a slow pace through the cold of winter," Vlagar responded. They are probably still two months out at their current speed."

"That confirms it," Geller turned to Gubuyis as he spoke. "We have much to do."

Without responding to Geller, Gubuyis asked Vlagar, "What else did you learn?"

"There appeared to be a weather enchantment that enveloped the entire army. It is providing protection from the elements as the winter storms have been harsh on their path," Vlagar explained. "The weather enchantment is not only protecting the troops from the outside weather, but it is providing warmth inside it."

"I'd be willing ta bet that Shamakul is the one that controls the weather enchantment," Fink stated.

Gubuyis nodded in agreeance. It was obvious to Jack that Gubuyis was thinking about his next step. Jack was curious himself, though, too.

"Where is Shamakul? Is he leading the army?" Jack asked.

Vlagar looked at the whole group as he answered, "Shamakul is in the center of it all. He is good with weather enchantments and could probably control it from any position in the ranks, but his other spell needs him to be in the center."

"He's got a protection spell, doesn't he?" Selini asked, but it was more of a statement than a question.

"You are quite right," Vlagar replied. "Shamakul has a protection bubble surrounding his troops as well. In order for him to cover all of his troops, he must remain in the center."

"What troops does he command?" Gubuyis asked.

Without hesitation, Vlagar spoke as if he already knew the question was coming, "It would seem the Reign is not done with the use of dragons and fironi."

"Great!" Gink said sarcastically.

Vlagar continued, "The front of his army is probably a thousand deformed troll axe throwers whose weapons are enchanted. Mixed within them are hundreds of fironi. There are various troops of sword wielders as well, but not too many from what I could see. Behind them is Shamakul in the center of everything. Behind him is the reason they must move so slow, there are hundreds of dragons."

"So," Geller spoke, "it sounds like we have dragons who breathe fire, fironi who throw fire, trolls that throw axes, Shamakul himself, a weather enchantment, and a protection bubble. Am I missing anything?"

"Sword wielders!" Gink shouted out.

Thinking of the axe throwers, Jack remembered that Geller had told him the dummies in the barracks courtyard would fight back when he was ready for a higher skill level. Jack suddenly thought that he may need to start training as if something or someone was going to be throwing things at him, particularly axes.

"We need to train in defense more," Jack said to Anna.

"Tell me what you know about the axe throwers," Gubuyis said to Vlagar. "Could you see if their weapons were enchanted?"

Jack's eyes grew larger at the mere mention that the axes might be enchanted. It hadn't occurred to him that they might be throwing fire axes or lightning axes similar to his daggers. Then, he also worried that they might be poisonous.

Vlagar answered, "I can see quite clearly with my vision, and Shamakul and his army did not seem to care that anyone might be watching. They kept no secrets as far as I could tell. They did not seem to have a desire to keep any tricks untold. That being said, I saw the axes were enchanted to return to the thrower. The deformed trolls threw them like toys as they walked. I noticed that the edges of the axes were reddened, which I assume means something but I'm not sure."

"They are enchanted to inflict wounds that don't stop bleeding," Geller said slowly as if he was remembering something. "I have seen a similar enchantment before on a different blade."

"How can you be so sure?" Selini asked. "Couldn't they be enchanted with fire?"

"Maybe," Geller responded, "but they already have fire with the fironi and the dragons. My bet would be that the enchantment is one of bleeding."

"I saw Shamakul issue the occasional shockwave through the troops that made the trolls become more enraged and larger," Vlagar added.

Gubuyis looked curious at that remark and asked nobody in particular, "Bloodlust?"

"What? What is that?" Anna asked.

"When ya have sumthin' like them trolls, grumpy and all, ya find a way to make them even madder!" Fink said happily.

"Yes," Selini rolled her eyes at his contentment, "a bloodlust spell would serve to enrage the trolls so they fight harder and more fiercely than normal. They would become filled with a thirst for blood."

"What makes them move so slowly?" Jack asked but immediately felt like his question was easily answered by the fact that the army was trudging through the deep snow.

"It is mostly due to the dragons," Vlagar explained. "They cannot fly in both the protection bubble and the weather enchantment. Both are too low for the lot of them to fly around in. That means they have to walk the entire way. And dragons are not really built for walking, especially over long distances. If they were to fly outside of the weather enchantment, they'd surely freeze."

"Don't they have to walk through the snow, too?" Anna asked.

"Their weather enchantment takes care of that," Vlagar replied. "It is melting a large swath of snow and ice. This is the other reason they are slowed down. It takes a lot of power to continually melt that much snow."

"The snow must be twenty feet deep!" Geller exclaimed. "They are just trapping themselves in an ice canyon."

"We thank you greatly, Vlagar," Gubuyis interjected. "This news would surely have found us much later, had we enlisted our traditional scouts."

"You are very welcome," Vlagar responded. "I am happy to have volunteered but I am sorry the news is grim, though. It makes me feel a little better knowing that you have more time to prepare this way. Now, if you are through with me, I must rest."

Gubuyis nodded. Vlagar turned to face Jack and Anna. He gave them a small smile and took off loudly into the darkness of the cavern before quickly disappearing from view.

"We will need to convene the Govilian Council tomorrow morning," Gubuyis said to the group. "As for now, I am heading back to my study."

Gubuyis grabbed at the necklace around his neck and looked at it for a moment.

"What is it?" Jack asked.

"There may very well be a story that connects you, Valkog, and this pendant. I am not sure, though," Gubuyis explained. "It is something that will require me to read more. There must be a connection between you and your protector, Valkog, that offers some meaning to this pendant."

As the group headed back home, they spoke about what they had learned from Vlagar. As they did, they attempted to conjure up ideas on how best to defeat Shamakul. One such suggestion came from Selini.

"We could shoot thousands of rocks at his protection bubble," she contemplated. "I could then enchant them in their flight through the air so that they'd be huge – like the size of hills. Surely, the protection bubble can't withstand all of that."

"The amount of magic needed to enchant the number of rocks like that would be magically exhausting," Valkog pointed out.

"I don't see how you could do much of anything else if you've exhausted yourself," Geller added. "What would we do without you when the actual fight happens?"

"It's just an idea," Selini continued. "I don't know what the next steps would be or who would do what, but at the very least his protection bubble might be down."

As they walked up to the house, Geller said, "We have much to figure out. Like, what if we could destroy the weather enchantment, too? We could nearly wipe them out by freezing them out of their will to fight."

Once they all ended up in the main room, Fink set his witchle on the table. He had been messing with it after Selini spoke of using so much magic that it might exhaust her mana. The witchle was a full, bright yellow. Intrigued by the gadget, Valkog picked it up and looked it over.

"What does it do?" Valkog asked.

"It's a witchle," Anna answered for Fink. She remembered it from before on their way to Wyvergia several months prior. "It measures one's mana level."

Valkog looked it over with a sense of awe. It changed from all yellow to just a small sliver of yellow. He nodded his head and placed the witchle back on the table.

Jack noticed the change of color and asked, "What happened to your mana?"

Valkog took a seat and let out a small sigh. "I have almost entirely exhausted my mana. As you can see from that nifty little device there, I have very little mana left. I cannot perform anything substantial right now. That unfortunately means I will be of little use during the battle."

"Won't your mana regenerate?" Anna asked.

"A flindishk's mana is a lot. So much so, I can perform many many portal spells over time or at the same time," Valkog explained. "But I did just that. When I performed tens of thousands of portal spells at the same time to save Jack's life in the cavern months ago, I nearly exhausted myself entirely. I have been reduced to simple spells for the time being until I can rejuvenate my mana."

"Why does it take so long to regenerate your mana?" Anna questioned.

"He needs a special food in order ta do it fast," Gink called out.

Geller chimed in, "That's a food I can't make. And there aren't too many I can't make."

Fink added, "He'll need a special ingredient, he will."

Jack smirked. It always seemed Gink and Fink felt the solution to everything was to concoct something with special ingredients. There had to be another way, Jack thought.

"Root of flindishion," Valkog said, agreeing with Fink. "I will need most specifically some root of flindishion in order to make the mana rejuvenation food. Once I have that, my mana will regenerate rapidly."

"Is there any of that here?" Jack asked, looking at Fink and Gink in particular.

"Sorry, fresh out," Fink replied. "We could use a little o' that there root, too."

"Yeah," Gink added. "Me in particular!"

"If anybody's getting some root of flindishion," Selini nearly shouted out, "it's Valkog. We could use his powers during battle. You two probably have some stupid concoction you want to sell if you get your hands on it. I haven't heard of any potions using root of flindishion anyway. What are you planning?"

Gink said happily, "It's an experiment."

"I doubt we have any in the storehouse here in the Panthyun," Geller stated. "It is an ingredient that is supposed to be nearly fresh when used and there hasn't been any demand for it since ...," Geller paused because he knew it was a delicate situation, "... since there have not been any flindishk around for some time."

"Where can we get some, then?" Anna asked.

Responding to Anna and the group as a whole, Valkog said, "It used to be found in ample quantities near my hometown. But I do believe the crops were destroyed when Flindishia was overcome by Shamakul. However, if I recall correctly, it grows naturally in small quantities in your Wellwood Forest."

"That's a wee bit difficult," Gink said, "as the forest is only about twenty feet under snow and ice right now. Ye'll have ta wait until springtime ta get some o' that."

Interrupting the conversation, Geller spouted out another idea for defeating Shamakul, "What if father were to drop the ground beneath Shamakul? If Selini here was able to destroy the protection bubble, maybe he could then destroy the ground they walk on."

Jack could tell Geller had just come up with the idea and hadn't spent any time thinking it through. He could see Selini's look of doubt as she slightly shook her head.

"I don't think father would be able to do that much damage from that far away without exhausting himself," she explained. "He is definitely the one we don't want to exhaust. He'll be doing all kinds of magic for sure."

Deciding to change the course of the conversation and to answer a few burning questions, Jack asked, "Where will the battle happen anyway? Here in the cavern? Out in the open? Do we have a weather enchantment, too?"

"The most likely scenario for where the battle is to take place will be at the cavern opening," Selini stated. "That is, of course, up to the Govilian Council to decide, but I cannot imagine any other location."

"Why there?" Anna questioned.

"We can fight from within the cavern as best as we can if we can get Shamakul to meet us at that point," Selini explained.

Continuing for her, Geller added, "It'll be naturally warmer in the cavern, which will provide us protection from the elements of the winter weather outside. And it'll create a bottleneck that will prevent Shamakul's forces from overrunning us all at once. They won't be able to flank us either. It will be a battle head on!"

Anna looked worried as she spoke, "It seems like that is really close to the city. What happens if we lose?"

"My dear Anna," Selini chimed back in, "losing is not really an option. We have to fight to the death. His forces will probably outnumber ours, but we have something we fight for and that is for the good of Lunia. Greatness becomes us when we strive for it."

"May I ask," Valkog interjected, "what happens if Gubuyis is hurt or killed in combat? It seems like you are relying on his powers to fight Shamakul. Is there another plan or will there be another strategy that is exercised in case of his demise?"

Silence befell the group. At that moment, Jack realized that the battle at Ezjuin was ultimately won by Gubuyis and he expected that it would be the same in this battle. He now wondered what they would do if Gubuyis was unable to fight Shamakul.

"Perhaps one of you two?" Jack broke the silence as he motioned to Geller and Selini. "Would one of you be able to fight him?"

"If Selini exhausts herself fighting off the protection bubble," Geller explained, "then it may be up to me to fight Shamakul if father is unable to."

Making fun of Geller's cooking ability, Gink abruptly stated, "You could cook 'em!"

"No, no," Fink said laughing, "you could skewer 'em!"

"Oh, oh I got it!" Gink exclaimed in excitement. "You could ..."

"Stop it you two!" Selini demanded.

Continuing as if uninterrupted, Geller stated, "I have powers and abilities to fight against Shamakul, but I am not the right one for the task. Maybe if Selini and I were to fight together we could defeat him, but that's just a maybe. I need much more training."

Jack saw how well Geller could fight and felt nervous by him saying he would need more training. He remembered how powerful Ghowla was and how hard Gubuyis had to fight against him. It made him feel weak and useless just to think of how there was another wizard that was just as powerful coming their way. He concluded in his head that they absolutely needed Gubuyis.

Over the course of the evening, the group discussed different options for battle strategies. Some were absolutely ridiculous, mostly the ones coming from Gink and Fink, and some were not that bad. It seemed as if they were getting somewhere with some of their strategies at times, but then they would be faulted for one reason or another. Eventually, the night got late, and they still had to meet up with the Govilian Council in the morning. So, they headed to bed without coming up with a strong strategy.

Chapter 8: Exhaustive Plans

Once again, Jack awoke to the smell of Geller's delicious bread. His room was lit much like as if the sun were beating in. As usual, he walked over to the window and looked out, hoping for a sunny day. All that greeted him was the normal bustle of the street below and the brightly burning lampposts scattered throughout the underground city. It was a familiar scene and one that somehow comforted him, but he longed for the daylight above.

A slight twinge of fear came over him as he thought about the unavoidable battle that was already coming their way. It was something that he spent all night dreaming about. In fact, he had come up with an idea while he slept. The idea had been churning in his head for hours and it made it difficult for him to sleep.

Jack only spent a few moments at the window before deciding to get ready for the day. He wanted to present his idea to the rest of the group. Normally, Jack's day clothes were folded and ready for him at the foot of his bed. This particular morning, however, they were not there. Just as Jack began looking for something to wear, his door quietly creaked open.

"Ah," Gryan's rough voice called out as he saw Jack up and about in his room. "Captain Jack, I have your clothes ready here. You are up earlier than I expected. My apologies."

Gryan handed Jack his folded clothes and quickly left the room before Jack could respond. Jack knew he was probably up earlier than normal because he was having trouble sleeping, but he didn't think it was that much earlier than normal.

The comforting and familiar sights and smells of the main room were quick to welcome Jack as he entered it. Geller was obviously cooking something, and the fireplace was already fully ablaze. A couple books remained strewn about the table from the night before. The only one other than Jack that looked to be awake was Geller.

"Good morning!" Geller shouted out as Jack entered the main

room. "Would you like some bread to start the day off with? Or, I have some eggs if you'd like some of those. And, I have your favorite from Bolar, some Prunklesnider!"

Eager to have some Prunklesnider to start the day off with, Jack immediately responded, "I'll definitely take some of the Prunklesnider and some bread, please."

Geller wasted no time in pouring a warm glass of the drink and breaking off some bread for Jack. It wasn't very normal for Jack to be one of the first individuals in the main room in the morning.

"Where is everybody?" Jack inquired.

Geller smiled and responded, "Well, you're up a bit earlier than you normally are. I suspect the others will be in here shortly."

The fact that both Gryan and Geller had mentioned his early wakening gave Jack the realization that he must be up quite a bit earlier than normal. He usually got to hear about how late he slept in. The idea that grew in his head and stuck there for most of the night had made its way back to the forefront of his mind.

"I had trouble sleeping," Jack replied. "I came up with an idea while I was sleeping, and I can't seem to unthink it. If it would work, I think we could win the battle."

Geller hadn't forgotten about Jack's last idea about freezing the arbolion tree, Ezjuin. Without hesitation, Geller leaned in to hear what Jack had to say.

"It is risky, though," Jack continued. "It would require us to go out in the cold of winter into Wellwood Forest."

Just as Jack finished his statement, Selini and Anna walked into the main room. It was apparent by the look on Anna's face that they had overheard what he just said. She looked very inquisitive.

"Well, good morning!" Selini exclaimed. "I'm surprised to see you up already."

"Good morning to you, too," Jack replied. "I was having a hard time sleeping so I decided to get up early, I guess."

Unable to hold her thoughts in any longer, Anna questioned Jack immediately, "Why were you talking about going into Wellwood Forest? It's way too dangerous out there for doing that right now."

Without letting her shoot down his idea too soon, Jack responded, "I have an idea." He moved to the table and sat down while he explained himself to the three of them, "It kept me up most of the night. I think it could work if we can manage to find some root of flindishion in the forest. I'm sure there has got to be a way to be able to move the snow out of our way in some fashion."

"Get some of that root of flindishion, eh?" Fink was moseying into the room with Gink in tow and had overheard Jack's comment.

"We are in!" Gink exclaimed. "We could use some root of flindishion in our stores. Plus, if we can get some, we have plans for creating a potion with it!"

"Nobody's 'in'," Geller chimed back into the conversation. "My father would, under no circumstances, let us all risk our lives like this. It is too risky and too close to battle to have us wander off into the dead of winter, in search of a root that may prove to be difficult to find. If I know my father, I'd guess he'd want us to hone our battle skills more in the time that we have rather than trace down a specific magical ingredient."

Fink and Gink looked devastated. Anna was nodding in agreeance with Geller, and Selini was paying more attention to getting something to eat than to what Geller had to say. Jack knew she probably agreed with Geller anyway.

"What's your plan with getting some root of flindishion anyhow?" Geller asked.

That's when Valkog entered the room. He was dressed in much better clothes than the day before. They were clean and were in good repair. He was the tallest in the room and he towered over Selini as he walked by her. He looked well rested, but still a little groggy.

Jack pointed at Valkog and simply stated, "Him. He is the plan."

Before Jack could divulge any more information, there was a knock at the door. Gryan could be heard answering the door and mumbling with someone about something before finally shutting it.

Gryan entered the room and before he spoke, Geller spoke for him, "It is time for us to go to the Panthyun. The Govilian Council is meeting this morning and we would be well to attend."

They were all already prepared for the day, so they did not waste much time gathering miscellaneous items before heading out the door. The walk to the Panthyun took about ten minutes from the house. The whole time was filled with Gink and Fink singing about how they were going to get some root of flindishion. Fink skipped as best as he could with Gink riding on his back. The two seemed very cheerful. Selini would occasionally correct the two of them by interjecting with disapproval at their false sense of giddiness.

Jack wanted to tell them his plan more in depth, but the truth was that even though he felt as if he had a plan it was more of an idea at best. He didn't want to get too in depth in explaining his idea until he had more time to think it over, so he decided not to mention more about it for the moment.

The walk to the Panthyun was filled with street goers going about their daily routines. It didn't take too long for the Valindi to start realizing there was a flindishk walking the streets. It occurred to Jack that this probably happened to him when he was new there, too. Maybe it was even worse for Valkog because of his apparent extinction. Either way, many Valindi temporarily stopped what they were doing just to watch as Valkog walk down the street with them.

As they approached the Panthyun, their view was filled with the presence of Vlagar at the bottom of the grand staircase. He was situated oddly amongst the steps and the street below. Jack recalled how scared he was when he first met Vlagar. Primarily it was because Vlagar was talking about eating him and the others, but also because of his sheer size. His large build and toughened scales gave him a rough but also majestic look.

Gubuyis stood not far from Vlagar. It was obvious the two had just been speaking when they saw the group coming up to them. Gubuyis wore his usual robes of various colors which were sometimes quite odd to Jack. The colors of his robes were at times like patchwork similar to that of a quilt. Today, though, his robes were more formal looking. They had glittery gold and purple stripes around most of the seams and the rest of the robes were comprised of various shades of brown.

Anna expressed her delight in seeing Vlagar, "Vlagar! How are you doing? Are you going to the meeting, too?"

Jack tried thinking where Vlagar would fit in such a space. The Govilian Council room was rather large and could probably fit his large body somewhere at the bottom, but it would be cramped for him for sure. Plus, there wasn't really a good way for Vlagar to get into the building or down the steps in there. Jack did remember, though, that things seemed to change based on the size of the creature. He figured maybe it could work out for Vlagar to attend, but it would look awkward.

"Our dear friend, Vlagar, must take his leave and scout for us again," Gubuyis stated. "It is important for us to get the most updated information as possible before the attack and as we attempt to put together a strategy."

"Before I head back, I plan to return to Wyvergia and inform Zarx'l of what is happening," Vlagar said. "He will need to know everything. He will also need to be informed that we need to amass our Frost Bird army as soon as possible."

"You are a great warrior," Valkog said out of nowhere. "I thank you for all you have done for Jack and the Govilian Alliance."

"It is my pleasure," Vlagar straightened up a little as he spoke. "Without them, we may very well still be struggling through a great drought in our lands. We are all very grateful for their help."

Jack felt like he should add something to what Vlagar had just said, so he stated, "It was our pleasure to inform you of what was going on."

"We wouldn't have done it any other way," Geller interjected. "It was our duty to inform you of such a great calamity."

Vlagar chuckled and responded, "I was sure it had more to do with building an alliance between the two nations! However, with Jack releasing a lake full of water right beneath the great den, we knew you all had the right hearts and minds within yourselves."

"You did what, Jack?" Valkog looked impressed and curious.

"That is a story you must share," Vlagar stated. "I must be going now. Zarx'l awaits my findings and is eager to help however he can."

Gubuyis gave a wave goodbye to Vlagar and he turned and loudly flew away. There really wasn't a way for a Frost Bird to take off quietly as far as Jack could tell. They were so big and their wings pushed so much air that it roared past his ears when he was close to one taking off.

"We must be getting to the Govilian Council room," Gubuyis said as he turned and began walking up the steps.

As they all walked up the steps, Fink got close to Jack and said with a grin on his face, "Make sure ya mention the root o' flindishion idea, Jack. We could really use ... er ... Valkog could really use some o' that them there root!"

The whole group entered the Govilian Council room together. Jack thought they probably looked like a group of misfits, with Gink and Fink the way they were, Valkog's towering height above the others in the group and the fact that he was a flindishk, and Jack and Anna being human and having no magical abilities at all. As he looked around, though, there were creatures of all kinds and his group was nothing much out of the ordinary it seemed, except for Valkog. As they found some seats, Valkog's presence garnered murmurs from other attendees in the room.

Gubuyis let the group find their seats and headed down to the main floor where he usually sat. There was a lone table there. Sometimes there were other delegates or even Geller sitting at the table down on the floor, but this time it was just Gubuyis. The meeting did not seem too formal. Jack figured this was because the meeting was called on such short notice and was more of a preliminary meeting to discuss Shamakul and possible strategies.

With Valkog's presence, the room had gone from light conversations to a dull roar of amazement. After securing his spot on the floor, Gubuyis waited for a brief moment before finally motioning for the room to quiet down.

"My Govilians," Gubuyis addressed the room, "you have been called here today to be updated about the whereabouts of Shamakul."

"I say let him rot where is he," one member of the attendees called out.

"Unfortunately," Gubuyis continued, "he is on the move. He and his forces have been making their way to this great city of Gargantulua. Shamakul is heading this way as we speak. He has amassed a sizeable army and there does not seem to be anything that is stopping him. But he is slowed by the winter weather."

"How is he ferrying an entire army in the dead of winter?" Another voice called out.

Gubuyis spent the next fifteen minutes explaining the weather enchantment large enough to cover an entire army and the protection bubble that would serve to prevent Shamakul's army from taking any damage. He described to the room what he had learned from Vlagar the day before regarding the troops Shamakul employed. The biggest shock to the room seemed to be the fact that Shamakul was moving his forces during winter. Jack wasn't too surprised at this response, though, because most of those in the room belonged to nations that also had to find ways to live outside of winter's reach.

Gubuyis finished explaining by saying, "One purpose of this meeting today is to see if we can begin developing a preliminary strategy. The fight is coming to us, so we cannot avoid it. We must develop a way to defeat Shamakul."

Another voice from the room called out, "What if we use the Frost Birds to freeze the weather bubble?"

Geller responded back, "If we were to utilize the Frost Birds in this manner, we would surely weaken them so much that they would be unable to assist in the remainder of the fight. What I mean to say is, the Frost Birds would nearly exhaust themselves trying to break through an enchantment of that strength and size. If we needed them at any other point during the battle, we would be left in the dark. Plus, we might get through the weather enchantment with them, maybe, but there would still be the protection bubble to get through."

"I think that's where I could come in," Selini said as she stood up. "I have the ability to quickly enchant things into smaller and larger objects. I could enchant rocks to the size of hills above the protection bubble and have them land on it. It would be worth a try, as we will have little in our inventory to destroy such a powerful spell."

Looking exasperated and worried, Geller stood up and looked at her as he spoke, "You would exhaust yourself, too! And, you don't know if it will work. You may spend all your mana on enchantments that may ultimately do nothing. What will you do when we need you to fight? You are too strong to leave you out of the fight. There's gotta be another way to break through that bubble."

Seemingly ignoring Geller's disapproval, someone chimed in from nearby, "You could enchant boulders that we launch from the catapults! Enough of that kind of damage will surely destroy the protection bubble."

"So," Geller said to the room, "let's say we use the Frost Birds to destroy the weather enchantment and likely exhaust their ability to fight with frost. Then, let's say we use Selini here to enchant rocks and boulders to the size of hills to break through the protection bubble. She would almost certainly become magically exhausted in her attempt to do so. How then do we plan to destroy Shamakul?!"

Gubuyis spoke as if continuing for Geller, "He will still be unscathed as will his army while our side will have already lost Selini and the Frost Birds. I may be the one who is needed to defeat Shamakul, but he is quite powerful, and I will need to keep my focus on him. For this reason, I will be unable to assist in the fight against his army. So, we must develop a strategy for fighting his army once the protection bubble is down. I agree that the weather enchantment should also come down as the freezing cold of winter will make it very difficult for his troops to fight."

There was a bout of silence as the room's occupants tried to think up of ways to fight Shamakul's army. It seemed like they had a strategy in place to get to the point where they could actually fight, but no plan yet on how to fight once the battle began.

"I think that settles it," Gubuyis said. "We have a strategy for destroying the weather enchantment and the protection bubble. We will use the Frost Birds to take down the weather enchantment, which will cause a sudden rush of freezing cold air into his army. It will prove very useful once the fight begins if Shamakul's forces can hardly move due to the cold. Then, we will have Selini enchant rocks into boulders the size of hills as they are launched from our catapults. I am sure this will work to destroy the protection bubble. But we will exhaust both the Frost Birds and Selini. It will be up to us to fight his army face to face. During that time, I will need a group of dedicated fighters to help me move my way through into the center of his forces where I can meet Shamakul."

Geller looked saddened and somber as he heard his father agree that Selini should be utilized in such a way that she would become exhausted. Not even Selini seemed too excited about the idea, but she had a look of determination on her face.

"I will fight with you," Geller stated. "And I will gather some of my best fighters to go with us, too."

Fink stood up and Gink sat up straight in his chair, "We will fight with ya, Gubuyis! We're sure ya could use our potions!"

"I might be exhausted by that point, but I can still fight," Selini said. "I will surely go with you! My skills in weaponry are not to be left unused in such a time of need."

Valkog stood up hastily, "I may already be exhausted, but I can still fight as well. I am sure there are ways in which I can assist."

Without saying anything, Jack and Anna stood up at the same time. Jack wanted to be able to help in any way he could, but he wasn't sure just how he'd be able to. He had gotten better at using his blades and felt he could do some damage with them if needed, but he still felt nervous. Jack didn't think Anna should join them, though, since she wasn't too good at close combat. But he felt comforted by her inclusion.

"That settles it," Gubuyis said, "we have the beginnings of a group to assist me as we fight our way to Shamakul himself."

Gubuyis tapped his staff on the floor and a small puff of purple magic expanded outwards in a ring around it.

"We have the beginnings of a plan, it would seem," Gubuyis stated. "If anyone else has an idea for a different or more comprehensive strategy, please speak up now. It is not the time for timidity."

After a few moments of silence, Gubuyis finally motioned that the meeting was adjourned. The group made their way back to the house. Geller was mostly quiet, having looked like he had been defeated. Jack could tell Geller didn't like the idea of Selini becoming magically exhausted. He also didn't seem to like the idea that the Frost Birds would not be as useful after just the beginning of the battle. Jack could also see on Selini's face that she was worried. He wondered if she was worried that the plan wouldn't work, and she would fail at the attempt to break through the protection bubble.

Jack had an idea, but he didn't want to mention it in front of the Govilian Council. He wasn't sure if it would really work and he didn't quite know enough of the details to make it a workable strategy yet. One thing was for sure, though, they needed to come up with a better plan than what they had so far.

Chapter 9: Jack's Idea

Back in the main room of the house, they all sat in front of the fire. Geller didn't look pleased at the outcome of the meeting. It wasn't long before Anna spouted out a question.

"Jack?" she asked. "What was your plan from earlier? You know, the one you said had to do with Valkog."

Jack responded what he had been thinking in regard to his idea, "I have more of an idea than a plan."

"Well, why didn't you mention it in the Govilian Council room?' she inquired.

"I didn't want to just shout out something and have everyone question if it would work when I wasn't so sure myself," Jack said. "But I think it would work. We just need to get the root of flindishion for Valkog here. That is the primary objective of my idea in order to make it a plan. Does anyone want to help me go to Wellwood Forest?"

"I seriously doubt with the fact that Shamakul is already on his way here," Geller contested "that my father will allow such a mission. Especially since time is very limited right now."

"Aha!" Gink shouted out. "We can go without mentioning it to Gubuyis and be back before anyone notices we're any of us gone! I'd certainly love to get my hands on some o' that them there root of flindishion."

Gink was rubbing his hands together and smiling as he spoke. Both Gink and Fink had made it pretty clear that they wanted some of the root for themselves for some reason. Jack knew very little about potion making, so he couldn't even begin to guess as to what they could use it for. Selini was obviously perturbed at Gink's suggestion to go without mentioning it to Gubuyis, and probably even more so that he only cared about getting that ingredient.

"I agree," Fink stated. "I think we could get back before anyone was the wiser!"

"Even if you were allowed to go," Selini spoke up, "I'm too critical a part of the plan with destroying the protection bubble. It wouldn't be wise for me to go at all. What if something went wrong? What if you all got held up for some unknown reason?"

"Well, um," Jack chimed in, "I was thinking that maybe just Valkog and I could go. And before any of you think otherwise, consider this. I am not magical and Valkog is nearly out of mana, so we are both pretty useless in the battle anyway. Even if things did go awry for us, the battle could still go on and you all could still have a victory without the two of us, without noticing a difference by the lack of our presence."

Anna quickly replied back, "If you're going, I'm going. You need all the help you can get. And, you haven't been reading enough about this world to make it out there in the wilderness."

Jack shook his head. He was not reassured that her reading would suffice in a time of need. It was one thing to read about some kind of deadly magical creature and another to actually encounter one. Plus, he thought, bringing her along would just mean another magicless person to watch over.

"You need help, Jack," Anna said responding to his disapproval. "You're not going without me!"

Fink decided to chime in as well, "Obviously, Gink and myself will be going! We need some o' that root for ourselves. Gotta be there ta make sure we get plenty of it."

"Again," Geller replied to the group, "We should not be planning on this. I really think this is a bad idea. Someone is bound to get hurt out there in the middle of winter and there'd be no help from Gargantulua because they'd be preparing for a ... what is it? ... oh yes, a battle! What is it about your idea that makes you want to go so badly, Jack?"

Before Jack could reply, Selini interjected, "It's not just cold and ice out there, you know. There are some creatures that live in the wild in the winter and they would love to find a meal walk right up to them.

Food is scarce out there, so the creatures that do exist are not likely to give you a chance to get away from them. You definitely need someone with magic abilities to go with you. And Gink and Fink there may be good with potions, but I seriously doubt that in their condition they are able to help fight off some dangerous creature if one happens to come your way."

Fink looked shocked and offended at her words but offered no rebuttal. Gink simply smiled and nodded. He looked like he completely agreed with her. However, he also looked as if he still totally expected that they were all going.

Continuing, Selini said to Geller, "You'd have to go with them. You are very powerful and able to fight. They would be lost without you and your knowledge of Wellwood Forest, anyway."

"Eh-hum," Valkog interrupted, "I'm not too sure how we would get to the floor of the forest, but I can sense root of flindishion very easily. Even with there being twenty or more feet of snow, I should have no problem sensing it down to the bottom. I agree, with my ability to find the root, we should be able to be back in no time at all."

Gink and Fink both simultaneously sat upright in their seats.

"We could concoct a warming potion," Fink said looking at Gink. "This way everyone is warm for the trip! Ya wouldn't even notice the cold o' winter."

Geller looked uneasy that they were all seriously considering going to Wellwood Forest. Jack knew Geller wouldn't want to defy Gubuyis. He still felt that only he and Valkog should go to the forest.

"Maybe only Valkog and I go," Jack said trying to reassure Geller. "Gink and Fink can make us various potions, like the warming potion."

"I still do not agree with this plan," Geller said. "There is too much that could go wrong. All that risk just to replenish Valkog's mana seems out of place."

Valkog nodded. It was evident that he was not too sure of the idea behind this plan either.

Geller walked to the hallway and called for Gryan who came fairly quickly.

"Please check on the status of Wellwood Forest, particularly the weather," Geller requested of Gryan.

With that, Gryan left the room and could be heard trotting down the hall. Jack heard a door open and what sounded like a sudden rush of wind. After a moment of the rushing air, the door shut closed again and there was silence. Then, Gryan could be heard walking back down the hall towards the main room. He entered looking more miserable than usual and he was covered in snow.

Gryan spoke in his rough voice, "There has been a storm in Wellwood Forest for several days now, sir. The snow is more than twenty feet deep and is mixed with blowing ice shards."

"Thank you, Gryan." Geller dismissed him. Then, he turned back to the group, "You see? This mission would be doomed from the start."

"Do not forget, though," Gink hollered out, "we can make some warming potions. Ya wouldn't even know it was snowing."

"How long would a warming potion last?" Selini asked. "If I recall correctly, they only last maybe a day."

Both Gink and Fink nodded in agreeance, but they still looked determined.

Jack decided to speak up, "I don't think we'd need any more than a day. Maybe we could find it within a couple of hours and be done with the whole trip altogether. What do you think, Valkog? Is it possible to be back within a day?"

Jack was beginning to get excited as his plan seemed like it might work. He thought of how Valkog could be more useful during the battle if he was able to produce magic.

Nodding, Valkog replied, "I am very capable of finding root of flindishion. But I do agree that a guide who knows the forest well would speed things up."

Valkog was looking at Geller as he spoke his last comment. Jack could see that Valkog would be more willing to go if Geller went. It made sense to Jack. Neither of them really knew the forest well and it would be even harder while it was under so much snow and ice.

"What would we do if it did take more than a day?" Anna asked.

"There's not much to do once those warming potions wear off," Geller responded. "Especially in a storm like that. The cold will overcome you quickly, in a matter of hours with the proper clothing."

Jack knew that all he really needed to do was to convince Geller and he would have Valkog on board with him. Anna seemed as if she was going to go no matter what but might be more willing if Geller went along. He knew Gink and Fink didn't need much convincing. They were dead set on getting some root of flindishion no matter what the weather was like.

"How long is the storm expected to last?" Jack asked. "Maybe we could go once it has died down.?

Selini spoke up, "Time is not your friend, Jack. Shamakul is on his way now and any delay would only prove to disserve you. If you are to go, you will need to go soon. You may not have the luxury of waiting out the storm."

"These kinds of storms," Geller said answering Jack's question, "can last for days to weeks at a time. I still disagree that we should go on this mission. But, if you were to go, now would be the time. There is too little time to waste. Perhaps the most important question here is: What is the benefit of such a mission?"

Jack still didn't have a complete plan based on his idea, but he was sure it would be beneficial no matter what. He hesitated for a few moments so that he could gather some of his thoughts.

"Valkog risked his life to save me," Jack finally said. "I am grateful for that. He has proven to be very powerful and if we can find a way to regenerate his mana, he will be able to assist during battle in ways we couldn't. Instead of focusing on protecting me during the battle, maybe Valkog could focus on keeping Gubuyis safe."

"I am not sure how you would want me to help," Valkog said. "I am here to protect you, Jack. If I focus my efforts on Gubuyis, I might not be able to keep you safe."

"Without Gubuyis," Jack explained, "the battle is lost. We need him to be able to make it to Shamakul. If things are getting too intense, you could create a portal and get Gubuyis away from Shamakul."

Geller looked intrigued, "It's an interesting idea, but what is the use of teleporting my father out of the battle? Shamakul would just be able to keep fighting everyone else and wouldn't be distracted any longer. He would be able to cast the bloodlust spells and maybe even recast his protection spell that we would have fought so hard to destroy."

"Maybe Valkog could cast multiple portals that would teleport Gubuyis in and out of the fight," Jack said. "Every time a spell is cast at Gubuyis, Valkog could teleport him away from where it is heading and then put him behind Shamakul to surprise attack him."

"It sounds like it could work," Geller pondered aloud, "but Valkog would definitely need to be fully charged. I still don't like the idea of going out into Wellwood Forest on such a whim. Like Selini said, time is against us. If anything were to go wrong, we could put our friends in a tight spot without us."

Selini spoke back up, "Although I agree that time is against you, I do fear for the safety of my father. There is so much that he would be expected to do in battle and he always wants to protect everyone else the best he can. It would be nice to be able to provide him with some strong protection and Valkog can do that with his portals. I think you should all go and get this root as fast as you can. Maybe just enough to be prepared for battle."

Gink's eyes had lit up and were wide when Selini mentioned that she thought it was a good idea to go, but he quickly looked disappointed when she mentioned that they might only get enough to work with before heading back home.

"What are you saying, Selini?" Geller asked in surprise.

Selini responded, "I will be magically exhausted before the real battle even begins. Plus, the Frost Birds will likely be exhausted and unable to breathe frost during the battle either. I can fight for sure, but I won't be able to fight using magic to protect father, which will prove very hard to do since everything coming at us will be some form of a spell. It would be of great help if Valkog could help us fight magically. Jack's idea sounds good. If we can get Valkog rejuvenated, we will be able to better protect father."

Jack was starting to feel like his idea was about to happen. It didn't take as much effort to convince the others as he thought it would. He figured that maybe it was just a good idea, or they remembered his last idea with the freezing of Ezjuin. Either way, he was starting to think they might actually go out into Wellwood Forest. That suddenly made him feel a little nervous, as Selini had just spoken about deadly creatures moments before. And the fact that they would have to figure out a way to get to the bottom of twenty or more feet of snow was a daunting thought.

"I agree," Valkog said, "Selini is right. I can provide protection for Gubuyis. I would need the root of flindishion, though. Once replenished, my mana will last for a long time. It is not likely that I would become magically exhausted during a single battle. I guarantee that I can sense the root, even through twenty feet of snow and ice. I can sense it while flying, so this shouldn't be a problem."

Anna questioned the group, "Let's say we do find this root of flindishion. How would we get to it? Won't it be under a bunch of snow? Are we supposed to dig it out?"

Jack felt a little relieved that she asked the question he was thinking. There had to be some way they would plan on getting to the bottom of twenty feet of snow, and he was hoping it wasn't going to be just by digging.

"I've got just the potion for ya!" Fink shouted out. "It's a melting potion good for somethin' just like this. Once we pour it out, it'll be just like as if we poured out a very large cauldron of lava. It'll be almost instantaneous!"

Jack smiled at Fink's enthusiasm. Although he knew both Gink and Fink were mostly in it for their own purposes, he felt as though they would be useful to have along on the trip.

"Yeah," Gink chimed in, "it would just be up ta Valkog ta tell us where ta pour it!"

Shaking his head, Geller said, "I don't see how you all will be able to get along without me. I know the forest very well. And I can provide some magical assistance, too. I only say this because I feel like it is necessary, I will go with you. But know this, I still disagree that this plan should even be executed in the first place. There is so much that could go wrong and so little time to act if it does go wrong."

They all sat there for a moment in silence as the mission sounded like it was a go. Eventually, they confirmed with each other what roles they would play. Gink and Fink reassured them that they could make enough warming potions by morning for the lot of them. Jack could tell Valkog was almost delighted that he would have his magic back.

After a while, Geller instructed Gryan to gather their warmest clothes for a trip into Wellwood Forest. Gryan looked astonished and had to be told again before leaving the room.

"When do we leave, then?" Anna asked.

"Once we have the warming potions ready," Geller replied, "we should go immediately. We cannot waste much time on this mission, and we cannot delay going. If the warming potions weren't such a vital part of this plan, I'd say we should leave now. The sooner the better. So, we shall leave in the morning."

Selini looked saddened, "I am sorry I will not be able to go with you all. But, if something were to happen that held us up, the battle might be lost without me there. I look forward to the success of your mission, though, as I firmly believe that we will be in a better position with Valkog fully recharged."

Anna got up and walked over to Selini and gave her a hug. Geller was now chatting with Gink and Fink, presumably about potions. Jack looked at Valkog and smiled. He was sure this idea would work. He figured to himself that if he made it all the way to Wyvergia while someone was trying to kill him, he could easily go out into the forest in the winter and search for a root.

Valkog looked at Jack and smiled back. Jack wanted to hug Valkog, but he didn't know if that would be something he'd appreciate. He had only just met him the day before. It hit him, though, that he had so much to actually talk to Valkog about. There were the stories of his own parents and the stories of what happened after the dragons attacked in the cavern and Valkog lost him.

Although he wanted to know more about his parents, Jack decided to fill Valkog in on the story of his trip to Wyvergia and the battle at Ezjuin. They talked for a great deal of time throughout the rest of the day about this. They were interrupted on numerous occasions by someone wanting to confirm something about their upcoming trip. Fink came up to Valkog at one point and pulled out a magical tape measure that measured Valkog's size. Apparently, he needed to know how much potion to make for him.

Eventually, they all made it to bed for the night. Jack was incredibly excited and nervous for the upcoming day. He felt bad that they weren't telling Gubuyis about it, but he knew in his heart that this was needed to protect Gubuyis. He drifted off to sleep while watching the flickering street lights outside of his window.

Chapter 10: Wellwood Forest

Anxious about his plan to go to Wellwood Forest, Jack awoke early once again. He got out of bed and looked at the street below his window. His clothes were already laid out for him at the foot of his bed. They were warmer clothes, much warmer clothes. His heart nearly skipped a beat as he thought of their plan for the day.

Jack got dressed for the day remembering his conversation with Valkog the night before. Valkog seemed very impressed by Jack's idea on how to give the Frost Birds plenty of water to last for some time. He also seemed impressed by the idea Jack had about freezing Ezjuin in order to defeat Ghowla's forces. Valkog had even asked about his ability to wield more than one weapon at a time. He was as perplexed as Gubuyis and wanted to know more on how Jack could do that. Jack didn't have any answer to offer, though, as he was not well versed in magic and magical things.

Without hesitation, Jack finished getting dressed and headed straight for the main room. He figured he might be the first one in there since he had awakened so early. When he entered the main room, Geller and Selini were already sitting near the fire. They were discussing something when they noticed Jack enter the room.

"Jack!" Selini shouted out with delight. "Good morning to you."

"Good morning," Jack responded, a little surprised that he wasn't the first one in the room.

Geller got up from the table and headed over to the kitchen counter. He broke off a piece of bread for Jack and handed it to him. The bread felt intensely warm and was darker than his usual spiced bread.

"Eat," Geller instructed Jack. "It is a special warming bread. It'll help to keep you warm on our trip."

Jack was confused. He thought they were going to be taking warming potions for the trip. He took a bite and it tasted wonderful, like eating a sweet butter roll right out of the oven at the bakery back home. His fingers immediately started to feel much warmer than normal, then his toes and feet. Soon, his whole body felt like he was sitting in a cozy hot bath, and he felt suddenly relaxed.

Noticing Jack's confused look, Geller clarified for him by explaining, "You'll still be taking a warming potion, of course. This bread will make you feel warm for just a little while, but it won't stand up to the test of a heavy winter storm. It should provide us a little extra time, though, before we have to take the warming potions."

From behind Jack, there were the sounds of footsteps. It was Anna entering the main room. She looked anxious. Without even acknowledging the others, she went straight for the bread on the counter and broke off a piece. She quickly began eating and then stopped for a moment and looked at the bread as if studying it. She gave a brief smile as the warmth filled her body.

"Good morning," Selini called over to Anna. "I see you've already found the warming bread."

She looked just as confused as Jack did at first.

"We're still going to be taking warming potions, too," Jack explained to her.

"I'm not eating this too soon, am I?" she asked while holding out the bread in her hand.

"Eat up," Geller told her. "It will last for some time before we find the need to take the warming potions. Once we get into the winter storm, though, it will wear off faster than it normally does. Jack is right, we will still need to take the warming potions when this wears off."

"Whew," she replied, "I was scared that I ate it too soon. Good morning, Selini. Good morning you two."

"Why do you look so concerned?" Jack asked her.

Anna walked over to the table and sat down.

A worried look came over her as she began to reply, "What if something does go wrong? It will just be us out there in the dead of winter in the freezing cold. Nobody will be coming to our aid if we need it. Everyone will be too busy prepping for battle."

Selini reached her hand over and gently placed it over Anna's hand as if to comfort her. It looked like Selini was going to talk but she just sat there for a moment in silence. Anna looked up at her and smiled, but it was obvious there was still concern in her face.

"Remember," Selini started, "Geller is an expert in navigating through Wellwood Forest. He knows it very well and can guide you through it, even with all the snow and ice covering it. And, Valkog has a very strong sense that can detect the root of flindishion from far away, even through the snow. The only thing that will likely delay you is finding the root itself."

Geller walked over and chimed in, "That's right, Anna. We won't get lost with my knowledge of the forest, and it won't take long to find the root with Valkog at our side. Once we find it, we will use the melting potion to get quickly to the forest floor. Then, we'll be on our way!"

Fink and Gink entered the room. They looked very happy. Fink walked over to the counter to grab some bread for himself and Gink. While he did that, Gink pulled a small wooden box out of one of his many pockets and set it on the counter.

With his mouth full of bread, Fink turned to the group and said, "Good morning to the lot of ya! I couldn't help but overhear that you are a bit nervous, Anna. Well, even though Selini here forgot ta mention us two, we will be there right by yer side to help with potions!"

Jack pointed at the small wooden box that Gink had just set on the counter and asked, "What is that?"

Gink smiled one of his big ear to ear kind of smiles and responded, "We worked late into the night ta concoct these little fellas." He flicked with his finger one of several small vials sticking out of the top of the box.

"Are those the warming potions?' Anna asked.

"Right ya are!" Fink replied. "And they won't take long ta kick in, so it'd be wise if ya'll waited as long as ya can before taking one."

Gink held up his piece of bread, "This is nice! I like this very much!"

"You like it, eh?" Geller asked, surprised. "I figured it'd be a nice addition to our trip. It might help stave off the need for the warming potion for just a little while."

"How will we know when's the right time to take the potion?" Jack asked.

"Oh," Selini called over from the table. "You'll definitely know. You do know when you're cold, right?"

"Well, yes," Jack stated, "I just don't want to take it too soon, that's all."

Geller walked up to the wooden box and grabbed a vial from it. Fink quickly corrected him and pointed to another vial that appeared to be made specifically for him. Geller took that vial and stowed it in a pocket on his chest. Taking Geller's cue, Jack and Anna also both retrieved a vial each for themselves that was pointed out by Fink. Jack's hand was already warm from the warming bread made by Geller, but this vial of potion felt incredibly warm in his hand. He put it in his pants pocket.

Valkog walked into the main room. He looked cheery, but uncomfortable. The clothes he wore were much heavier than the day before. Gryan had made him special clothes for the trip, but apparently Valkog did not like how restrictive they were on his body.

"It is a good morning!" Valkog exclaimed as he walked over to the counter to retrieve some bread. "I very much look forward to a successful mission today."

As he grabbed some of the bread, he noticed the small wooden box with a single vial of warming potion in it. It was about double the size of Jack's vial. Valkog must have recognized what it was immediately, because he grabbed the vial and held it in his hand for a brief moment before looking for a pocket to put it in.

"Remember," Gink said to Valkog, "take it only once the time comes and ya find yerself needin' it."

Valkog took a bite of the bread and looked at Geller and said, "Oh, this is just delightful."

Geller smiled. It was quite common for others to enjoy Geller's food preparations. He was very good at enchanting food to taste in ways that even the most skilled bakers and chefs could only desire to do.

Looking around the room as if he were making sure he wasn't forgetting something, Geller said to the group, "We should be going as soon as possible. We don't want ..."

There was a loud, interrupting knock at the door. Gryan could be heard answering it and then heading down the hall to the main room.

"Sir," Gryan addressed Geller, "that was a messenger of Gubuyis. He requests your presence in his study at this very hour."

Geller looked shocked! Jack wondered if Gubuyis knew what they were up to or if this had something to do with Shamakul. He then wondered if it had something to do with Jack, since Gubuyis had said he was going to read more about how Jack had the ability to wield two enchanted weapons at the same time. There was no way possible, Jack thought, that Gubuyis could know about their plans for the day.

"Well," Geller said slowly, "I guess we've got a little meeting to go to first. We should not keep father waiting. If we hurry, we can still make good time on our mission."

Everyone including Selini headed for the Panthyun. The streets were busier than normal and Jack knew the city was preparing for battle. The blacksmith's shop near the house seemed louder too. He could hear clinks and clanks of metal against metal in rapid bursts. The group was slowed down on their path to the Panthyun by all the busyness of the street. Several times a cart would block their way and they would have to either squeeze by it or wait until it passed.

They headed straight for the library when they got to the Panthyun. The trip down the long halls and the hidden doors was becoming very familiar to Jack. He observed the flindishk statues more intently than before. It was intriguing to him that there was probably a story behind each one of them. Maybe, he thought, the statues were of those who helped design and build the Panthyun. It wasn't long before they found themselves at the door of the library.

They entered the room casually. It was unclear as to what the meeting was about, so they decided not to mention their plans for the day. Jack quickly saw Gubuyis sitting in his chair behind his desk. He was studying a leather map of what looked like the cavern opening. Jack figured Gubuyis was studying the battleground. The map was much like the one they studied before heading to the battle at Ezjuin. It looked lightly animated in areas and there was a snowstorm crossing almost all of it.

As the group entered, Gubuyis looked up and smiled. His eyes quickly scanned over each of them and their clothes. Jack realized they were still wearing the heavy clothes they planned to go out in.

"I haven't been out today," Gubuyis stated, "but perhaps it is a bit colder out there than usual?"

He motioned to what they were wearing. Then, he looked at Selini and seemed confused as she was not wearing a heavy set of clothes. Jack felt foolish. He began to think that they should have just mentioned their plans to Gubuyis in the first place.

"What do you think of the strategy we came up with yesterday?" Gubuyis asked the group.

Geller stepped forward and replied, "I am uncomfortable with exhausting Selini and the Frost Birds before the battle has even started. I am confident that we will win the battle. It would just be better to have Selini able to fight magically by our sides for the duration of the battle."

"I am ready, and I know we will win," Selini said. "We still need a strategy for the actual battle, though."

Valkog looked saddened as he spoke, "I am disheartened that I will not be much use during the battle. I know I could be very useful if only I had my mana back."

"My friend," Gubuyis said to Valkog, "do not fret. There will be a time and place where you will be of great assistance. As for you, Jack and Anna, do you have any thoughts on our plans from yesterday?"

Jack was surprised that they were being asked this question. There was very little they could do to help in battle, he thought. Without being magical, Jack couldn't see any reason his opinion would matter. Anna, on the other hand, must have been waiting to be asked because she quickly answered the question.

"I also don't like that Selini will be drained of her mana," Anna responded. "What if she is needed later in the battle? Also, I don't like the idea of depleting the Frost Birds of their ability to breathe frost. Will that hurt them? What if we need them later, too?"

"I assure you," Gubuyis replied back, "the Frost Birds will not be hurt from the action to destroy the weather enchantment. Unfortunately, we have not come up with an alternative plan to destroy both the weather enchantment and the protection bubble. If any of you that think there might be another way, please speak."

"Well," Anna quickly answered, "we don't have another idea for how to destroy the weather enchantment or the protection bubble, but we do have another idea that could prove very helpful during battle."

"I wonder," Gubuyis said aloud to no one in particular, "if your attire is indicative of an intent to travel somewhere very cold."

Gubuyis picked up his staff and lightly tapped the slowly spinning, floating globe above his desk. It spun quickly until it got to a certain spot. It then stopped and a portion of the globe enlarged in front of itself. Jack couldn't tell at first what the map was presenting, but Geller recognized it well.

"Wellwood Forest," Geller whispered.

Jack could see there was an indication of the weather above the map. It was a fierce looking snowstorm. The ground was all white and the trees looked bare. As he saw the strong storm, Jack felt a sense of unease. It was right where they were planning on going and it looked miserable.

"Perhaps," Gubuyis asked aloud, "your group is planning on going to Wellwood Forest? From the looks of it, maybe even soon."

Geller asked, "Why would you think that?"

Gubuyis laughed and pointed at the clothes they were each wearing, "Maybe I'm guessing, maybe. Or, perhaps I've been clued in by the 'borrowing' of some essence of fire breath from the royal storehouse."

Both Gink and Fink laughed nervously.

Selini looked furiously towards the two of them and said, "I thought you two said you had all the ingredients you needed."

Pointing at Valkog, Fink quickly replied, "We just needed a little extra fer the big guy here."

"Might I ask what your plans are this day?" Gubuyis inquired of the group.

Anna opened her mouth as if she were about to say something, but stopped. She looked at Jack. Jack figured it was already too late not to explain his idea to Gubuyis. It seemed like Gubuyis already knew what the plan was anyway, or at least he seemed to know where they were headed.

Jack began to explain, "I think if we can quickly go to Wellwood Forest and find some root of flindishion for Valkog, we can regenerate his mana and he could be useful in battle. Since Selini and the Frost

Birds will be unable to fight magically, I think it would be very important for us to be able to provide more protection for you, sir. With mana, Valkog could make portals that move you in and out of battle."

Jack had spoken quickly as he was nervous and unsure if his plan would be well received. Geller had picked up where Jack left off and explained their plan to go to Wellwood Forest to find the root. He assured Gubuyis that Valkog could easily detect the root and that he himself could navigate the group around the forest, despite the storm and snow.

After some explaining from the group, Gubuyis finally replied back, "I agree that this plan sounds useful. However, we just don't have the time to dispense. If anything were to go wrong, we would be out some strong fighters."

Geller spoke again, "I think all we need is a day at most. Remember, I know the forest and Valkog will find the root. We could be back by dinnertime."

"I will need some time to deliberate," Gubuyis responded. "For now, please return to your home."

The group headed back to the house. For the most part, they didn't really speak on their walk home. There was the occasional "I told you so" from Geller. Jack paid more attention to his own foggy breath in the darkness of their walk than to the others. He was lost in his own thoughts. His idea seemed like a great one and he was sure it would work if they could just go as soon as possible. The warmth of his body from the warming bread was still going strong. He was feeling like the time to go was now when they had everything ready. Jack wondered if Gubuyis had figured out their plan from the missing essence of fire breath, or if there was some other way he found out. It wasn't really that big of a deal to Jack that Gubuyis found out, but he didn't want to get stuck not going on the quick trip to Wellwood Forest.

When they returned to the house, everyone quickly shuffled in. Jack took off his coat. The walk home had made him even warmer and getting into the house out of the cool cavern air was stifling. Everyone looked somber like they had just been given bad news. Jack felt the warmth of his warming potion in his pocket. He shook his head in disappointment that they were not likely going anywhere.

The silence was broken by Selini who said, "I was nervous about this idea from the beginning. Don't get me wrong, Jack, I think it's a good idea, but it just comes at such a horrible time."

"You were the one that told me I should go," Geller said. "I repeatedly stated that we should not go because father would not be likely to offer his blessings for such a mission at this time. If anyone was nervous about this idea from the beginning, it was me. I feel awful that we didn't include father from the beginning."

Knowing that his plan was likely to be canceled at this point, Jack began to wonder to himself about his original plan. He had first planned to just go with Valkog and the two of them could search out the root themselves. He was sure 'that plan' was much more viable than bringing everyone else along anyway. They could all be used in battle, even if Valkog and Jack got caught up on their mission and couldn't get back in time. There was no way they were going to be missed in battle.

Speaking up, Jack said, "I still feel like Valkog and I could go alone. We're not useful right now anyway, but if we succeed then Valkog could be very helpful. If we don't succeed, then there's no difference anyway."

"I disagree," Anna spoke out. "If you could go, then I would go, too. I just don't think you are well enough prepared to go out in the wild. I've been reading and studying ever since we first got here. I can be helpful, and if I weren't able to fight in battle either, I wouldn't be missed since I can't fight magically."

Fink chimed in immediately after Anna, "We need ta go, too! What if ya need a potion? Plus, we really want some o' that root. I trust ya'll would bring us back some, of course, but it is better for us to be there to retrieve it ourselves."

"There you all are," Selini said sounding a little upset, "back at it again. You are trying to plan the smallest mission you can and yet the group size keeps growing. We just need to wait for father's word and see what he has to say about it."

Jack realized that his efforts to do a small mission were futile. No matter what he would have to say about going alone with Valkog, someone was bound to say they needed to go along as well. If anyone else was going to go, he thought, it would be Geller. Jack would feel much better if someone with great powers and knowledge of the forest was with them.

Saddened, Valkog responded, "I don't like being powerless to help my friends who are in need. I have sworn to protect Jack and without mana, that may prove difficult. Of course, I want to be able to assist in any way I can during battle, too."

"That time will come," Selini said trying to reassure Valkog. "One day you will have your mana back, and your abilities will come in great use for everyone here."

"That time is now," Valkog responded. "I should be helpful now! This mission of Jack's is good and I know I can find the root quickly. My senses have not gone dull over these past years. They are as sharp as a needle, and I am in dire need of the root of flindishion. Maybe, did either one of you," he looked at both Gink and Fink, "see some of the root in the storehouse while you were in there?"

Gink replied back, "I ain't seen any in there. Trust me, I looked for my own sake."

Gryan walked into the room and approached Geller who was sitting at the table. He whispered into Geller's ear for a few moments before finally leaving the room again. Everyone watched Geller. They all knew it had to be the message from Gubuyis.

Geller stayed somber for a moment, leading Jack to believe they were disallowed from going on their planned mission to find the root of flindishion. Then, after a moment, Geller stood up and walked over to his bag and grabbed it before turning to the group.

"We have been given permission to go!" Geller finally said with the look of excitement filling his face. "We only have one day max, after which point we are to return home regardless of whether we have found the root or not. Obviously, that means we are to leave immediately for the sake of having as much time during the day as possible. The mission is to be kept a secret in case there are any spies in the ranks."

Geller began to lightly pack his bag. Valkog followed suit and left the main room to go grab his bag and pack for the upcoming day. Jack was still trying to grasp what had just happened; the mission was a go. Gubuyis must have believed the plan was a good idea, he thought. It made Jack feel a little uneasy, though, that there was the possibility of spies in the ranks of the Govilian army. He remembered how he had been in danger before, because of a similar situation, and felt nervous that someone or something might try to hurt him again.

Gryan came into the main room with a bag each for Jack and Anna. They were already packed for them, which made Jack feel better. He was not sure what he would need and he was positive, despite her readings, that Anna did not know what she needed either. Valkog returned to the main room with his bag. Gink and Fink looked as if they had been prepared from the moment they woke up. They didn't really carry a bag. They had tons of magically enchanted pockets in their clothes that gave them plenty of storage space. Within minutes of getting the news that they could proceed, they were ready to go.

Selini had already left the room and was waiting by the door in the hallway that led to the heart of Wellwood Forest. She stood there anxiously awaiting the group. Jack and Anna had been closest to the door of the main room and hadn't needed to pack, so they were the first ones to arrive at the door.

"Won't the door be blocked by snow?" Jack asked Selini.

Selini simply smiled and responded by opening the door. It opened to a ferocious windy snowstorm. Jack remembered the door having been at the bottom of the tree when he had opened it before, but this time the door opened much higher up in the tree. She closed the door immediately. Jack and Anna had gotten to see a sneak preview of what they were about to get into. Jack still felt warm from the bread, but he put on his coat as he prepared to walk into the storm.

"I hope we find that root fast," Anna said, sounding worried after seeing the treacherous environment they were about to go into.

Valkog came trotting down the hall as he clumsily adjusted to wearing a bag on his back. As he came up to the doorway, it grew larger in size in order to fit him through the opening. Only a moment later Fink came skipping down the hall with Gink in tow. They were both, obviously, very happy to be going on this mission.

"Where's your bag?" Anna asked them.

"We have very large pockets," Gink sang out in a weird tune.

It was apparent that both Gink and Fink were delighted, even gleeful, that this mission was indeed happening.

Finally, Geller walked down the hall with his medium-sized bag strapped to his back. It was fairly large for his build, but much smaller than what Jack had seen him carry on their previous venture.

"This is much lighter than our trip to Wyvergia," Geller stated as he approached the group. "I only had to pack for one day!"

Selini opened the door to Wellwood Forest. As they reluctantly began to step forward and into the raging storm on the other side, she gave them each a hug.

"Remember," Selini stated, "you have only one day. You cannot waste time. No matter what, you must return by this time tomorrow if not sooner."

With that, they each one stepped into the forest and were immediately greeted with the pounding force of snow and ice driven by immense winds. There was no sun, all was white and grey.

Chapter 11: Not Alone

For a brief few moments, they all struggled to find their bearings in the wind and snow. The sudden change of environment made for a confusing mess of thoughts. Jack saw Geller pull out his wand shortly after the doorway was closed. The door slowly disappeared into the tree until it was completely gone. Curiously, it wasn't the snow and wind that made it disappear. Jack felt a small sense of nervousness overcome him as he watched the door fade away.

Geller used his wand to create an air shield in front of him in order to see better. It wasn't very big and only really blocked a small area. But, it was quite effective at blocking the wind and snow coming at him. Jack tried to position himself behind Geller to get a reprieve from the blasting winds.

Jack looked at the others and noticed Fink and Gink had sunken into the snow a bit. Anna was already expressing a look of discomfort in the cold and wind. Valkog looked out of place. His height put him much higher than any of the others, and the wind was hitting his face full force. He attempted to block the wind on his face by using one of his wings, but he was having problems with how his bag was fastened to his back which prevented him from being able to do so.

Gink and Fink certainly looked warm, though. They wore numerous coats that Jack knew had to have tons of pockets. The wind was driving the cold between the fibers of Jack's clothes and coat. He still felt warm from the warming bread, but he knew it wouldn't be long before he was going to need his warming potion. He could tell Anna was feeling the same way, as she was already shivering. Valkog looked cold almost immediately from the moment they arrived in the forest. His thin skin and light fur did not appear to be adequate for helping him adapt to winter weather of any sort.

The sudden rush of freezing cold wind was already starting to overcome the warming bread's effects. Jack reached into his pocket that held the warming potion and grabbed it. It felt wonderful to his fingertips as they surrounded the vial. He started to lift it out of his pocket when he noticed Anna giving him a look that said not to mess with it yet. He let it drop back into his pocket.

"We have to wait as long as we can!" Anna shouted over the wind to Jack.

Jack nodded in agreement but did not reply back. As he thought about it, he realized he definitely felt warmer than he should for the environment they were in. The warming bread was working, at least for now.

After the door faded away, Geller began to look around the area some. It was not clear to Jack what he was looking for, but it seemed as if Geller was getting a feel for where they were. Everything was white or some shade of grey. The sky melded into the ground with the help of the storm. They were all clearly well above the ground as they were in a forest of branches all around them. It appeared the tops of all the trees were where their path was going to be.

Seeing the door disappear into the tree, Anna shouted to Geller, "How will we know where to come to?"

Geller motioned for all the others to come in close so he could explain the plan to them. "The door will be nearly impossible to find in this storm," he said. "So, we will plan on using a portal summoned by Valkog here to get back home."

Alarmed, Anna then asked, "What if we don't find this root of flindishion? How will we get back home then?"

"That's still not a problem," Geller reassured her. "If we don't find the root in enough time, Valkog can simply carry the lot of us back to Gargantulua by way of flight."

Everyone looked at Valkog as if to ask if he was okay with that. Valkog simply nodded and smiled. Jack was sure Valkog's face was nearly frozen.

"Are you going to be able to see where you're going in this storm?" Jack asked, slightly concerned that these details were not discussed earlier with the whole group.

Valkog replied back loudly over the rushing wind, "I can fly back there with my eyes closed. I have unique navigation senses that allow me to know very easily where I'm going. In fact, that is most likely the way we will be returning home."

Geller stood up straight and looked content with the plan. He then began looking around once more and stopped in his steps as he looked in one particular direction.

"This way!" Geller hollered back to the group.

Jack noticed Geller situating his cap all the way on. Anna followed suit and motioned for Jack to do the same. Once he did, he realized he could hear everyone in the group with ease. He had forgotten about the enchanted headpieces that allowed communication between members of the group. This not only allowed him to hear everyone easier, but it deadened out the loud howl of the wind rushing by his ears.

They all walked for a while through twisted treetops and heavy snow. Jack was beginning to feel the cold creep over him as the warming bread was wearing off. He kept a hold of the warming potion in his pocket to keep his one hand warm. Every so often, he would move the potion to his other pocket so that he could also warm the other hand. It wasn't very long before Jack began to wonder if he should drink his potion. He wondered if maybe the others were able to stay warmer longer than he was.

Trying to keep the cold out of his thoughts, Jack looked around for something to distract him. He was surrounded by white snow and the daunting grey of the storm, but in contrast, there were some things that stood out from everything else. Those were the treetops they were navigating through. The snow must have been at least twenty feet deep, maybe even deeper. All that was left of the trees were the tops of them. There were tens of thousands of branches covered in ice swaying in the wind. As they swayed, they collided with each other making a wonderous sound similar to what Jack could only think of as a crystal chandelier clinking together in a breeze.

"We're nice n' toasty," Gink said to Jack.

Jack looked over to Fink and Gink, who looked like they weren't bothered by the cold at all. He wondered if they had already taken the potions, or was it just that they were so close together that had something to do with it. In any event, Jack's thoughts were now back on the cold. It was easy to focus on it, though, as it was a hard and sudden cold that kept driving itself into the fabric of his clothing covering his body.

"How will we ever find anything out here?" Anna asked nobody in particular.

"I assure you," Valkog replied, "I can sense the root quite easily. I have no worries, and we won't miss the chance when it comes our way."

Geller spoke up, "We have everything we need to get this done fast. All we need to do is walk around some until Valkog senses the root. Then, the rest is easy."

"Um," Gink chimed in, "I may have forgotten the melting potion."

Everyone stopped in their tracks and looked at both Gink and Fink, particularly Fink. They were hoping he had grabbed it instead. After all, they were 'potion masters' and should definitely be the ones in charge of making sure they had the potions needed, Jack thought.

Fink started laughing. His laugh appeared to Jack to be as if Fink was accepting the fact that they didn't have it. Geller looked annoyed but Valkog started laughing as well. Jack looked back from the direction they came from. He was not sure what it was he was looking for, maybe the route back to the tree they came from? There was nothing but a disappointing view of white and grey mingled with glassy looking branches.

"Well," Valkog finally said, "we'll just have to dig. It will slow us down some, but we're still okay."

"Just kidding!" Gink shouted out. "I only said I *may* have forgotten it."

Upset and annoyed, Geller said, "You're lucky Selini isn't here to listen to such a dumb joke."

They all began walking forward again. Gink and Fink began to sing out loud like they always did. Their songs usually had to do with stories of their past. The words rarely made sense together and the tunes were even worse. Jack had gotten used to listening to the two of them singing all the time, but occasionally, it was difficult to listen to.

"How does this sense thing work?" Anna asked Valkog as they marched on. "Will there be a sign for all of us to see?"

"You mean like my ears perking up?" Valkog asked with a smile.

Anna immediately lit up and said, "Yes! Something like that!"

Valkog replied back, "It won't work like that, I'm afraid. I will just sort of know when we get close. It will be similar to if you were to smell something as you got closer to it. As we get closer, my sense will let me know by becoming stronger."

Anna looked disappointed at Valkog's remarks. It appeared as if she wanted some outwardly sign from him that she could watch for.

"I could make ya a potion that will let ya sense the root," Fink said to her. "Buuut, it requires some root of flindishion. So, that's not happening."

Anna's face was contorted in a confused look as she grappled with what Fink had just told her. Jack could tell she was trying to make sense of why Fink would even mention it to begin with. It wasn't uncommon for Gink or Fink to do this, though. They were pretty intent on acting or being senseless most of the time. Jack smirked as he watched Anna's confusion.

After nearly more than an hour of walking, the group was stopped by Geller. He reached into his pocket and pulled out his warming potion. His hands were shaking from the cold.

"At this time, you may all want to take your warming potions," Geller suggested through chattering teeth.

Jack noticed that the warming bread's effects had indeed worn off some time ago. He was very uncomfortable, and his fingers and toes were hurting. He had not used his potion yet because he was unsure of when the best time would be. Although, the thought had occurred to him several times in the last fifteen minutes or so.

"The wind is picking up," Geller continued. "It's only going to get colder from this point on."

Jack's eyes opened wide at this news. It was already too cold and trekking through the snow was nearly unbearable on his legs and feet. He hurriedly took out his potion and waited for someone else to take theirs first. He wasn't sure what to expect and wanted to see how the others reacted to it before he took his. Anna also quickly pulled out her vial of warming potion. She was finally just as eager to take it as well.

After only a brief moment, Geller took his vial of warming potion as if he had done it before. It only took a second before his face turned a bright, glowing orange. This same effect happened to his hands and feet. His whole body was glowing orange. Geller shuttered as the orange glow began to subside. He smiled and motioned for the others to take theirs.

"Ahhhh!" Gink said while celebrating with Fink. "We made it right this time!"

The two of them pulled out their potions and drank them. They reacted in much the same way as Geller. Their faces turned orange, then their hands and feet, and then their whole bodies. Within a moment, they too shuttered.

Together, the remaining others in the group raised their vials like drink glasses and then drank them in unison. Valkog turned orange all over, but his shiver and shutter resulted in a small burst of orange flames that shot out from the tips of his wings.

When Jack took his, he instantly shuttered at the taste. To him, it tasted as if it was made from rotten pumpkins. He turned orange all over as well, but for a little while longer than the others. A welcome warmth soon came over him. He felt pleasantly cozy now, as if he had just gotten into a hot bath. He was somewhat relaxed by this new feeling. It almost felt like the clothes he was wearing were too warm now that he had the potion in him.

"How long do you think this will last?" Anna asked.

Gink replied back to her as the group began walking again, "This should last most of the day, I would expect. It really depends on how cold it starts gettin'."

Jack appreciated the warmth against the starkness of the cold that insisted on trying its best to hinder his every move. He was very relieved that he wasn't going to have to experience the cold from this point on.

Geller seemed like he knew where he was going. He walked with intent and made deliberate turns every so often. Jack felt like they were actually heading somewhere specific.

"You seem to know where you're going," Jack said to Geller. "Are we going somewhere in particular?"

"Just one more snow hill to go!" Fink shouted out.

Valkog laughed. There were endless hills of snow in every direction. Jack knew Fink had no clue where they were or where they were going, and Anna looked annoyed at Fink's remark. Jack could tell she was getting impatient. It had already been a couple of hours since they started out and it didn't look like they were close to being 'somewhere specific.'

Geller replied to Jack, "I am heading for a clearing in the forest. It is more likely that we will find the root there than in the middle of the forest. It is a plant that typically needs more sunlight during the summer months when it grows. So, a clearing makes the most sense."

"What does the root look like?" Anna inquired.

Valkog responded, "It is a fairly plain looking root. It is light brown and looks somewhat dusty because it is covered in little hairs."

"So, when we find this root, do you just eat it and your mana regenerates?" Anna asked. "Or do you have to stew it up or something like that?"

Valkog chuckled at Anna's inquiry.

"There's a little bit of a process involved," Valkog explained. "It will need to be fermented somewhat before it's brewed into a sort of stew, as you will. This is particularly why we will be flying back home instead of me summoning a portal. Most likely, I won't have enough time to ferment the mixture before making it into its final product."

Without missing a beat, Anna asked, "How much of this root do we need?"

It just occurred to Jack that he never asked that question. Now he wondered, if they did find some, would it be enough or would they have to keep searching for more throughout the day? It was already a little discouraging that Valkog had not even once mentioned that he felt like they were close to some.

"Well," Valkog answered, "I would say I need roughly fifteen pounds of it to fully rejuvenate my mana. Plus, of course, any extra needed for Mr. Gink and Mr. Fink there."

Anna's eyes opened wide in panic! She looked at Jack for some kind of reassurance, but he had none to give her. He too was feeling like the amount of root needed seemed like a lot.

"Where are we going to find that much root?" Anna asked out loud for everyone to hear. "We've already been walking for quite some time. We're wasting the day as we speak!"

Jack replied back, trying to reassure her in any way he could, "I have a feeling this root isn't as small as a carrot."

Jack hoped he was right. Otherwise, he hoped that they would find a lot of it in the same place and not have to search all day in other areas for smaller amounts.

"A single root," Fink chimed in, "can weigh up ta fifty pounds!

There's no reason to fret."

"Are most roots nearly fifty pounds?" Anna asked Fink.

"Well, no," he replied. "They're typically more like ten to twenty pounds."

A sense of ease came over Jack at hearing those words. Even if they could only find one root, it sounded like it would cover most of what Valkog needed. Jack figured Valkog didn't need to be 'fully recharged' in order to fight in battle, but he wasn't sure.

"Will you need to have the full fifteen pounds?" Jack asked Valkog. "In order for you to be able to fight, I mean?"

Reassuring both Anna and Jack, Valkog replied back, "I guess not. But it would sure be nice to be fully recharged."

"We're hopin' ta find a fifty pounder!" Gink exclaimed. "That way there's extra left over for us."

Gink was nudging Fink and they both had big smiles on their faces. They were the same smiles they usually had when they were up to no good.

"Well, here we are," Geller said to the group as they approached a break in the tree branches.

Valkog stood up straight as he focused his efforts on sensing any roots. He almost looked as if he was smelling the air, but Jack knew that was not how his root of flindishion sense worked.

Geller suddenly stopped and quickly motioned for the others to do the same. He looked alarmed! Jack could see that Geller was at attention to his surroundings.

"Everyone down!" Geller whispered loudly as he dropped into the snow.

Jack and the others hastily did the same. He felt bad for Fink and Gink as they were bound to each other, and getting down and up again was not an easy task.

Whispering, Geller stated, "I don't think we're out here alone. I think something or someone is already here."

Chapter 12: Icy Tunnels

Geller lifted his wand out and cast a large air shield in front of him. The shield was big enough to stop the surging cold of the wind in front of the group. It only lasted for several moments, but Jack appreciated the reprieve from the cold and gusty wind. He didn't feel cold because of the warming potion but the sudden silence was nice.

The wind shield was big enough to clear the air for about fifty feet in front of the group. It didn't take long for each of them to see a large hole dug into the snow right in front of them. The hole was deep enough that it went all the way to the ground and it was approximately sixty feet across. Jack felt the hole would have been large enough to fit his house in from Pumpernickel Drive.

At the bottom of the snow hole was a large fire near a boulder. That's when Jack recognized that it was the same boulder he and Anna had traveled to this world through. He suddenly felt a sense of fear. He wondered what anyone might be doing with the boulder, and it seemed as if whoever was messing with it was not part of the Govilian Council. Gubuyis would have certainly mentioned it, he thought.

"This cannot be good," Valkog stated.

Anna asked quietly, "Is there anyone from Gargantulua out here?"

There was no answer as the group remained silenced. Geller crawled through the snow from his position to a point at the edge of the hole. He peered down as if he was searching for something. Jack felt uneasy, and the idea that their mission had just been sidetracked made him very nervous. He wondered if there was still someone down there and what it was that they were attempting to do with the portal. If something nefarious was going on, Jack was sure they would have to end their mission and report back immediately. There was no chance the group was going to be allowed to come back out for a second time, due to the time crunch and the possibility of something bad happening.

"There are no missions out here that I am aware of," Geller finally replied to Anna's question. "My father would surely have mentioned something."

"Maybe whoever was here is gone?" Anna asked as if Geller knew the answer.

"I am looking as best as I can," Geller said while scanning the ground below him.

The air shield was diminishing and making it difficult to see again. Geller continued to look for any signs of activity. The brightly burning fire was a good indication that someone had been there recently. It shone a bright reddish yellow in a haze through the blowing snow.

Valkog whispered, "I can sense the root here. If you can determine the coast is clear, General Geller, I would very much like to retrieve it."

At this point, all the members of the group had crawled over to the edge of the hole and were looking down as best they could without falling in. They were all scanning for any signs of movement or life. But, unfortunately, the blowing snow made it nearly impossible to see anything.

"I could quickly fly down and get the root," Valkog explained to the group as he looked for permission to go. "It would be much easier to get with an opening like this, and I do not see anyone down there."

"There!" Geller whispered to the group.

He was pointing to a spot behind the portal boulder. All of them immediately looked in that direction. Jack saw some movement from the general direction of the boulder. It was extremely difficult to make anything out, but there was clearly someone or something moving around down there. The wind shield collapsed entirely at this point, making any details of the hole's occupants impossible to see.

"Can you make another shield?" Anna asked Geller.

"It might clue them off to us being here," Geller responded. "And

I would be very surprised if they hadn't already seen us from that shield."

Geller backed away from the edge slowly as he tried not to let any snow fall into the hole. He motioned for the others to do the same and they each followed. Jack watched as the glowing haze of the fire below was the only thing that filled the air in front of them.

Although no one made a sound or disturbed the snow around the edges of the hole, it seemed as if they had been spotted. A single fireball flew right past their heads.

Quickly getting to his feet, Geller exclaimed to the group, "We have been detected!"

Suddenly, several other fireballs flew past the group. None of the fireballs seemed to be directed at anyone in particular. They appeared to be sort of scattered. Jack thought to himself as he and the others got up, whoever was shooting at them couldn't see them either.

"It's got to be fironi," Geller said quickly. "It could be an ambush. We need to get away from this place right now!"

As the group began to run, Jack wondered if they were running in a specific direction or if they were going to become lost. It did not look like Geller was following a particular path and they weren't following the same path they came in from either. Although the snow was blowing hard, Jack would still have noticed their footprints in the snow from before, and he would know if they were backtracking.

Jack found it difficult to run with any speed. He was not the only one either. It seemed as if everyone was struggling to run in the heavy snow. Fink was quite possibly struggling the most with Gink riding on his back. He looked like his movements in the snow were very cumbersome and difficult to make with any amount of speed.

Through his heavy breathing, Jack asked, "Can Valkog fly us out of here?"

He thought that would be the ideal scenario in this case. Obviously, they were all struggling to get away from the hole. Now that the mission was over for sure, it seemed like the perfect time to simply get out of the area by flight.

"We'll be easier targets in the air," Geller called back to Jack and the others. "We need to get out of this area first and then we can fly the rest of the way home."

Geller's last comment cemented Jack's concern that this meant the end of the mission. Now, it sounded as if the plan was to get home as quickly as possible. Jack knew that made the most sense, though. They needed to let Gubuyis know that there was an enemy in the forest close by, and was in a spot of great significance.

Jack wondered as he struggled to continue running what they were doing with the boulder portal. He grew concerned that they may be trying to take it out of the forest and back to the Reign for some reason. Maybe they wanted to be able to use it for themselves like others had suggested, he thought. Whatever the reason was, Jack felt concerned that the only way he knew of getting home was now under enemy control.

After running for what seemed like an hour, but what was more like fifteen minutes, Geller finally stopped. Jack was sweating and out of breath. The warming potion seemed to have an even stronger effect after all that running, and he wanted to take his coat off. He decided otherwise, though. The storm was stronger now than when they first set off earlier in the day. It didn't make much sense to take his coat off in a storm like this, even if he was hot.

Still catching his own breath, Geller asked out loud to no one in particular, "What would the fironi be doing in the middle of Wellwood Forest?"

Nobody answered.

Geller then took out his map and began to look it over as he tried to determine where they were. Jack could see that Geller was trying to figure out their location. It seemed impossible to determine where they were, based off of what Jack could see, but Geller knew the forest well and it appeared that he was able to still navigate through it regardless of the snow storm.

"That was the same boulder we came through from Earth," Anna finally said through heavy panting. "Why would they be there? What are they doing?"

Gink chimed in and suggested, "Maybe they're tryin' ta move it. That sort o' thing could fetch quite of few valins!"

"Only a flindishk can move such a portal with ease," Valkog spoke up. "Portals made by the flindishk are not to be tampered with. Only a very powerful being could move such a portal, and the fironi are not powerful enough to do anything with it."

This news made Jack feel a little relieved. He still wondered what was going on with the portal, but he knew once they got back to the city Gubuyis would send some reinforcements to the area. Valkog had even mentioned that there was some root of flindishion near the area. Maybe, he thought, they could still get some of the root after chasing away the fironi.

"Whatever the case may be," Geller stated, "we need to get back to father and inform him of what is going on here."

Valkog nodded in agreement. Even though Jack figured that maybe they might still have a chance to get some of the root for Valkog, he felt disappointed. There was a very real chance that any mission to get the root would be cast by the wayside.

Geller motioned to the group to come together as he said, "Everyone come here."

Pulling out a net, Geller began to lay it on the ground near their feet. It was evident that they were going to step onto it. Then, Valkog would grab hold of the net and they would all go flying away back to Gargantulua.

They only stood together for a brief moment before the snow beneath their feet caved in. The whole group struggled to climb up and out of the growing hole, but it was all in vain. The hole grew deeper and faster than any of them could fight against. Eventually, they fell deep into the snow. Jack could see that the snow had dumped them into a tunnel. Behind them was the collapsed portion they had just fallen from, and in front of them was a long, tall tunnel.

Without hesitation, Anna and Jack began attempting to dig themselves out, trying to find an opening to climb back out of. The lack of wind and blowing snow made it much easier to see, except for the fact that they were deep under the snow. There was darkness all around them. Everything was some shade of blue or white.

After a few moments of fighting against the ever-collapsing snow mound, Jack and Anna finally stopped digging. Jack turned in the direction of the open tunnel and took in what he saw. The tunnel was large enough to fit Valkog, so he figured it must be nearly eight feet tall from floor to ceiling. The sides of the tunnel were hard and made of ice, and there wasn't much more to it than that as far as he could tell.

Geller reached into his bag and pulled out a small, floating orb that glowed brightly. He released it into the air, and it stopped several feet in front of them. Jack saw that the lights inside of the orb were the same ones from his tent on their way to Wyvergia. In the dark, it was easy to see that the small lights were actually little bugs of some kind that huddled close together, making a bright light. As the orb floated in front of them, it glowed a warm orangish-yellow. The tunnel filled with the light, and where it did not reach, the tunnel remained dark and blue.

"Kaboom!"

Everyone turned to look at where the small bang had come from. It turned out that Gink had just thrown a small vial of some kind at the tunnel wall in an attempt to break through it. Jack could see where the vial hit based on scorch marks and some small chunks of ice that had broken off.

"Well," Gink said calmly, "it seems as though the walls are made o' thick ice."

Anna looked shaken and upset, "Are you mad? You could have

killed us all! What if the walls had caved in?"

"If the walls are so strong," Jack asked, "how did we fall so far down and into the tunnel?"

Geller responded, "It could be that there was another tunnel that had been dug up near the surface and was only just recently snowed over from this storm."

Patting his pockets and then looking through his bag, Geller was evidently looking for something. After a bit of searching, he looked defeated.

"I have lost my map," Geller stated coolly. "But, have no fear, I know these woods quite well and should still be able to navigate us through them."

Sarcastically, Fink asked, "You don't happen ta know the name of the tunnel we're in, do ya?"

"Was this tunnel made by the fironi?" Anna inquired.

Geller looked around for a moment as if to inspect the tunnel. He knocked hard against the walls which returned a solid thud. Jack could tell the ice had to have been thick, otherwise it would likely have echoed or sounded shallow when Geller knocked against them.

"I'd say," Geller finally replied back, "that we're quite possibly in a snole tunnel."

Jack, fearing another type of enemy, quickly asked, "What is a snole? Is it going to try and kill us?"

Valkog let out a small laugh.

Before anyone else could answer, Anna chimed in, "Snoles are a lot like moles where we're from. You know, those pesky critters that tear up lawns by digging tunnels under them? Snoles, though, they're big and dig tunnels in the snow."

"Wh…what?" Jack asked Anna, confused as to how she would know that.

"Honestly, Jack, you need to read more in your free time," Anna said. "I told you that you were going to need me here with you."

Geller spoke up, "I don't know what a mole looks like where you're from, but I hope you don't have them digging tunnels under your yards and houses."

"They're much, much smaller," Anna replied. "One could fit in your hand."

Jack then asked a follow-up question, "Well, are they at least friendly like the ones from back home?"

Gink and Fink laughed in unison.

"They won't eat us, if that's what you're asking," Geller said.

"They ain't too friendly, though," Fink stated after he stopped laughing. "A single snole is about as high as Valkog there and would fill this tunnel from side ta side."

Geller asked Anna, "Maybe you learned some other information about these 'critters' that you could share with the group?"

Jack felt like they were wasting precious time. They could be searching for the root of flindishion or be trying to figure out a way to get back home. All he wanted to know was whether a snole was friendly or not and what they would need to do if they came across one. He looked down the tunnel as best as he could, hoping to see something that would signal a way out.

"Well," Anna started as she recalled what she had read about snoles, "their hair is white and hollow. The hollow hair helps to keep them warm. You have to be very careful around their hair, though, because it is extremely sharp. Their teeth are very sharp too, so they can chew through roots and tree trunks. Their eyes are small and beady, and they cannot see very well. You may find this comforting, Jack; they can't run very well either. They just aren't built for running at all, so if we encounter one, we should be able to outrun it if we need to. Hopefully that helps you a little bit, Jack."

Gink laughed and added, "Ya may have forgotten about the simple fact that they can breathe fire *and* ice."

"You're joking!" Jack said exasperated.

"Um, yeah," Anna responded. "I forgot to mention that small fact."

"Why do they breathe fire and ice?" Jack inquired, annoyed at the fact that they could end up encountering something like this at one point during the day.

"In order to create strong tunnels," Geller replied. "A snole creates the tunnel by digging it out and pressing the moved snow to the sides. Then, the snole will breathe fire all around the new tunnel to start melting the sides. And then, the snole breathes ice to quickly freeze the melting snow into a thick ice wall like the one you see here."

The fact that they could easily outrun one was somewhat comforting to Jack. It seemed as if the others were saying snoles weren't to be messed with, but they weren't going to intentionally try and kill them either. Jack felt the ice-covered wall and knocked on it himself. It was hard and obviously very thick. He knew they didn't have the tools to break through these walls, so they were going to need to find a way out, he thought.

"What can we do if we do encounter one?" Anna asked. "If we run, will it agitate the snole and make it angry?"

Valkog chimed in, "They may not necessarily be aggressive by nature, but I would recommend we run as fast as we can. Their hair is a weapon and it's their armor as well. If we needed to fight one, we would be at a disadvantage with hair that's like thousands of short swords swinging in every direction."

"I agree," Geller stated, "we would likely need to run. However, chances are that if we did come across a snole, it would back away and go in another direction."

Knowing that they didn't really have anything to break through the walls with, Jack remembered the melting potion.

"What about the melting potion?" Jack nearly shouted out as it came to his mind. "Could we use the melting potion to get out of here?"

Gink coolly replied back as if he had already considered it, "We could use it, yes. But ya have ta remember that it would only melt down. So, we would effectively make a big hole below us and then be stuck underneath the tunnel. Not a real big improvement in this situation, I'd say!"

"There's a little bit of good news," Geller said. "We may be able to find some root of flindishion while we look for a way out of here. We're closer to the forest floor inside the tunnels, and we may even be lucky enough to find some without having to dig it out."

Gink and Fink had big smiles on their faces as they heard this news. Jack liked the idea that they may still be able to get some root of flindishion, too. He looked at Valkog and noticed he too sported a small smile. Jack was relieved that they seemed to have gotten away from the fironi from earlier. Now, he really wanted to find the root and get out of this place. He still felt quite warm despite the freezing temperature of the tunnel. In fact, he felt much warmer now that they were out of the snowstorm with its heavy winds.

"Shall we proceed?" Valkog asked the group.

Geller walked to the front of the group and said, "We will have to go this way for obvious reasons. Keep your senses on high alert, Valkog, for we are likely to come across various roots as we travel."

Valkog nodded in agreement and replied, "I sensed some near the clearing before and I'm sure we will come across more. It is reassuring that I felt its presence earlier."

Just as the group began to take its first steps forward, a noise came from behind them. Everyone turned to watch as the crumbled wall of snow came down behind them. It began to shake and Jack thought he could hear sniffing like that of a very large dog coming from behind the snow. Several large chunks of snow crumbled forward to the floor. After a few moments, numerous other chunks of snow and ice fell away from the collapsed snow wall, and a large nose appeared sticking through the snow. Eventually, after enough snow had collapsed, Jack could make out what appeared to be a snole. Jack and Anna both gasped at the sight of it!

Geller moved to a position in front of the snole. It was still digging through the collapsed section of the tunnel with great efficiency. In a matter of moments, the snole had dug enough snow out of the way so it could now fit through the tunnel with ease.

"We mean you no harm," Geller said loudly to the snole. "We fell into your tunnel and are looking for a way out. If possible, we would also like to find some root of flindishion while we're here."

The snole moved forward aggressively, as if it didn't hear Geller or didn't care what he had to say. Everyone in the group backed up as the snole inched forward. It let out a thunderous growling sound. Jack could see its eyes and remembered Anna saying that it couldn't see very well. He wondered if it could see them at all, or if it could only smell them.

Repeating himself, Geller shouted, "We mean you no harm! We are looking for a way out of here!"

The snole moved forward again in a threating manner. Jack felt as if they were about to be in a very bad situation. Its hairs were pulsating from a smooth, shiny coat to looking like a porcupine ready for battle.

"I don't think it cares just how peaceful we are!" Gink shouted over the loud sniffing and growling. "I think it's angry at us for some reason."

Jack watched as the snole clenched its claws into the floor beneath it. The icy floor crumbled in its claws like loose gravel. Jack's eyes opened wide at this sight. He knew the ice was so strong that not even one of Gink's exploding potions could break through it. The snole stomped forward again.

"Perhaps we should not stay here," Valkog suggested to the others.

The hair on the snole began to ripple and pulsate changing from smooth to sharp, jagged pieces. The rippling of its hair sounded like hundreds of bamboo sticks hitting together. Each hair was like a sharp dagger, but much longer. Jack knew there was no way they would want to have a fight with this thing. He also knew that Anna mentioned that they weren't good at running either.

"I agree!" Geller shouted out to the others, "We need to leave right now!"

Slowly, at first, the group began to back away from the aggressive snole. As they picked up their pace, so did the snole. It did not seem like it was going to go the other way as Geller had suggested earlier. This snole was being quite aggressive and Jack saw Geller take out his dagger. No one in the group had turned away from the snole since it was obviously not intending to leave them alone. Jack pulled out his two daggers as well. He was not prepared to fight this thing, but it sure didn't seem like there was much of a choice.

Suddenly, a pink smoke filled the tunnel around the snole. Anna screamed as the smoke wafted upwards and around it.

Chapter 13: The Escape

The snole, now completely enveloped in pink smoke, suddenly became still and slouched against the tunnel wall. Jack watched as the smoke flowed into its nostrils as it breathed. It looked lifeless.

Fink quickly shouted out, "We need ta get out o' here away from the smoke, now!"

"Great job, Fink!" Gink exclaimed to his brother.

They all started running in the other direction. Eventually, they came to a fork in the tunnel and stopped to catch their breath while deciding which way to go.

"What happened back there?" Anna asked, while still catching her breath. "The snole looked like it just died or something."

Fink explained, "I used a small sleeping potion on it. It's just having a little bit of an unexpected nap."

Geller nodded his head and said, "That was not a bad idea. Selini would be very proud of you for sure! A peaceful resolution to a very scary situation."

The group stood there for a few moments while everyone caught their breath. Jack's feet hurt from running on the curved floor. He still felt warm from the warming potion but running just made him feel hot. Now that they were at a fork in the tunnel, he knew someone was going to have to make the decision which way to go. He wondered how much time they had before the snole came looking for them.

"How long will it be asleep?" Jack finally asked, breaking the silence.

Gink spoke up, "It was just a small potion, so it'll probably only be out for about an hour."

"We will need to work quickly," Geller said, "to find the root and a way out of here. Getting out of here is our first priority though."

"What do we do if we run into another one of those things?" Anna asked.

Geller looked around the tunnels before answering, "I'd say by the looks of this tunnel system, it was only built for one. I think we're in the clear for not running into any more of these guys."

Jack looked around the tunnel, too. It did look like only one snole could fit through at a time and that made him feel much better. This meant there was little chance of running into another one while they were down there. Now, they could focus on finding some root of flindishion and a way out of the tunnels. He wondered how they were going to decide which tunnel to go down.

"We should take the tunnel to the left," Valkog stated.

Gink looked giddy and Fink was smiling big again.

"Do ya sense the root?" Gink asked excitedly. "Is there a lot of it? I must know! What do you feel?"

Chuckling, Valkog replied, "I do not know how much of it there is, but I do believe there is some to the left. It must still be far away because although I can barely smell it, I can't sense it yet."

Nobody offered any arguments as to why they shouldn't go down the tunnel to the left, so that is the direction they took. They walked for what felt like most of the remaining part of the day. Jack knew they would be missed back in Gargantulua soon. He hoped that they would find something before long. His eyes had seemingly adjusted to the darkness of the tunnel, even though it was lit by the floating orb of light. The light followed behind them to make it easier to see without a glare.

There were no other branches in the tunnel throughout the day. The sights of blue and grey all day were bleak. The group moved at a quick pace. Geller explained that they needed to walk faster than the snole so they could keep ahead of it. Valkog led the group using his sense of smell. Occasionally, he would signal that it smelled stronger.

Eventually, Geller said, "It is getting late in the day. We need to begin focusing our efforts on ways to get out of this tunnel so that we can get back home."

"Awww," Gink complained, "We're too close ta give up now! We need that root!"

Fink chimed in, "I agree! Valkog, how close do you think we are now?"

"I think we're getting closer," Valkog stated. "I am starting to be able to sense it."

"We can continue for maybe another half hour," Geller explained, "before we need to seriously stop and figure out a way to blast through the tunnel walls and dig our way out of here."

Jack began to notice the cold air on his skin. The warming potion must be wearing off, he thought. He looked over to Anna and noticed her shivering a little.

Anna finally complained out loud, "It's getting colder down here in the tunnels."

"Yer warming potion is wearing off," Gink said. "All of our potions are wearing off. It is definitely late in the day."

The group continued to walk for another twenty minutes before Valkog, who was leading them, stopped. He stood there for a moment looking ahead in the tunnel. Jack saw what Valkog was looking at. There was a faint glow coming from the tunnel ahead.

"What do you think it is?" Valkog asked Geller.

Geller looked ahead at what Valkog was talking about and reached for his dagger. He pulled it out and held it in front of him. Jack knew that if there was someone or something down there, they would probably have already seen them due to the floating orb of light they were using. Geller moved to the front of the group.

"Be ready for a fight," Geller whispered loudly. "This could be a way out or it could be another fironi dig site."

Jack felt an instant shiver of fear come over him. He did not feel like fighting, but knew they might have to if it came to that. There was nowhere to go if they were found by the fironi. They would be trapped in the tunnel, running for the whole day trying to escape them. Even worse, they might run into the snole again if they had to run the other direction. They would be stuck fighting a snole and the fironi. He didn't feel good about this situation at all.

Geller moved forward slowly and the group followed. As they got closer to the dim light in the tunnel, Jack noticed that all the sides of the tunnel were becoming coated in a dark purple moss that lit up yellow as they walked over it. The farther they walked, the longer the moss became. Eventually, it was like a long grass that swayed ever so gently with the movement of the air. A light fog covered the floor and looked eerie to Jack as it picked up the glow of the moss beneath it.

"What is all over the walls?" Jack finally asked quietly.

Fink responded, "I ain't ever seen anything like it."

After a little more walking, Geller motioned for the group to stop. The dim light that had been so far ahead of them was now only about a hundred feet away.

"I will go and check things out," Geller said. "You will all remain here."

Geller proceeded forward walking close to the wall. The moss provided some sense of cover, but the fact that it lit up if touched made it difficult for Geller to stay camouflaged. The group watched anxiously as he got closer to the light.

"I can sense the root," Valkog whispered to Jack. "It is definitely coming from ahead. I really hope there is no danger up there because we're just too close to turn back now."

Jack felt anxious about what might be ahead. It couldn't be a good sign that it was lit up, he thought. He wondered if it was actually the moss lighting up the way ahead, or if someone was down there doing something. The worst possible scenarios were running through his head as they all watched for Geller to return. Although the light wasn't that far ahead of them, he could barely make out Geller through the seemingly ever lengthening moss coming from the tunnel walls. He looked down at his own feet and watched as the dark purple moss lit up yellow in a slow and swirling motion. He hoped as best as he could that there was nothing dangerous ahead.

"Well, it's definitely getting warmer," Anna commented. "I think the moss is warming up the tunnel the further in we go."

Valkog quietly replied back, "I have noticed that, too. It must be something to do with this type of moss."

"Look!" Jack whispered loudly to the others. "He's coming back."

Geller approached the group hurriedly. Jack watched as he came back to the group, looking for any signs of trouble in his appearance. It looked like Geller was rather upbeat and that made Jack feel a little better. Maybe, he thought, there wasn't any sign of anybody causing the light, or maybe they weren't there. Whatever the case, Geller wasn't signaling bad news.

Geller got back to the group.

"It's a den," Geller whispered.

Jack figured by the way Geller was still whispering that there must still be something in the den. He didn't look too worried, though. There was silence from the group except for a slight groan of disappointment from Fink. It seemed as if the rest of the group was still trying to comprehend what the situation was.

Finally, Anna broke the silence by asking, "A den? What does that mean?"

Geller motioned for the group to huddle together so that he could easily explain without being too loud.

"There are three baby snoles sleeping in the den right now," Geller explained. "They're all stacked on each other in a nest of sorts."

Suddenly, Jack felt the disappointment that Fink had already expressed. He wondered if that meant it was a dead end and they would have to turn back to the fork in the tunnel from earlier in the day.

Valkog inquired, "Did you happen to see any root of flindishion while you were up there?"

The fact that there were three baby snoles ahead wasn't deterring the others from wanting to get to the root if they could. Jack was somewhat okay with that idea. He still wanted to find some of the root and badly, but he was also nervous about what it meant to try and retrieve it with snoles in the way.

"Yes," Geller replied. "There was a bundle of various roots set aside as food for the snoles. It is located to the right of the babies."

Fink started to jump in happiness but was quickly calmed down by Geller's harsh look. His jumping made noises as his coat and Gink's coat were full of things that clinked together loudly in the silence. Jack felt relieved. They were so close to being able to get the root that he could almost feel it in his hands.

Geller, looking at Gink and Fink, spoke sternly, "I must remind you that we are not here for your inventory needs. If we are to get any at all, it will be for Valkog first."

"I could sneak in and grab some without the snoles ever knowing," Valkog stated to Geller. "I can do it quietly."

"Was there a way out?" Anna inquired, ignoring the fact that they found what they originally set out to find. "Does the tunnel keep going?"

Jack watched as Geller's face contorted as he struggled to answer the question. He wondered if his hesitation in answering was due to the fact that there was no way out and just wasn't sure how to say it nicely.

Finally, Geller replied, "It appears to be a dead end."

Another moan came from Fink, who was obviously not enjoying the long walks on the curved tunnel floor with his brother on his back. Anna's shoulders dropped as she realized what a dead end meant for them. It meant lots more walking, and hopefully not running into the mother snole again.

"But" Geller said with a little reassurance to his voice, "there appears to have been a small vent shaft above the snoles. I wouldn't recommend that we try exiting that way, though, as we would have to climb over the babies in order to do so."

It seemed as if Geller was against trying to use the vent hole to escape and Jack was fine with that. He had no desire to try and climb on top of snoles, babies or not. The hair of the snole they met already was sharp and deadly. There was little about the idea of climbing over the baby snoles that made him feel good. There must be another way out, he thought.

Geller continued to explain his reasoning, "Baby snoles may be smaller than their parents, but they're just as dangerous. And, there are three of them. Just imagine what would happen to us if one of us accidently slipped and woke them up?"

"I agree," Valkog said. "Maybe there is another way out or we can make our own way out. Regardless, though, I'd like to try and sneak in there to get some of the roots. After that, we can focus on getting out of here."

Looking uneasy at this suggestion, Geller replied back slowly, "I really don't feel good about that idea. If you were to wake even one of them up, we would all be stuck in a terrible situation. The last thing we need right now is for us to have snoles chasing after us in the tunnels."

"We're too close!" Gink whispered loudly. "There's no way we came this far just to turn away!"

Jack felt there was something he could do. He thought about how large Valkog was compared to himself. Then, he gazed ahead and decided to make a suggestion of his own.

"I could go," Jack stated plainly. "I am smaller than Valkog and can sneak in and out much faster, without being seen."

Geller flashed a small smile and then replied back, "You could go, yes. But you would have to make multiple trips. Remember, the roots are quite heavy. The more trips you make, the more likely you are to wake them up. If anyone is to go, it would need to be Valkog. If we were to do this, we would need to have a plan in place as to what we would do if the snoles did wake up. We can't just wander in there all 'willy nilly' and hope for the best. Where will we go if the snoles do wake up? We have no way of fighting three snoles, let alone just one. I should remind you that snoles are peaceful creatures and we should not choose to pick a fight with them on purpose. We are in their home and our intent is to burglarize it!"

Suddenly, a low growling sound came from behind them. It sounded familiar, much like the sound of the snole they met earlier that day, but further down the tunnel. Jack and Anna were both wide-eyed as they watched the darkness of the tunnel behind the group.

"It sounds as if the mother is on her way back to see her babies," Valkog mused.

Anna looked worried as she asked, "What are we going to do?"

"What about that vent shaft?" Jack asked hurriedly. "Does it go outside?"

Geller thought for a brief moment as he recalled what he had seen before saying, "I'm not sure where it leads to. There are three baby snoles sleeping directly underneath it, though. It will be challenging to get up there for sure. And we can't simply fly out because the snoles are too close to the opening."

Another growl sounded from behind them. Anna moved closer to Valkog, as he was the largest in the group. Jack's heart was beginning to pound as a slight bit of fear filled his chest. It was obvious that the snole they were hearing was definitely in the same tunnel and it was getting closer. He remembered that they couldn't run well, which made him feel just slightly better. He figured they had a little more time before it got to where they were in the tunnel. The growling sound came again and was louder this time. Jack began to panic as he thought of the baby snoles waking to the call of their mother.

At this point, the group was seriously in a difficult predicament. There was nowhere to go except into the den with the sleeping baby snoles who were likely to be awake soon.

"I don't think we have a choice," Fink said to Geller.

Geller looked concerned at their options, which were none. It seemed like the only option they could possibly try was to get up the vent shaft in hopes that it went outside. He looked behind the group down the tunnel as best as he could, to assess the situation, and he looked ahead of the group at the lit den. Finally, he sighed.

"Alright," Geller said while whispering, "we will go the only way we can. We must try and get up the vent shaft, but I haven't a clue how we are going to do that. We need to move forward quickly and quietly, though."

As they walked forward the last hundred feet of the tunnel, the moss got nearly a foot long. The temperature was rising, too. It must have been at least thirty degrees warmer than the part of the tunnel without moss.

When the group entered the den, Jack saw a mound consisting of three snoles in the center of the room. They were stacked almost directly on top of each other. The den room was about the size of the main room of the house back in Gargantulua. Dark purple moss swayed and rippled all around the room, lighting up as it did. The temperature in the den was like a cool spring day. Even without the warming potion, Jack felt warm enough to be able to do things without his fingers and toes hurting. The room was slightly higher than the tunnel leading into it and was a roughly shaped circle. Jack noticed a pile of roots and twigs to the right of the entrance. It was a rather large pile, nearly the height of his own body.

The baby snoles looked sound asleep, but Jack knew with the mother coming down the tunnel that was about to change. Each snole was approximately the size of a large baby bear, maybe five feet long and four feet high if they were standing. Jack could see the vent shaft Geller had mentioned. It was about the size of the snole they had met earlier in the day. At that moment, Jack realized just why Geller was so hesitant on attempting to leave through it. Jack wasn't sure how they'd be able to get out without waking up the snoles. Maybe, he thought, they would be able to escape if the baby snoles were magically moved out of the way.

Whispering, Anna asked, "How are we supposed to get up there?"

"Valkog can carry us up once we're up there," Geller whispered back. "We just have to find a way into the vent shaft first. That's the tricky part. We may all have to make a run for it and hope for the best before the mother snole returns."

From down the tunnel, not far away, came another growling sound. The mother snole was steadily gaining ground on them now that they had all stopped. It didn't sound as if she was charging them. Jack thought maybe she didn't realize they were in the tunnels still. He looked into the tunnel and watched as the moss lit up in a circle all around the edges maybe a hundred feet back. She was closing in on them and Jack was getting nervous. He scooted to the side of the tunnel mouth so that he was out of view of the mother. Although he knew she couldn't see well and probably couldn't see any of them, he felt better not being in her direct sight.

"Everybody get out of view," Geller whispered quickly as he saw the same thing Jack was seeing.

The whole group positioned themselves on both sides of the den opening. They were now pressed for time and needed to come up with a plan fast.

Jack, trying to think of an idea, asked Gink and Fink, "Do you guys have any more sleeping potion?"

Fink replied back quietly, "We only have a small vial left. Not enough ta put all o' them ta sleep. Even if we do put the mother ta sleep, we'd never be able ta get around her. She fills the whole tunnel!"

"Yeah," Anna interjected. "What good would it do to put her to sleep? We would just be trapped in a room with a bunch of snoles. The baby snoles could wake at any moment."

Ignoring their arguments, Jack whispered across the tunnel opening to Geller, "I have an idea!"

Chapter 14: Flying Blind

The mother snole was only about fifty feet away from the group. Everyone was getting very nervous, especially since they did not have a good plan of action before going into the den. They had been forced down the tunnel and into the room due to the lack of other options. Now, Jack had an idea and he decided to let the others know quickly before time ran out. The only other option they had at the moment, was to simply try to carefully climb over the baby snoles without waking them and exit through the vent shaft above them.

"I think we should use the last sleeping potion on the baby snoles," Jack whispered loudly.

Anna interrupted Jack in a louder whisper, "Are you mad?! The baby snoles are already asleep. Why in the world would we put them to sleep again?"

"The sound of the sleeping potion exploding open would certainly alert the mother snole that we're here," Geller replied. "That would just add to our current predicament. If the mother sees or hears us, she will be sure to come charging in here and we'll all be dead for sure."

Jack knew he had very little time to explain his plan, so he got straight to it.

"If we use our melting potion at the top of the entrance here it should collapse part of the tunnel. That would prevent the mother from getting in."

Valkog spoke up this time, "Snoles are incredibly efficient at digging. It won't take her long to get through the debris. And she'll definitely know something is in here with her babies. She'll work fast."

At this point the mother snole was about twenty feet away from the den opening. Her growling was loud, and Jack was surprised it hadn't woken the babies yet.

"It'll buy us a short window of time," Jack whispered frantically to the group as he tried to explain his idea. "We could keep the babies asleep with the sleeping potion and slow down the mother before she gets in here. Then, we could use the few moments she is slowed down to climb over the babies and get into the vent shaft."

They were out of time. The mother snole was mere feet away. Geller dashed across the tunnel opening.

"Get the sleeping potion ready!" Geller said to Fink in a loud whisper.

The breath of the mother snole could now be felt in the air around Jack's head. He was getting nervous. They were about to try something that if it didn't work would definitely give away their position. There was still a chance that the mother might turn around and never enter the den and therefore never see the group. But Jack knew that was extremely unlikely, and they needed to act fast.

"Quick!" Geller nearly shouted. "Give me the melting potion!"

Having been only about ten feet from the entrance, the mother snole heard Geller shout to Fink. It stopped for a brief moment while it tried to determine where the sound came from. Then, it began to charge towards the den. Jack could feel the ground rumbling under the weight of the mother snole.

Fink quickly tossed the melting potion to Geller who was only a few feet away, standing in front of the tunnel opening. Geller pulled out his wand and prepared to throw the melting potion at the top of the tunnel.

"Throw the sleeping potion! Now!" Geller commanded Fink.

At that moment, Geller threw the melting potion as hard as he could at the tunnel ceiling. Using his wand, he exploded it just as it found its mark. A small shockwave blew outwards from the vial causing the snole to stop in her tracks and back up a little. The tunnel cracked and shook, and then finally it collapsed in on itself. At the same time, Fink had thrown the sleeping potion straight at the baby snoles behind them.

"We must move fast!" Geller exclaimed without regard for the volume of his voice.

"It worked!" Anna nearly shouted. "Your plan worked, Jack!"

Geller was already heading over to the baby snoles. The sleeping potion seemed to be working. The snoles hadn't budged at the sound of the potions exploding or the collapse of the tunnel. Geller began to climb the first snole, slowly and carefully but as fast as he could go without getting hurt on their sharp hairs. The others quickly followed, knowing that the mother snole wouldn't be long behind them. They had no time to waste.

Fink was struggling to climb with the odd weight distribution of Gink on his back. Jack found it not too difficult to climb up the snoles as long as he was careful where he placed his footing. One slip could lead to disaster. As his hands gripped the hairs, he noticed they were slightly barbed as well, catching on his skin. He realized that merely brushing up against one of these things would be painful, even if he didn't get hit with the sharp points of the hairs.

As he got to the top of the snole pile, Jack reached back and gave a helping hand to Anna who was right behind him. Then, he helped pull Fink up. That's when he realized Valkog was trailing behind. Jack watched as Valkog struggled to climb. He looked as if he was in a stupor.

"Valkog!" Jack shouted. "You need to hurry!"

The mother snole was already breaking through the collapsed portion of the tunnel. Chunks of ice and snow were beginning to fall into the den. She could be heard clawing, digging, and pushing from behind it all. Her growls were louder and much more aggressive than what they were just a moment ago.

Valkog swayed as he spoke, "I seemed to have been too close to the sleeping potion. I was trying to collect some roots, you see? I'm terribly sorry, but I am feeling overwhelmingly tired right now."

A sudden panic overcame the group as they realized what was

happening. Valkog had breathed in some of the sleeping potion in his attempt to gather some roots. Now, he was fighting the urge to sleep, while trying to escape the den. It seemed impossible that he would be able to maneuver climbing up the snoles. They all watched as Valkog attempted to climb the pile and then stumble back to the floor.

Geller shouted down to him, "You have to try, Valkog! You need to get back up and do it again! You're our only way out of here!"

Jack looked up at the vent shaft above his head. It went straight up. It was made in a similar fashion as the tunnels, surrounded in thick ice. There was no way they would be able to climb up faster than the mother snole. Already panicked, Jack felt even more fear as he realized how much they were going to have to depend on Valkog to fly them out of there.

Another large chunk of ice and snow broke away from the collapsed portion of the tunnel at the den's entrance. Jack watched in horror as one of the mother snole's claws began reaching through. Valkog hadn't made any progress up the baby snoles. In fact, he was still mostly on the floor, trying to stumble back up.

"Isn't there anything we can do?" Anna asked in fear.

Gink fumbled through several pockets before finally pulling out a thin rope. He tossed it over to Geller who quickly threw down an end to Valkog.

Geller motioned for the others to help as he commanded, "Everyone, hold on! He's a big guy and we're going to need to do this together!"

Valkog, still in a daze, grabbed onto the thin rope. The group pulled as best as they could while Valkog climbed up the snoles. He wasn't far from the top of the pile when the rope broke from rubbing against the barbed and sharp hairs. He fell back to the floor clumsily and rather loudly. Jack looked beneath his feet and watched for any sign that the snoles were waking up. They appeared to still be fast asleep, which was the only good news at this point.

Slowly, Valkog got back to his feet. The mother snole was just about through the debris. Jack could tell Valkog was struggling to stay awake.

"So … tired …" Jack could hear Valkog muttering.

At this point, Jack decided to look through his own bag to see if there was another rope or something that he could throw down. He took the bag off his back and rummaged through it. He quickly found a thin chain that glittered yellowish green. He pulled it out, but quickly decided that it wasn't going to be strong enough to hold any kind of weight. He began looking for anything else and motioned for Anna to do the same.

Noticing the thin chain, Geller quickly said, "Jack, that's an enchanted chain. Throw it down!"

Jack quickly threw one end of the chain down to Valkog. The group once again rallied at the top end and held on while Valkog attempted to climb the pile another time. He fought sleep as he climbed.

Just as Valkog started to make it up the baby snole pile, the mother snole was starting to make it through. She had one of her paws all the way through and was attempting to swipe at Valkog. She just missed him by inches! Jack watched the collapsed tunnel. The mother's full face was visible at this point. She would be through entirely within a few seconds. He knew they didn't have another chance to get Valkog up the mound.

Everyone pulled as best as they could and Valkog held on as best as he could. He climbed slowly and stumbled along the way, but after a few grueling moments, he finally made it to the top. Without even acknowledging his presence, Geller took the chain and hurriedly tied it to Valkog's leg.

"Everyone, grab on!" Geller shouted to the group. "She's almost through!"

Jack looked back at the tunnel opening and saw the mother snole breaking through her last large chunks of ice. She shoved them aside like they were pebbles under her feet. Not even a moment after she broke through, she breathed in a large breath of air and exhaled a large fireball right at the group. Geller quickly cast a small heat shield that deflected the oncoming fire. Jack could feel the sudden, intense heat all around him.

"Valkog!" Geller shouted. "Go! Go! Go!"

Still stuck in a heavy daze, Valkog swayed while he stood atop the snoles. He looked like he didn't want to move or that he would even be able to move. Geller tugged at the chain and continued to shout commands at a nearly sleeping Valkog. Jack's eyes were wide. He knew they were out of options and time.

Anna pleaded with Valkog, too, "Valkog! Please! We have to go now!"

Struggling to keep his eyes open, a sleepy Valkog finally began to make his attempt to fly. He flapped his wings for a second, but only lifted a few inches. The mother snole at that moment breathed more fire at them. Geller shot out another heat shield.

"I won't be able to keep casting these," Geller said quietly to Jack. "We don't have all day!"

Valkog began flapping his wings again. Jack could tell he was trying hard to stay awake. This time, Valkog was beginning to make progress. He lifted into the vent shaft and the chain lifted with him. Jack made sure he was holding on tight. It looked as if Valkog was going to make it as the group started to lift off the ground.

"Everyone, hold on tight!" Geller shouted back to the others below him.

Another round of searing hot fire followed them up the shaft. Geller clumsily tried to deflect this one as well, but only managed to cast a small shield. As Valkog flew, he banged against the walls. It was difficult for Geller to properly aim his wand and cast a shielding spell with all the banging. Some of the fire flew right past all of them and up the vent shaft before disappearing into the sky above.

After a moment or two, the group finally made it out of the tunnels and into the outside air. Jack suddenly felt freezing cold, which was welcoming for a brief second after nearly getting fried just a moment before. The warmth of the den was long gone and now they were flying through a still raging snowstorm. Jack looked down and couldn't see anything other than grey and white. All around them was grey. He felt slightly concerned about where they were going. He remembered, though, that Valkog had said he could fly to Gargantulua with his eyes closed. A small sense of comfort came over him as he realized they were now heading home.

Jack's comfort quickly diminished as the seconds flew by. The flight was rather rough, he thought. Then, he recalled Valkog was still fighting the urge to sleep. He wondered if they might have to land for a bit to let Valkog sleep or wake up. Jack felt the chain swaying from side to side and up and down. He knew they were in trouble and hoped they would just land. There was no way they would make it back to town like this, he thought.

"Look at his wings!" Anna shouted.

Anna was above Jack on the chain. She had a better view of Valkog than he did. In between sways of the chain, Jack got a glimpse of his wings. He could see that they had recently been on fire and were still glowing red. They were badly singed around the edges.

Geller, who was closest to Valkog, shouted down to the group, "Prepare for a rough landing!"

The flight was definitely rough. They kept going from side to side and up and down. Jack couldn't tell how far up they were. For all he knew, they were close to the ground and he just couldn't see it in the storm. His hands were hurting from holding on to the small chain and from the freezing air. It certainly didn't help that the chain kept jerking around from Valkog's haphazard flying. They flew for several more minutes before Jack felt a consistent descent. He looked up and realized Valkog was almost entirely asleep. They were heading for a crash landing. He hoped they weren't too high up.

It wasn't long before the group crashed into the snow. Thankfully, it was not a rough landing as Jack had figured it might be. They all landed in a line based on where each one was on the chain. Valkog landed with a heavy thud. They each got up and brushed the snow off. Jack looked around and saw nothing but white. The snow was still furiously blowing at them. Even though he was wearing his leather armor cap that blocked out much of the outside sound, he could still hear the muted howling sound of the wind.

Geller was without his map, and Valkog was unable to fly. Jack could see Geller was struggling to get his bearings in the storm. He wondered if Geller knew where they were. There were no landmarks as far as Jack could see and there were no trees sticking out of the snow either.

"Where are we?" Jack asked, hoping for an answer that would ease his fears.

Nobody answered, though. Geller was busy looking around, and it seemed like there was no way of knowing where they were.

Anna finally asked, "What are you two doing?"

Jack looked over at Anna who was watching Fink and Gink. It looked like Fink was cutting something on Valkog's back. Jack walked over to them to get a better view of what they were doing and saw Fink cutting a piece of a root.

"Just stocking up!" Gink exclaimed happily.

"Well," Anna replied back to him, "can you two prepare it so that he can use it when he wakes up?"

Both Gink and Fink began laughing.

Fink finally said, "He'll have ta be awake for that!"

"Why?" Anna inquired. "Do you not know how?"

Geller interrupted, "We need to find shelter. This storm is only going to get worse."

"We're in luck!" Gink quipped. "There's a nice warm cottage just around the corner!"

Anna looked annoyed at his sarcasm. They were all freezing and knowing that it was just going to get worse wasn't exactly what any of them wanted to hear.

"Everyone check your bags for anything that we can use as cover," Geller said, ignoring Gink's comment.

Gink and Fink started patting their pockets heavily as they searched for something they could use. Jack took off his bag and decided to look through it, even though he hadn't seen anything useful for this situation when he rummaged through it earlier. He glanced up to Geller with a look that said he didn't have anything.

"Look!" Anna exclaimed as she withdrew another bag from within her backpack. "Gryan packed me a tent!"

Quickly, Geller grabbed the tent bag from Anna and threw it to the ground. He pulled out his wand and gave a small flick. The tent sprung up fully without any need for manual intervention.

"Get in," Geller commanded the others. "It'll feel warmer in there."

Then, Geller used his wand to levitate Valkog and bring him into the tent with them. Jack instantly felt warmer now that they were inside. He saw the same glowing orb as before floating in the center. Up close, he could see that they were a bunch of small bugs that lit up brighter as they got closer to each other. In one corner of the tent was a small stove with a chimney. Although it was warmer inside, they could all still see their breath. Jack was getting tired as the day had been long, but he knew there was no way he would be able to sleep in the cold.

Anna spoke up as they all huddled in, "Maybe we can make a fire."

She pointed at the stove with a small bit of excitement in her voice.

"We ain't got firewood," Gink replied. "Or … we could burn the root of flindishion."

"We're going to freeze to death if we don't do something," Anna replied angrily.

Jack's eyes were wide. He hoped that they did not come to the conclusion that they should burn the root of flindishion that they had worked so hard to get. The whole mission would have been for nothing and they would end up being in an even worse position than when they first set off that morning.

Geller spoke up, "We cannot burn the root. With Valkog's wings so badly burned, there's little chance we'll be able to fly home. We're going to need the root for him to take in order to rejuvenate his mana. Then, he can summon a portal and we can get back that way."

Geller looked lost as he spoke. There was something bothering him from what Jack could tell. It looked as though he was coming to the realization that they were going to be there for a while.

"What about you two?" Anna asked Fink and Gink. "Do you have a portal potion or something? I've seen you use portal potions before."

Gink responded, "We might have the ingredients ta make one, but not enough ta get us all through. We might be able ta go by ourselves, though. It would take some time."

Jack asked Geller, "Were you able to determine where we are?"

Geller shook his head.

"I couldn't find any landmarks," Geller said. "Without being able to see anything from the air or the ground, I have no clue where we've landed. I don't even know if we were flying in the right direction."

"So," Jack said slowly as he thought, "even if Gink and Fink could get home by using a portal potion, they wouldn't have a way to find us?"

Anna quickly interjected, "But, at least they would know we needed help and would attempt to find us."

"My dear Anna," Geller spoke softly, "by now, they probably

already know something is wrong. I doubt they will be sending anyone out to find us. They need all the fighters they have to focus on preparing for battle. Sadly, I do believe this means we are on our own. We must explore other options."

Anna looked a little disappointed, but decided to ask, "What about Valkog? Is there some way we can wake him up? Is there a such thing as a 'waking up' potion?"

Fink answered her, "There is such a thing, but we would need ta brew it first."

"And, to brew it," Gink chimed in, "we would need a fire."

Anna picked her bag back up and began looking through it. It didn't look like there was much in it from what Jack could tell by the way the bag sagged in her hands.

"What are ya lookin' for?" Fink finally asked.

Still searching through her bag, Anna replied, "I don't know. Maybe some sort of magical firewood box or something silly like that. I'm looking for something we can burn. Jack, check yours."

Jack shook his head and said, "There's not much else in my bag that we could use for burning. Sorry."

"Gryan would probably have concluded that we were going to be in a forest," Geller said. "And we would have been surrounded by firewood as far as he was concerned. Firewood would have been unnecessary weight. I'm quite surprised that he packed you a tent. This tent will protect us from the elements of the storm outside, even if it's still cold in here. We have much to be grateful for right now. Things may not be going our way, but it could have been so much worse than it is. Everyone is still alive and what we need to do now is try our best to get some sleep."

Geller took his bag and positioned it as if it was going to be his pillow. Anna looked shocked that everyone was giving up on the fire. Gink got off of Fink's back and laid on the floor. It was difficult to get to sleep because of how cold it was. Jack struggled for the better part of an hour to fall asleep and he could tell Anna struggled, too. The floor of the tent was freezing cold, being that it was sitting on top of twenty feet of snow. Eventually, they each drifted off to sleep.

Chapter 15: The Troublesome Cave

Jack awoke the next morning to the sounds of talking and some weird snorting noises. He sat up in a haste and his whole body was freezing cold. He could hardly feel his feet and his fingers hurt. It took a moment for him to figure out where he was, but it all came rushing back to him as he focused on the tent walls. Remembering Valkog, Jack's eyes darted to where he had been the night before. That's when he saw Valkog happily sitting in the center of the tent with both Anna and Geller. They were all chatting about the root of flindishion. There was still the issue of the other noise that Jack was trying to figure out. He immediately determined that it was coming from both Gink and Fink. They were snorting and snoring very loudly. He was surprised the others hadn't forced them to wake up yet.

By the way the tent was shaking, Jack could tell the storm was still raging outside. It seemed even stronger than the night before. The cold was nearly unbearable, and he longed for the warmth of the fire in the main room back at the house.

"Good morning," Jack said to the others as he slowly got up.

It felt as if his muscles and bones were too stiff to move.

Anna, looking concerned, replied back, "Likewise."

After a quick yawn, Jack asked Valkog, "Were you able to get enough of the root of flindishion to make what you need?"

Speaking loudly, so as to talk over Gink and Fink, Valkog replied, "I would think so. I grabbed as much as I could, as fast as I could."

"But" Anna chimed in, "we need a nice hot fire in order for it to brew."

She looked almost annoyed and mad at the same time. They were all in quite the predicament. Now that they had what they needed, they were stranded in the middle of nowhere with no way of getting home.

Geller interjected, "We will now need to make it our mission to find something to burn. I can't imagine we're too terribly far from the forest or at least some trees."

Valkog picked up a piece of root and began to claw at it. As he did, the root fell into little chunks at his feet. He continued to do this until the roots he had were completely broken into pieces. It didn't take him very long to accomplish this; his claws were rather large and the roots gave way to them easily.

"Why did you do that?" Anna asked Valkog as he was finishing up.

Valkog looked at both Anna and Jack and explained, "I need to chew the roots, and this will make it easier."

Trying to talk over Gink and Fink's snoring, Anna began to ask, "What would you need to ch…"

She stopped abruptly. Her eyes darted over to Gink and Fink. Anna looked agitated by their loud snoring noises. Jack could see that she was fed up with the noise.

"Oh, would you two just wake up already!" Anna shouted at the both of them.

Anna picked up her almost empty bag that was sitting near her and threw it directly at Fink, who was closest. It landed squarely on his face and he did not seem to notice, as his snoring continued.

"I believe you are using the wrong motivation, Anna," Valkog stated calmly. "What you need to do is to find the right incentive to wake them up. Here."

Valkog handed Anna a handful of the root chunks. She held out her hand to let him put several pieces in it. She looked confused, though.

"What am I going to do with this?" Anna asked.

Valkog smiled and replied, "Let them smell it or act like you're going to discard it, not sure. I think you'll figure something out."

Anna looked at the root chunks in her hand as she decided what to do with them. She got up and took a few steps over to Fink and grabbed her bag off his face. She then held out her hand above his head.

"Guess I'll just discard this root of flindishion," she said quietly.

Fink stirred and snorted. Then, he finally awoke and saw Anna's hand above him full of root pieces. His eyes opened wide.

"No!" Fink nearly shouted as he stumbled to get up from his sleep. "I can use that!"

Anna smiled. She looked at Gink and must have decided to be nicer to him, because she only nudged him a few times before he stirred awake. The tent was much quieter without the noises coming from their snoring. The wind blowing outside was the only noise that remained, which was quite loud. Anna walked back over to her spot near the rest of the group and sat down.

"Now," she continued with a pleased look, "Why do you need to chew up the roots?"

"Ahhh," Fink chimed in from behind them, "he needs to chew them in order to start the fermenting process. Then, he can brew it into a sort of stew."

Anna looked disgusted and confused at the same time. Jack could see that she had questions but was struggling with what to ask.

Finally, she inquired, "How will chewing the roots do *that*?"

"It's a simple process of his saliva reacting to the starch in the roots," Gink replied.

"That's disgusting," Anna said as she backed away.

Jack was curious about how the process worked and asked, "Do you have to spit it back out? What do you do with it after you've finished chewing it?"

Valkog reached for a decent sized brewing pot and held it up a little for Jack to see.

"Yes," Valkog replied. "I will be spitting it in here so that it can begin to ferment."

The process required for Valkog to get his root of flindishion was rather new to Jack and Anna. Both of them were somewhat taken aback at how gross it sounded. However, the others seemed to be well aware of the whole method and didn't seem to be bothered in the least. Geller was packing up his bag, Gink was already attached to Fink's back, and Valkog looked like he was nearly prepared to leave as he finished gathering all the root chunks into a neat pile.

Geller interrupted their conversation by saying, "We must get back on the move, now that everyone is up and in good spirits. We've lost a lot of time and we were supposed to be back last night."

"What about his wings?" Anna asked while pointing to Valkog's burned wings. "He can't fly like that, can he?"

Valkog was scooping the root chunks into a sack that was now hanging around his neck. He did not appear to be in pain, but his wings were in pretty bad shape from what Jack could tell. Maybe the cold was helping to keep it from hurting him so much, Jack thought. Either way, it definitely did not look like Valkog could fly.

"We will have to walk as far and as fast as we can," Geller explained. "Without a fire to brew over, the fermented mixture will be useless for rejuvenating his mana."

Still chewing, Valkog stood up and grabbed the pot he showed Jack. Then he took a piece of rope leftover from the den, and tied it around his neck so it hung down near his chest. Without regard for how gross it looked to both Jack and Anna, Valkog spit a chewed chunk of the root into the pot. It clanked with the sudden presence of the root from his mouth. He immediately took another chunk and continued the chewing process.

Obviously disgusted but still curious, Anna asked, "How long will it take to ferment?"

"It will probably take a whole day in these temperatures," Valkog explained. "If I had a way to keep it warm, it might only take a few hours. I'll do my best, though, to keep it against my body so it can stay warmer than the outside air."

The group didn't waste time getting ready. They packed up quickly and headed out of the tent into the freezing cold air. Jack certainly felt a lot colder than when he first woke up. The strong wind was driving the cold air into the fabric of his clothes that were supposed to be keeping him warm. His toes were already numb, but now his feet were sunken deep into the fresh snow. He felt miserable without the warming potion.

Once they were all out of the tent, Geller flicked his wand and it folded neatly up into the bag. Anna quickly grabbed it and shoved it into her bag. She looked just as miserable as Jack felt.

"Which way?" Geller asked Valkog.

Valkog stood for a second as he looked around. Jack wasn't sure what he was trying to see, because there was nothing to see as far as he could tell. As he turned on his spot, Valkog stood up straight and almost looked as if he was smelling the air.

Finally, Valkog said, "This way."

Without hesitation, Valkog began walking. Geller quickly followed behind him and the others fell in line as well. Jack wondered how Valkog could see anything in the storm. He knew Valkog could navigate back home in flight, but he wondered if it was possible to navigate the same way on land while walking.

It was frustrating for Jack to walk in the storm as his hands and feet felt heavy and they hurt. The snow and ice pelted his face like sand. He looked over at Anna and saw that she was having difficulty traversing through the snow as well. He then glanced over at Fink and felt bad for him too. Not only was he somewhat shorter than Jack, he also had the burden of carrying Gink on his back. It didn't make Jack feel any better or any warmer, but it did make him realize that it could be much worse. And, he couldn't forget that it was his idea that brought all of them out here in the cold of winter. But, he also remembered that Gink and Fink insisted on coming. He wondered why they wanted the root of flindishion so badly.

Gink was facing away from the blowing wind so he wasn't getting hit as hard as the others. Then, Jack realized that they were both wearing goggles. They wore goggles so much that he didn't even notice them at first glance.

"Hey," Jack said to Gink, "you don't happen to have any extra goggles, do you?"

Gink laughed. Then, he reached into one of his many pockets in his coat and pulled out a couple pair.

"We've always got goggles!" Gink said cheerfully.

Jack quickly snatched both pair of the goggles and thanked him. He put them on and felt instant relief to his eyes, which were watering so badly that he had frozen tears on his cheeks. He handed the other pair to Anna who also hurriedly put them on. It wasn't much, but it was one less thing he had to be concerned about.

The group walked for roughly twenty minutes before Jack felt like they were beginning to make progress. It seemed like forever before Jack's legs got in sync with walking through the thick snow. Every step he took his feet sank deep into it. That meant every step he took required him to lift his legs higher than normal. He was now in sort of a rhythm with his walking.

"How far do you think we've got?" Geller asked Valkog.

There was a brief moment of silence from the whole group as they anticipated the news. Jack wondered if it would be good. He hoped for the best.

Valkog finally answered, "I'd say we have about a week at our current pace."

"How did we get so far away?!" Jack asked, exasperated.

Valkog was still chewing. In fact, during the silence and in the moments between wind gusts, Jack could hear the chewing through his cap.

"I can fly at great speeds," Valkog replied. "I remember trying to fly as fast and as far away as possible from the danger of last night. But I do not recall if I was paying attention to which direction I was flying."

Geller chimed in, "It sounds like we went too far in the wrong direction!"

Jack felt a bit of disappointment. He didn't want to talk much either because his lips and jaw were nearly frozen. It was difficult to talk without sounding like he was falling asleep.

The group walked on for several hours, mostly in silence. Jack figured no one wanted to talk because their mouths were probably just as frozen as his. Eventually, Valkog stopped in his tracks. He was looking at his brewing pot hanging from his neck with a concerned look on his face.

"What is it?" Geller asked. "Why are we stopping?"

Valkog held his pot up a little and said, "It has frozen over."

"Does that mean it's ruined?" Anna asked through shivers.

Valkog tried to smile through frozen lips as he answered her in reassurance, "No, it will be fine. But I need to find somewhere that's out of the cold where I can warm it back up to get the process going again."

"There!" Gink shouted out. "What's that over there?"

Gink was pointing to a place in the distance. It was a dark point on what looked like some rocks, but Jack could hardly see what it was. Valkog squinted his eyes a little as he attempted to peer through the storm as well.

After a moment, Valkog said, "It looks like it may be a cave in some rocks."

"It wouldn't be a bad idea to stop and rest out this storm," Geller said. "There's not much sense in continuing on if the mixture is frozen anyway. Let's head over there."

The group turned and headed toward the dark opening in the rocks. As they got closer, Jack could see that it was a very large hill. They were headed toward the cliffside of the hill. Eventually, he was able to make out that it was indeed a cave, and he was relieved. It was going to be a good feeling to get out of the cold wind and snow, even if just for a little while. He longed for warmth or still air at the very least.

Jack recalled his recent luck in caves and began to feel a little uneasy about the prospect of being in another one. His fear was overcome by the fact that he wanted to be outside of the storm. However, it was still in the back of his mind. As they approached the cliffside, Jack noticed that they were going to need to climb at least fifteen feet in order to get in.

With lots of help from Valkog, the group made it into the cave. He was much larger than the rest of them and stronger, too. He lifted each of them halfway up the rock face so that they all had less to climb. After a few moments, they were all in the cave. The sudden absence of the wind was refreshing to Jack. His skin burned like it was on fire even though he had just been freezing cold. The wind had caused him to get so cold that in that moment he felt very warm.

Valkog didn't waste any time. He took off the pot from around his neck and set it down on the cave floor. He then sat in front of it and wrapped his singed wings around it while blowing air onto the pot.

"Do the two of you have any more melting potions?" Anna asked Gink and Fink.

Gink answered back with an apologetic look, "We have the ingredients, but we need a fire to brew it over."

Anna snapped back, "Well, we don't need a melting potion if we have a fire!"

"Maybe," Geller suggested, "we could look around here for something to burn."

Jack looked around and saw that the cave went back further than he could see. It just seemed to disappear into darkness. He didn't expect that they would find anything down there. The only way wood could possibly be down there, was if someone had brought it in previously.

Fink very enthusiastically skipped toward the darkness while both him and Gink sang. The others followed as well, but not as cheerfully. Geller summoned the glowing orb in order to see as they walked around.

After half an hour of searching, the group concluded that they found all they were going to find. The cave was bare of wood, but they did manage to find some small sticks and roots. It wasn't much and wouldn't make a big fire, but it could possibly be big enough to melt the fermenting mixture.

Geller started a small fire with the scraps they found. He took the pot and levitated it over the fire. After a short while, the mixture began to thaw out and heat up a little. As it did, it released a horrible stench that made Jack's nose wrinkle.

"Is something wrong with it?" Jack finally asked.

Valkog chuckled and answered, "Unfortunately, that's just the way it smells when it's fermenting."

"Well, it smells just plain awful!" Anna said.

Fink and Gink laughed.

"I rather like the smell," Gink said while laughing.

Geller looked at Gink and said, "That's simply because it means money. That horrible smell is just the precursor of earnings for you two."

Gink stopped laughing, but he was still smiling.

Jack was feeling rather hungry now that they were warming up a little. They had all been walking for hours without eating. There was no way Jack would have wanted to eat while they were walking, though. It would have been painful to chew with his mouth seemingly frozen in place from the storm. He hoped Geller had brought something to prepare.

"You don't happen to have any food, do you?" Jack asked Geller.

Sitting up in surprise, Geller stated, "I had totally forgotten about food."

Geller reached into his bag grabbing for something. Jack felt relieved that there was something left to eat in the first place. He knew they had only planned on a one-day trip, so the fact that Geller had extra food was encouraging. After a quick moment of searching, he pulled out what looked like crackers. Geller then handed them out to all the members of the group.

"I didn't have the time to produce a meal, nor did I have the forethought to do so," Geller explained to everyone. "Fortunately, I brought some of these crackers in case we missed our timeline to get home. They're not much, but they'll fill you right up."

Jack looked at what Geller handed him. There were only two small crackers resting in his palm. Each one was smaller than his hand. He felt a sense of disappointment as he looked them over. They were fairly plain looking with a light orange tint. Although Jack remembered that Geller was good at making food that would fill them up, he still couldn't get over the small amount he had been given. He figured Geller was rationing the food in case they found themselves being delayed even longer.

Finally, after staring at the crackers for a moment or two, Jack decided to take a bite of one. The flavor was wonderful! It reminded him of Prunklesnider. His eyes opened wide as he savored the taste.

Then, he recalled that Anna disliked Prunklesnider. He shot a glance over at her and noticed that she was not liking her snack. Her face almost looked as if she had sat on a tack, but she must have been hungry because she took more than the one bite.

"This tastes just like Prunklesnider," Jack said between nibbles. "It's delicious!"

Laughing, Geller explained, "They're called Prunklesnider crackers. They are exceedingly difficult to make because Prunklesnider is supposed to stay warm. There's quite a technique into making these."

Jack was very content with his small meal. As he ate, he began to get full and was only beginning the second cracker. Soon, each member of the group had their fill. Jack decided not to eat all of his second cracker and save some to nibble on later. He stuffed it into one of his pockets.

The storm outside the cave was blowing hard. The wind howled past the cave opening like air being blown over a bottle. It was making a dull, constant noise. Suddenly, a strong wind blew just the right way and made its entrance into the cave. It chilled them all to the bone! The small fire went out and Jack immediately felt cold again as the cave went mostly dark.

Geller got up and took out his wand. He attempted to restart the fire, but there just wasn't enough wood to relight. Eventually, he gave up. Sitting back down and looking slightly defeated, Geller put his wand away and pulled out the glowing orb again.

"I suggest we stay in the cave until the fermentation process is complete," Geller stated with a sigh. "Otherwise, we'll just be in the same situation again.

Valkog took the pot of fermentation mixture and wrapped his singed wings around it to keep it warm like before. He didn't look too bothered by the fact that the fire was out, which offered a little bit of comfort to Jack. If Valkog didn't look concerned, then it must be working just fine, Jack thought.

As they sat there, cold took over the cave. Even the glowing orb didn't offer a feeling of warmth. Jack shivered. He noticed Anna was shivering, too. He got up and walked over to sit down, right next to her, so that they could keep each other warm.

Slowly, a green gas filled the floor of the cave. Jack looked down at the river of smoke flow between them. It acted much like slow moving water, making its way all around each of them. At first, he thought either Gink or Fink had dropped a potion out of one of their many pockets.

Geller jumped up and yelled, "Everyone, out! Now!!!"

The group barely had a chance to move when the green smoke lifted into the air and filled the cave all around them. Jack couldn't see a thing.

Chapter 16: Gary

Waking up again from a deep sleep, Jack tried to determine what had happened. He struggled to remember what transpired in the cave. He recalled the green smoke, but nothing else. The fact that he was alive made him feel relieved. It must have been an accident, he thought.

Then, as he tried to stand up, he realized his hands were bound together with some silverish string. He fumbled around trying to free his hands but without success. Looking around, he saw that he was in a cage of sorts.

Jack stood up to take in the surroundings. There were many cages made of wood, tied together with the same string that was holding his hands together. In some of the cages were the other members of the group. He quickly looked to make sure everyone else was there.

In the cage to Jack's right was Anna and she was just stirring awake as well. To his left, in a corner, was Geller who was still asleep. To the right of Anna was Valkog. He was also still asleep. Across a path in the middle of the room was Gink and Fink. They were snoring and snorting loudly.

The room was made of large chunks of cobblestone. The spaces between the rocks were filled with the silverish string substance that Jack was now seeing everywhere. There was only one door leading into the room with a couple of lanterns hanging on each side. He noticed the temperature in the room was rather warm.

It was nice being out of the storm, but he felt a sense of fear coming over him. He wondered who tied all of them up and put them in cages. As fear set in, he began to struggle. He wriggled around trying to break the string that held his hands together. His erratic movements caused the cages to start bumping together. Geller awoke to the commotion.

"Are you okay?" Jack asked Anna as he noticed her becoming aware of their new surroundings.

Anna struggled for a moment with her bindings too before settling down and answering, "Y-yes, I think I'm alright."

Jack continued to look around the room for anything that could help them escape, but he saw nothing useful. In a corner near the entryway were their belongings, all stacked on top of each other. The bags were too far away to reach.

Standing up in his cage, Geller said, "Everyone remain quiet. We're in danger here."

Geller scanned the room and looked like he was also assessing the situation. He tried pulling his hands apart for a brief moment before giving up. It looked as if he knew what it was. Jack looked at his bindings and saw that it was much different than string. The bindings seemed more like a thick, stringy glue.

"Can you break it?" Anna asked Geller, motioning toward his bindings. "What is it?"

Geller responded, "If I had my wand with me, maybe. But, even then, it would be tricky. This stuff here is araknolian silk. It is inherently magically strong. Very tough to break, and very handy to use for many reasons."

"What is araknolian silk?" Anna asked, confused.

From behind her came a loud crashing sound as Valkog began to come out of his slumber. He was also just realizing that he was bound and stuck in a cage and he struggled against it as he tried to break his hands free.

"Quiet!" Geller whispered loudly over to Valkog.

It still took another moment or two before Valkog calmed down. He too looked around to assess the predicament they were in as he determined that he was unable to free his hands. Once he gathered what was going on, he stopped moving and the crashing of the cages subsided.

Valkog looked over at the other three in his row of cages and asked, "How long was I out?"

Geller whispered back, "I'm not sure, but an araknolian petrification gas can last for weeks. I am hoping that is not the case, though."

Wide-eyed, Jack asked, "What does that mean? What is an araknolian petrification gas thing?"

"We are in an araknolian dungeon," Geller explained. "We must have been in an araknolian cave before. By the looks of it, it means that we have been captured by one."

Anna quickly interrupted Geller by asking, "What is an araknolian? Why would it want to capture us?"

"An araknolian, in the simplest explanation, is much like a very large spider with goblin-like features," Geller explained. "It uses petrification gas to essentially put you to sleep."

"Why would it do that?" Anna asked in a scared tone.

Valkog replied quietly from behind her, "We are most likely meant to be several meals."

Anna's eyes opened as wide as they could, as she was suddenly overcome with fear! She didn't say anything else, but Jack could see in her eyes that she was full of questions. Jack wondered how they would ever get out of the room without one of the araknolian things finding out. Anna looked like she was thinking something similar.

From across the path, the snoring stopped abruptly. Gink and Fink were beginning to wake up. They had been bound the way they were found, which was with Gink still attached to Fink's back. Their cage swayed and bumped up against other empty cages as they also struggled against their bindings. Once they came to the same realization that they were trapped, they stopped moving around. Fink looked over to the others with an uncharacteristic stern look on his face.

Now that Gink and Fink were awake, the room was nearly silent without their snoring. A loud thumping sound could be heard down the hall leading into the room. It was getting louder and closer. After a few minutes, a large spider the size of Jack entered the room. It was a shimmery silver color. Anna screamed at the sight of it and fell back in her cage. Everybody else backed up in their cages as well.

In a high pitched, growling, menacing voice, the araknolian spoke, "Welcome to my humble abode!"

Jack saw a small smirk on its face as it welcomed them. On its face were many small, black beady eyes. Its face was scrunched up and puffy. Jack could see why Geller said they were goblin-like spiders. It was standing there in front of them looking like it had nefarious plans for them. There were two large fangs sticking out of its mouth. The flickering light from the lanterns caused its skin to shimmer as if it was covered in glitter. It looked much like Jack would expect a huge spider to look like, except for the face. There were large hairs that covered its legs and it stood on top of the same type of hairs, lifting it a couple inches off the floor. They must be really strong, Jack thought.

Speaking out, Geller said, "We mean you no harm. We were merely passing through."

The araknolian laughed and walked over to Geller's cage. He lifted one of his many legs and gave a push against the cage and let it swing around.

"I am pleased to meet such a delightful dinner!" the araknolian said menacingly while laughing. "I am not sure what kind of harm you think I fear from you. You have no way of injuring me even if you wanted to."

Valkog spoke up, "We are on an important mission from the Govilian Council. There is a war coming this way. You would be wise to release us and let us continue our mission, so that we can prevent the evils that are intended to destroy our ways of life as well as yours."

Smiling, the araknolian asked, "Do you mean there is an all-powerful wizard named Shamakul coming this way?"

"How do you know that name?" Geller inquired, showing no fear of what was standing in front of him.

Still smiling, the araknolian stopped what he was doing and looked at the whole group. Jack disliked its smile; it seemed somewhat pleasurable, but he knew it was smiling only because it had control of the whole situation. Nothing they could do would change the fact that they were bound and locked in cages.

"Where are my manners?" the araknolian asked. "First things first, I should introduce myself. My name is Gary and my wife's name is Emsters."

Fearing that there were more than one of these things, Jack asked, "Where is your wife?"

"Ha! She has been out hunting for some time now," Gary said. "I have lived here in this cave for nearly a century. My wife and I dug it out ourselves over time. We added each room as needed, as the years passed us by."

Geller interrupted Gary, "That's great information, Gary, but I'm still curious as to how you know Shamakul. How do you know who that is?"

The group watched as Gary walked over to Gink and Fink and tapped on their cage. It swayed and thumped against the cages around it, but they remained silent. Then, Gary walked over to Anna's cage and tapped it hard. She struggled to stay standing as it swayed and bumped into the other cages. Jack could see that Gary was toying with them. He had absolutely no fear that anyone in the group could cause him harm. Jack realized that Gary's fearlessness was correct; none of them had any way to disable him much less break free of their cages.

"It's been a good winter this year," Gary finally stated. "It has been oddly in our favor. One of the best yet!"

Jack noticed several staffs in the corner near their belongings that weren't theirs. He began to realize that others had likely been in these same cages, and he wondered if they were able to get free or be let go.

"Have there been others here?" Jack asked as he motioned toward the staffs in the corner.

Chuckling, Gary explained, "Like I said, it has been a great year for us."

He wasn't sure how, but Jack knew they needed to stall as long as they could before anything bad happened. Maybe they could tire Gary out, he thought. He felt somewhat helpless, though, because he wasn't sure if it was late or early in the day.

Looking at the staffs as well, Geller inquired, "Have you come across any fironi?"

"I do not care what they were," Gary smiled. "They were tasty and maybe even a little spicy! They were the ones who spoke of this Shamakul character; telling me that if I were to eat them, I would surely experience the wrath of him."

Geller moved forward in his cage and asked, "Why does it not bother you that a war is coming? Shamakul is very powerful, indeed. And we intend of taking care of his threat."

Gary gasped in astonishment.

"Of course I care!" he replied. "All that food ... er, I mean ... all those dead bodies ... who could possibly benefit from that? No matter who wins, I will stand to benefit. I won't have to hunt for food for ages!"

Jack was taken aback. He looked at the others in the group and saw they had similar looks of shock on their faces. It didn't seem as if Gary intended on fighting in the battle or participating in any other fashion except for scavenging the battlefield after it was over. All Gary cared about was getting a ton of free food.

Then, Gary continued, "While we're on the subject of food ... we should discuss this evening's dinner plans."

"We aren't the enemy!" Anna exclaimed. "Our mission is to protect these lands. That includes protecting you from Shamakul!"

With a sigh, Gary responded, "I do not care who is on whose side. My concern lies in whether they are tasty and delicious to eat. I do

---

love food!"

Geller, attempting to change the subject away from Gary's dinner plans, asked, "How long have we been asleep?"

Gary laughed once again. His laugh was almost shrieky and not very pleasant to Jack's ears. It made Jack feel uneasy about what Gary was going to say.

"I don't keep track of the days!" Gary said, still laughing. "That kind of stuff doesn't matter to me. I just care about eating."

Jack quickly asked, worried, "Has it really been days?"

The group had already been late getting back. If they had really been gone for a few more days, Selini must be worried sick about them. He knew from what Geller had said before that there was no search party underway. They were stuck out there without any help to get them home.

"Ha! It may have been weeks for all I know!" Gary said with a smirk on his face.

It was obvious Gary didn't care about time, nor did he care that they were pressed for time. Their mission was essentially a bust. It had its bumps early on from the fironi doing something near the portal to the snole's tunnels, and then this predicament. Jack felt sick to his stomach about how long they may have been asleep.

The members of the group looked at each other in horror and surprise as they all realized the seriousness of the situation. Fink could be seen patting himself down as he looked for something, but his coat with many pockets was missing from his attire. Jack wondered if he was looking for a watch or timepiece of some sort. Valkog looked saddened, and Geller looked astonished and angry. Anna had a single tear roll down her check as the news set in.

"Look, is there anything we can do to convince you to let us go?" Jack asked Gary in desperation.

Gary took a couple steps so that he was standing in front of Jack.

He observed Jack for a moment and smiled big. He then shook the cage until Jack fell down. Gary laughed as he watched Jack struggle to steady himself again.

"There is nothing my food can do to convince me to simply let it go," Gary stated cheerfully.

Gink shouted over to Gary, "You need ta let us two go! We won't taste any good. You are stressing us out and that makes us gassy. Trust me. You wouldn't want that! Not in the least!"

Without turning to look at them, Gary simply replied, "I am well aware of your gas issues. I have had to deal with the stench for some time now. For that reason, you two will be first. That way, I get rid of the worst stuff first. Then, I'll move on to the desserts. Look at all that meat!"

Gary was still looking at Jack as he spoke. Jack's face dropped as he realized Gary was talking about him. His heart was starting to pound as the realization that he was going to be food for this spider thing began to set in. Gary watched him intently and continued to smile, but menacingly.

"Hey, over here!" Geller said to Gary as he tried to get his attention. "I can help you have food for an entire season. Whatever food stores you have, I can enchant them to last for longer than they normally would. The food will be tasty and fill you up fully before you've finished eating. It will taste delicious, every single bite!"

Valkog nodded and added, "Yes, there's no reason to eat *us*. Especially with an offer like that! He can make your food taste nice and fresh until the very last bite."

Jack could see that Gary looked intrigued. His heart was racing now. There was a chance that they could get out of there and this seemed like it was the only way. They needed to convince Gary that he no longer needed to hunt for his food for a while. Surely, Jack thought, this strategy could work!

"I will remind you," Gary said after a moment of silence, "I have had a great season. I know how to prepare my food just as well. Maybe it doesn't always taste the freshest near the end, but it serves me well."

Geller rebutted, "I can prepare enough food for you and your wife for *two* seasons! Just think of all you can do with your free time if you're not having to constantly hunt for food. Think of all the time you can spend with Emsters."

Silence filled the room as everyone waited for Gary's response to this enticing offer. A smile left Gary's face and intrigue filled him. Jack was getting nervous as the moment dragged on. Finally, Gary backed up a little to Geller's cage and looked him over intently.

After the extended moment ended, Gary spoke slowly and quietly as if to himself, "I don't particularly like eating food that can talk. It makes my stomach squirm some."

Jack slowly moved to the front of his cage so he could see and hear better. He wondered what Gary meant. Maybe, he thought, he was actually considering Geller's offer. He was still pretty nervous, his heart still pounding in his chest, and his hands were sweaty under their bindings. He listened intently to what Gary had to say.

"I do have a stockpile of meat," Gary explained slowly. "Like I said before, it has been a great season. I do like to eat the fresh food first because it tastes so much better. It's like having a treat that I rarely get to have."

Gary hesitated for a moment as he considered Geller's proposition. Then he turned completely to face Geller. He sighed and he looked like he'd finally made his decision. He inched closer to Geller's cage and spit on the bindings on Geller's hands. The stringy substance dissolved instantly. It dropped down like wet paper pulp to the floor below the cage. Then, Gary opened the cage door.

Geller cautiously climbed out and landed on the floor of the room. He watched Gary carefully, looking for any sign that it may be a trick. He glanced around the room at the others and then focused on their belongings in the corner.

"I will need my wand," Geller stated, plainly. "I cannot enchant that much food without it, at least not very effectively."

Gary thought for a moment. Then he sighed and motioned for Geller to get his wand. Gary watched him closely as Geller retrieved the wand from his belongings. Jack could feel the tension in the room. It occurred to him that this may be the first time Gary had let his food loose.

As Geller got his wand, he then stated, "I will also need to gather some seasonings from my bag. That's the only way this will work."

Jack knew Geller was a man of his word, meaning he would fulfill his promise to Gary. Jack also knew that Gary didn't know any of them so he would certainly be cautious. He watched as Gary kept guard of Geller, staying close to him the entire time.

"Fine," Gary responded to Geller, "get your seasonings. Set your wand down on the ground and move slowly while you get them."

Geller followed Gary's instructions and grabbed a small box from his bag. He opened it up showing Gary the contents, to let him know that he was definitely getting the seasonings he needed. Jack thought that was a good idea. Maybe it would ease Gary's fear that this might just be a ruse to escape.

"I will need some help," Geller stated firmly. "I am of small stature, and unless your meat chunks are small, which they probably aren't, I won't be able to lift them by myself."

Gary sighed heavily.

"You are pushing it," Gary said with anger. "You may choose … him."

Gary had pointed to Jack. Now, Jack's heart was beating at full speed. He thought Valkog would have been the better choice, but also figured Gary didn't choose him because he was bigger. Valkog would be much harder to keep under control if they were to try and escape.

"Where is your food storage?" Geller finally asked as he slowly picked up his wand.

Gary motioned for Geller to stay in front of him as he released Jack. Then, he positioned himself directly behind Geller and Jack, motioning for them to move forward into the hall. Geller looked at the others noting a look of comfort and reassurance. Then, the two of them began walking down the hall and out of the room where the others were. Within seconds, the three of them disappeared from view.

Jack and Geller walked down the hall. They passed several different branches where other halls and rooms were attached. After a short while, Gary motioned for them to turn left into a room. This room was similar in construction and looked a lot like the room where they had just come from.

As he entered the room, Jack noticed that it was much colder than the cage room. There were piles of meat neatly stacked from floor to ceiling all around the room. Jack kept quiet, thankful that he was 'somewhat' free, but also very aware that something could go wrong at any moment. He feared that Gary may be playing tricks on them, or that he may change his mind and just decide to eat them!

"There's so much food in here," Geller said to Gary.

Gary replied, "Like I said, this season has been very favorable for me and my wife."

Geller then asked, "I thought that araknolian ate their food alive?"

Jack's eyes opened wide! Why in the world would Geller say such a thing? In Gary's eyes they were food, and they were also *alive*. Both conditions were favorable for Gary but definitely worked against Geller and Jack. He certainly wouldn't remind Gary that they were ripe for eating!

"With as many animals and creatures that have come through the cave this year," Gary explained, "there has been more food than we could eat. I do desire fresh food, though. It is much tastier. So, you'd better be able to do what you said you could do!"

Geller looked around the room, inspecting the food supply. He looked as if he was counting and assessing while he walked around. There was way more meat than Jack could have imagined. The meat stacks were neatly separated by the size of the chunks. Some piles were massive meat chunks, while other stacks were of medium or smaller meat pieces. As far as Jack could tell, it was going to take some time to work through it all.

Finally, Geller stopped and said to Gary, "This is going to take some time, but I know I can do it."

"Very well," Gary stated, "I have other things to attend to anyway."

With that, Gary backed out of the room. His face was stern and much less 'smiley' than before. Jack did not like his menacing smile, but his stern looking face was even less tolerable. He was not sure how to interpret it. Gary then sprayed araknolian silk all across the door creating a thick barricade.

The two of them were now trapped in the meat dungeon. The coldness of the room was uncomfortable, especially knowing that they were now stuck in there with no way out.

"Can't you use a levitation spell to lift the heavy meats?" Jack finally asked Geller.

"Yes, I can," Geller replied, "but I wanted to see if Gary was truly willing to work with me on this. If he had said 'no', that would have been a clue he was just taking me out of the room for his dinner. If he allowed someone else to come with me, it meant otherwise. I doubt that he would eat two dinners. I really didn't care who came along, but I am glad it was you! Now, I must really be getting to work here."

Geller quickly began to prepare the meats in his special way. Jack was hoping that Gary would consider letting them go once it was all done. He wondered how long they had really been out, and if there was still time to get back to the city before the battle. There was so much meat that needed preparation; it made Jack nervous to think that even more precious time was being wasted in doing so. However, Geller was not wasting time getting started. He opened his spice box, pulled out his wand and brought a piece of meat to the center of the room.

Chapter 17: Battle March

Thousands of torches broke the darkness of the cavern as the Govilian army made its way through on the road to battle. High overhead were hanging roots that swayed and twinkled in the fire's glow. Chants of various kinds filled the air, and the creaking of large wooden wheels filled in the gaps between chants. There were heavy thuds of the Govilian Beasts' feet hitting the ground. Thousands of smaller feet stomped rhythmically as they moved forward. All of these sounds echoed throughout the cavern, bouncing off the ceiling far above and blending together to make a deafening roar.

Selini marched next to Gubuyis at the front of the army. They were leading the Govilian army to battle. The cavern was cold, but nothing like the cold of winter outside. Very few fighters were wearing heavy clothes to protect themselves from the elements if they were to be engaged in fighting outside. Heavy clothing would slow all of them down hindering their ability to fight. Gubuyis wore a colorful robe, just as he did on many occasions. His attire would certainly keep him warm if he found himself fighting outside the cavern. Selini was dressed for outside fighting as well. Under her armor, she wore a heavy set of clothes to protect against the raging winds. The two of them were prepared to battle wherever they were needed.

As they walked, Selini couldn't help but think about her missing brother and the others. A tear rolled down her cheek. She feared for what may have happened to them. She had not heard any news at all. Knowing that Valkog could have easily flown all of them back if they hadn't found the root of flindishion, or made a portal if they had, she worried what went wrong. She struggled trying to imagine what had happened but she knew something did. She also knew that Gink and Fink could have made a portal potion and let at least someone through to alert everyone as to what had happened. That made her even more concerned. Something really bad must have ensued she concluded.

"If we win," Selini asked Gubuyis, "will I be able to put together a search party to find them?"

Knowing exactly who she was talking about, Gubuyis nodded and said, "Warmer weather is just around the corner. I have high hopes for the group. You will take a team of your choosing and seek them out."

Selini nodded and gave a small smile as she thought about finding the others. She continued making her way through the cavern away from the underground city of Gargantulua. As she walked, she fought internally to remain focused on the coming battle. She could not let herself get distracted by the absence of her brother and the others. Once before, for a long time, she had thought he was dead but Geller had proven otherwise. She knew in her heart that he was a fighter and would be able to remain alive.

Gubuyis and Selini followed the same path the group had followed on their way to Wyvergia several months earlier. It glowed its bright, watery blue. The glowing water flowed between the cracks of the rocks and went on for as far as anyone could see. The path reminded Selini of the trek before. She recalled meeting Jack for the first time, down in the depths of the cavern, and the dragons they encountered. It was such a recent memory that she still felt like there could be dragons roaming around somewhere.

From overhead came a loud rushing noise as a single Frost Bird flew low. It was Zarx'l. He landed loudly about fifty feet ahead of both Selini and Gubuyis. He wore shiny, rainbow and silvery armor that coated his scales. Although it was dark in the cavern, it was easy to see the detail of such a large being as the torchlight reflected off him. Selini and Gubuyis approached Zarx'l.

"My army is ready to fight!" Zarx'l informed them. "We are prepared to do our part and more."

Selini looked around into the darkness and asked, "Are they already here?"

Zarx'l smiled a big smile; he was happy to see that his army had been able to be 'stealthy enough' not to be detected. He stood up straight and let out a loud, booming roar into the cavern. The sound of his roar shook Selini's clothes. The metal armor of nearby fighters rumbled and vibrated together. As he roared, frost flew from his mouth.

From the dark regions of the cavern above them came a thunderous sound, as many hundreds of Frost Birds roared in return. The air suddenly felt chillier. Selini looked up and saw the faint movement of numerous Frost Birds flying above them. As she focused her eyes on the ceiling of the cavern, she could see the shimmering of large scales as the Frost Birds crawled across it. Had she not known they were there, she may have disregarded the shimmering as simply just a part of the cavern.

Zarx'l then looked back at the two of them and smiled.

"As you can see," Zarx'l stated, "we are ready and with you all the way to victory!"

Gubuyis raised his staff and said to Zarx'l, "We thank you for your service to this cause. We are in a much better position with you and your army by our side. With your assistance, we will win. We will prevail!"

The army had stopped as they spoke. Zarx'l knew he would need to move soon in order for all of them to get back to their mission. There were several cheers from fighters close enough to overhear Gubuyis as he thanked Zarx'l.

Before taking back off, Zarx'l asked, "Have you heard anything from Jack and the others?"

Selini looked sad and replied, "No, we have not heard anything since they left nearly two months ago."

"I am very sorry Vlagar was unable to find anything on his reconnaissance missions," Zarx'l said. "They just weren't anywhere near where we thought they'd be."

Gubuyis stepped forward and said, "They are sure to be okay. I can feel it in my bones."

Selini felt a little comforted by this news. She knew her father was usually right about these kinds of things. She actually felt somewhat enthusiastic that her father was willing to openly convey such a thought.

"That is great news!" Zarx'l responded. "I hope for the very best outcome. Now, it is time for me to address my troops and tie up any loose ends. I agree with you, Gubuyis. We will win this battle!"

Zarx'l then took off loudly into the air. He flew straight up and nearly disappeared into the shroud of darkness above. Several roars could be heard as he began to address his troops. Once again, Selini, Gubuyis, and the army began to press forward.

As they walked, Selini spoke to her father, "Just to make sure we're planning on the same thing happening, I would like to go over the plans for destroying the shields. First of all, the Frost Birds will destroy the weather enchantment by freezing it until it collapses. While that is happening, we will be focusing on tearing apart the protection shield. We will use the catapults to launch large rocks from the cavern. As the rocks approach the protection shield, I will cast enchantments to enlarge them as big as they can get. They will smash against the shield. Hopefully, the barrage of boulders will end up destroying the protection shield."

"This is what we have agreed upon, yes," Gubuyis replied. "But, it is quite unfortunate that you and the Frost Birds will likely become magically exhausted in the process."

Selini responded, "I am disheartened knowing that I will not be able to fight magically if this goes the way we think it will. You need more protection than we can give you. Is it still your plan to fight Shamakul, one-on-one, without a magically strong posse?"

"Do not fear for me," Gubuyis replied. "I have a few tricks up my sleeve that even you haven't seen before. There will be a strong group of fighters, including you, to assist me on my way to Shamakul where I will face him head on. We will need to ensure the rest of the army provides the reinforcements required to defeat the fighters protecting Shamakul. Once I begin fighting Shamakul, I believe we will see a dedicated group of fighters that will focus on solely protecting him. This will be our biggest challenge outside of fighting Shamakul himself."

Selini and Gubuyis walked for a while without saying anything.

Selini couldn't help but worry about her father. She knew he was powerful, but to have to fight a powerful wizard in the middle of a battle was very different and dangerous. He would be right in the middle of an area where everyone around him was trying to kill him. She wondered if he had any plans to retreat if things weren't going his way.

Finally, Selini broke the silence and asked, "Do you have any concerns that Geller won't be by your side in this?"

"My dear daughter," Gubuyis stated reassuringly, "even though I am old, I have some very strong magic left in me. We will just have to focus all our efforts on Shamakul, as soon as possible, once the shields are collapsed. Remember, when we fought Ghowla? His forces gave up almost immediately after his defeat. I anticipate the same thing here. We need to focus on Shamakul. He has done many terrible things in his position. And Shamakul supports Karakaziem's efforts to do many terrible things to the inhabitants of Lunia. Of course, I agree, without you and Geller fighting magically by my side, it will be a very tough win. But the conditions are the way they are. We will have to work with what we have been given. I am comforted by the fact that you will still be able to fight in combat by my side."

Selini, Gubuyis, and the army pressed forward for quite some time. As they walked, Selini talked with her father about different strategies and scenarios that might occur during the battle. No strategy seemed new, though, as over the last couple months, they had contemplated numerous outcomes. Selini just wanted to make sure everything had been thought of before they got into battle.

Soon, the air began to get cooler and fresher. Ahead of them in the distance was a dim light. They weren't too far from the cavern opening and large bangs could be heard coming from ahead of them. Selini and Gubuyis slowed down, knowing that soon they would be approaching the battlegrounds.

Vlagar landed a short distance ahead of them and waited for Gubuyis and Selini to get to him.

"Shamakul's army has amassed outside the cavern mouth," Vlagar explained to the two as they approached him."

More booms and bangs could be heard. They were louder now that they were getting closer. They could hear the dull roar of chants coming from afar. The frequency of the banging increased as well. It sounded as if Shamakul's army was already attempting to destroy the opening.

Vlagar continued, "His army is full of axe throwers and fironi. And, Shamakul has enchanted himself to be on fire. He is standing in the middle of the whole group."

"Why would he enchant himself to be on fire?" Selini asked her father.

Gubuyis simply responded, "He means to be the source of the fironi's fire needs in this battle."

More large bangs continued from ahead. The Govilian army quieted down. They were only about a thousand feet from the opening. There was a loud murmur of concern coming from the troops behind Selini and Gubuyis.

"Thank you, Vlagar," Gubuyis said. "Thank you for all your help these last few months. It seems as if the battle is about to begin!"

Vlagar gave a slight bow and took off into the darkness ahead. Gubuyis then turned to face the army behind him. He watched as they slowly quieted down. After a few moments, the army was completely silent. The booms from ahead of them continued. Vlagar reached his army brethren and joined them at the ceiling on the inside of the cavern opening.

"My dear Govilians," Gubuyis said as he addressed the army. "We fight today not out of malice or desire to expand our territories, but out of necessity. We fight because we have to. Evil has brought itself to our doorsteps this day. I must tell you; we are stronger and much more magically powerful than Shamakul will ever be. We are more powerful than his army. Gargantulua will see the sun rise in a glorious spring once again!"

There was a roar of shouts and cheers from the troops that filled the cavern.

After they settled down, Gubuyis continued, "I must remind you that you are all that stands in the way of Shamakul and your loved ones. We must persevere regardless of the intensity of the battle. You each have your mission; focus on those missions and we will win this battle! I ask that you try at all costs to merely disable our opponents. Stun them. Put them to sleep. Do whatever you can to avoid killing them. We are on a mission to save lives, and that includes their lives as well."

A large bang came from ahead. It was louder than the others. Selini knew they must begin fighting soon or the cavern mouth may be collapsed before they get there.

"You must not lose focus of the good in you," Gubuyis continued. "You must not lose focus of your mission. You will live to see the sun rise on another warm summer morning. Today is not the day for evil to prevail!"

The army erupted into cheers. They clanked their shields and swords together. Gubuyis turned and began to walk forward toward the constant bangs at the cavern opening. The glowing water rippled between the cracks at each boom and the heavy footsteps of the army marching.

"We will have our victory today!" Gubuyis finished saying as he walked.

The chanting of the army behind them was loud in the cavern. There were bangs of drums followed by the sounds of battle horns. The stomping feet of foot soldiers and Govilian Beasts alike were much louder than the drums. Many members of the army slammed their shields and weapons against each other, making a loud, metallic ruckus. There was an occasional shot of magic in the air, temporarily illuminating the cavern all around.

The army was led by Gubuyis and Selini, who walked together. Behind them were thousands of foot soldiers wielding swords, pikes, spears, and wands. Many, but not all of them wore metal armor. Interspersed within them were about the same number of archers with plenty of arrows to spare. Some of the archers had quivers that self-replenished. Many of the archers had no magical fighting abilities or armor which was the reason they were what they were. They all followed Selini and Gubuyis intently.

The Govilian Beasts marched diligently behind the archers and foot soldiers. On their backs were three riders each, and one of these three riders controlled the direction of the beast. Another rider sounded the battle horn that charged the troops and also directed the beast as to which magical ability to discharge, or which action it should take. The last rider held a very large drum. The beat of the drum helped to fire up the troops, almost like a spell being cast to energize them. The drum beat also acted similarly to a battle horn, and its sound directed specific actions from the Govilian Beasts. There were nearly a hundred of these beasts, each ready for battle.

Between each of the Govilian Beasts were large, wooden catapults. The wheels creaked and whined under their weight. Each catapult weighed more than a ton. They would be instrumental in the fight to bring down the protection shield. The Govilian army was counting on their effectiveness. The wheels of the catapults were aglow in a purple haze. Behind each catapult were several Valindi with wands drawn and pointing at the wheels. They were moving the catapults with their magic, making it much easier than dragging or pushing them through the cavern. They kept pace with the army quite well.

After a short while, the army made it to the cavern opening. Selini and Gubuyis stopped along with everyone else. Gubuyis motioned for the catapults to move forward into position. The army cleared paths for the catapults to park in a center line. Shamakul's army sat not far outside of the opening.

The Govilian army was abruptly greeted by thousands of green skinned troll axe throwers. They all had long, black hair. Many were in ponytails, some wore fancy braids, and many others just had a heap of a mess for their hair. Their bare chests revealed how very muscular they were. Each troll had on light colored shorts and shoes. Their eyes glowed red and small horns protruded from all around their heads. Grunts and indiscernible chants could be heard coming from the entire troll army. Many of them were tossing their axes menacingly into the air and back and forth in their hands. The axes, including the handles, were entirely metallic and very sharp. Each blade was trimmed in a reddish substance. The sheer number of axe throwers was intended to instill fear in their enemy, the Govilian army.

If the axe throwers weren't enough to cause panic and fear in the Govilian army, the fironi was there to add to it. All throughout the axe throwers were hundreds of fironi. They tossed fire high into the air and between themselves as if they were playing a ball throwing game. As they tossed around the fire, it would eventually dissipate. They would simply conjure up more fire and do it all over again. The fironi looked pleased to be in battle.

Behind the fironi and axe throwers were hundreds of sword wielding creatures of all sorts. They weren't very well trained for war, but were sure to be a menacing force, nonetheless. Some were short and stubby with shields that were nearly the size of their entire body. There were also some creatures that stood towering high above the axe throwers. Much like the Govilian foot soldiers, they also clanked their shields and weapons together making a taunting ruckus.

Right in the center, behind the foot soldier creatures, stood a large being brightly ablaze. It was Shamakul. He was much taller than any of the army ahead of him and it was very easy to make him out in the crowd. Although he was on fire, his features could still be seen in some detail. He wore a thick, black and white speckled robe with red cuffs. It was also noticeable that he was bald under the fire. Shamakul stood resolute while laughing and watching Gubuyis ahead of him.

Several hundred dragons stood behind Shamakul. They were the same type of dragons Selini had fought in the cavern with Jack and Geller just months prior. The protection shield was not too far overhead for Shamakul's army, which kept the dragons on the ground. It was too difficult for all of them to fly. Occasionally, one would jump up into the air and fly over the others for a moment before landing again. They were all moving in an erratic fashion, eager to fly again.

Every so often, one would let out a loud roar. Their scales were thick, like planks of wood and it appeared they were not wearing any armor. But, all looked ready to fight!

Suddenly, the fironi acted in unison and cast a large fireball right at the cave's entrance. The fireball was massive and headed directly towards Gubuyis and the army behind him. It came at them fast and ferociously. Gubuyis gave a quick flick of his wand and the fireball veered upwards. It crashed into the rocks above the cavern opening. Everything shook and rumbled. Many large rocks fell from the ceiling and into the army. The fireball had missed its target.

Selini looked behind them and assessed what little damage was done. No one seemed to be badly hurt and the Frost Birds remained on the ceiling.

"There will be no shortage of rocks," Selini said. "The catapults can go all day long like this."

Gubuyis remained standing still. He kept his eyes on Shamakul, allowing Selini to do her assessment of the damage taken. After a short bit while the Govilian army situated itself again, Gubuyis called out to Shamakul.

He shouted in a magically enhanced voice, "SHAMAKUL! SHAMAKUL! STOP THIS MADNESS! TURN AWAY NOW! YOU STAND TO LOSE SO MUCH!"

Shamakul began laughing at Gubuyis's words. As he laughed, his army erupted into a loud roar of chants and taunting noises. The dragons behind him blew fire into the air. The fironi cast fire into the air as well. The axe throwers threw axes between themselves to display their dexterity with the blades. Shamakul made a motion with his hands for his troops to quickly quiet down. He stopped laughing.

"There is nothing you can do to stop me," Shamakul said in a loud but calm voice to Gubuyis. "There is nothing you can do to stop what is about to happen, except for one thing. I would like to inform you that we have had a recent opening for a wizard! You, Gubuyis, have been sought out by the Reign of Karakaziem to fill this position. You can fill that need for us. Ghowla was very powerful, and you have gained the respect of Karakaziem. If you accept this offer, I will stop our forces from annihilating the Govilian Alliance this day. Karakaziem will grant you limitless powers and you and your family will want for nothing ever again! Your puny little army will be granted the ability to surrender and assimilate into ours. This offer is extended to you from Karakaziem herself!"

Silence covered the battlefield on both sides. Shamakul's army snickered and chuckled as the moment grew longer. They looked eager for a fight. Shamakul looked irritated that Gubuyis wasn't responding but remained quiet.

"There would be no peace in war and eternal struggle for power!" Gubuyis called out. "I should let you know that I, too, have an offer. You can stop the carnage of this day if you simply surrender now. You will be granted the right to live peacefully for the remainder of your days in the catacombs of the Panthyun. You will be under lock and key and guarded until you've taken your last breath on our beautiful Lunia."

Shamakul recoiled in disgust and discontent at Gubuyis's words. He stood in silence, but not because he was considering the offer. He was silent out of anger. The Reign was not accustomed to being rejected and Shamakul was furious at the insubordination exhibited by Gubuyis.

Still angry, Shamakul finally replied, "I take it you are rejecting Karakaziem's offer, then?"

"There is only one deal that will be made today," Gubuyis said forcefully. "You surrender and live in the catacombs, that is it."

Numerous taunts came from Shamakul's army. There were boos and murmurs. The occasional show of fire came from the dragons behind him, and a rhythmic banging started from the foot soldiers who were clanking metal against metal once again. The noise grew steadily as Shamakul remained silent. Then, he motioned for them to quiet down.

"I hoped you to be a fool!" Shamakul said with a big grin on his face. "I didn't think you were a good pick. You are too weak! You believe too much that there is good in this world. You and your Govil friends are too soft!"

Gubuyis turned to Selini and said, "We are out of time. We must be at our ready."

Chapter 18: No Deal

Shamakul appeared quite happy that Gubuyis rejected his deal. He didn't travel all the way to Gargantulua just to present a simple job offer. There was blood to be shed as far as he was concerned. Ghowla was powerful, and Shamakul felt it was more luck than skill that overcame him. He intended on proving that through success in battle.

Raising his hand high into the air, Shamakul gestured to his army to be ready for his commands. He then dropped his hand, and the axe throwers began to march forward until they got to the edge of the protection bubble. All the way there they chanted and hollered while holding their axes into the air. They were very close to the edge and watched Gubuyis and the Govilian army intently.

Gubuyis looked at Selini who knew exactly what he wanted. She turned and signaled for the catapults to get locked and loaded. Selini then pulled out her wand and readied herself for what was about to come. She watched as Gubuyis raised up his wand as well.

"Zarx'l," Gubuyis called out, "be at your ready! Wait for my command."

They all stood ready to fight. The battle drums and horns were going in full force on both sides of the battlefield. The axe throwers waited eagerly at the protection bubble's edge, swiping their blades together in an intimidating fashion. The Govilian archers were stretching their bows and the foot soldiers were swinging their swords around to show their abilities. Gubuyis did not move.

"Why aren't we attacking?" Selini asked. "He has said he won't surrender."

Gubuyis watched the battlefield ahead of him and replied, "We are here to defend ourselves, not *start* a war. We will wait for as long as it takes for them to issue the first strike. At which point, we will issue our firm reply."

After a few minutes of the noise of cheering and taunting, a lone axe thrower walked up to the very edge of the protection bubble. He appeared to be in a position of command, possibly a captain in his army. The axe wielder smiled at Gubuyis threateningly. He held an axe in each hand. While still watching Gubuyis, the individual ran the blade of one of his axes across the protection bubble. Small sparks glittered off the axe and fell like drops of molten metal to the ground. He then motioned for Gubuyis to come to him.

Gubuyis remained still. The axe thrower then took another step forward and was at that moment outside of the protection bubble. He motioned for Gubuyis to come over to him once again. Gubuyis still did not move. Then, the axe thrower began to taunt everyone in front of him by swinging his axes back and forth in a very methodical manner. It was obvious that he had skill with his blades, and he intended on displaying that for all to see.

Without turning his back, Gubuyis spoke to the Govilian army, "Do not attack unless we have been attacked. We must remain disciplined."

Finally, the axe thrower must have had enough. He was in the middle of swinging his axes back and forth when he suddenly threw both of his axes. One was headed straight for Selini, and the other was headed for Gubuyis.

With a small flick of his hand, Gubuyis cast a small shield in front of him and Selini. The oncoming axes hit the shield and bounced off and up into the air. Eventually, they corrected course and headed straight back to their owner. Gubuyis shook his head in disappointment.

Suddenly, an arrow from the Govilian army flew past Gubuyis and Selini. It was headed straight for the axe thrower who saw it coming. He smiled and backed up so that he was back inside the protection bubble. The arrow struck the shield directly in front of the axe thrower and disintegrated on impact. The axe thrower laughed. He then hollered back to his companions in a sort of chant. They returned the chant. The fight had begun.

Within moments, hundreds of axes were flying through the air.

They flew right through the edge of the protection bubble and headed for various targets in the Govilian army. The soldiers in the front line put up a mix of physical and magical shields to protect themselves from the oncoming axes.

Hundreds of loud clanks and clunks could be heard as the axes met the shields. Sparks flew off the magical shields and dents formed in the physical shields. A few hollers of pain meant that some axes had found their targets, and several soldiers fell to the ground. None were badly hurt, but the axes were enchanted to cause unstoppable bleeding and the soldiers were quick to be in dire need of attention. Immediately, several medics ran to the soldiers' aids and issued counter spells to stop the bleeding as best as they could. All the while, the axes that had been lobbed at the Govilian soldiers were now making their way back to each troll. Some axes had even become lodged in the physical shields but wriggled free as they also returned to their throwers.

Without any hesitation, the trolls returned their barrage of axes back at the Govilian soldiers who stood ready at the front line once again. As the axes began their short journey through the air, Shamakul's fironi also began shooting large fireballs. The fironi had targeted numerous spots throughout the Govilian army. As the axes flew straight ahead, the fireballs split in many different directions once they were about halfway to the Govilian army's front line.

The soldiers had their shields prepared for the axes. As the fireballs made their way to various points in the army, the battle horns from the Govilian Beasts sounded the alarm. The fireballs quickly descended upon the army and the Govilian Beasts raised up on to their back legs, stomping back down to the ground with their front legs. As they did this, the haze of an orange shockwave rapidly released throughout the army, stopping the fireballs from making it to their targets. There were numerous loud booms as the fireballs impacted the temporary protection shield. The sound was nearly deafening as the fireballs crumbling on impact sounded much like thunder.

Not much time passed before another round of fireballs made its way into the cavern. As they flew through the air, Gubuyis motioned for Zarx'l and Selini to begin their tasks. He then pointed his wand at the small stream of iridescent blue water that flowed between the rocks on the ground beneath their feet. With a small flick of his wand, the water raised like an upside-down waterfall filling the air above the army and extinguishing the newest set of fireballs in their paths. This time, they could hear the sounds of hundreds of steamy extinguishments much like that of a blacksmith's hot iron meeting an icy cold bath.

The axes were still making their rounds into the frontline soldiers. No longer were the axes being thrown in a methodical pattern or order. They were being thrown almost as soon as they made their way back to each troll. This haphazard way of firing caused the air to be filled with axes, and the Govilian soldiers were having a hard time keeping from being struck by one. While magical shields could be replenished before the next attack, the soldiers holding physical shields were dealing with the degrading integrity of the iron that was keeping them safe. Axes were beginning to break through the iron faces of the shields.

Gubuyis was beginning to see the escalating issue at hand in his frontline soldiers, as they grappled with maintaining a barrier to the rest of the army behind them. He made several motions with his wand that caused some of the axes to veer off their paths and back into the air before returning to their masters. As he did so, it gave a very brief chance for some of the soldiers to switch out with those behind them to provide a renewed defense with new shields.

Suddenly, there were loud whooshes from overhead. Some of the soldiers looked up. The first of the catapults had just released their payloads. The catapults had been loaded with rocks of varying sizes, the smallest being a mere three feet across. Gubuyis, who had just deflected another round of axes, turned and watched Selini for a brief moment.

The fironi had just released another barrage of fire that descended quickly into the Govilian army, where the Govilian Beasts had once again released a protection shield that destroyed almost all of the fireballs. One fireball, however, made its mark and hit a Govilian

Beast, killing its riders instantly.

Gubuyis wanted to help Selini in any way he could, but his attention needed to be on the troops for the time being. Since there was virtually no way for them to return fire, all the Govilian army could do was to be on the defense. Shields of all kinds were raised above heads throughout the ranks. Many of the archers huddled under magical shields. The Govilian Beasts issued defensive effects to counteract many of the fireballs from the fironi. Almost all of the soldiers on the frontline had cycled through positions at least once or twice. Shields were weakening, soldiers were taking hits, medics were being stretched thin, and Shamakul's protections were still strong. There was no way to stop his army from their attack while the protection bubble was still up.

As the first of the catapulted rocks was about to hit the protection bubble, Selini took in a deep breath and waved her wand. A large purple and green magical stream of energy quickly released from the tip of her wand and shot directly at the rock. Immediately after getting hit with the magic, the rock grew to nearly a hundred feet across. It was just above a group of the troll axe throwers. They had been laughing at the seemingly feeble attempt of the Govilian army to try and damage the protection bubble. However, once the rock grew to a hundred feet and blocked out the light of day, they all began to cower and run in different directions. The hill-sized rock fell heavily onto the protection bubble. On its collision with the orange energy of the bubble, the huge rock disintegrated into a flurry of fire, ash, and molten rock that slid down the bubble's edge all the way to the ground. There appeared to be no damage at all to the protection bubble itself.

There was a small moment of silence from both sides as they watched the rock hit and fall apart into nothingness. Then, the once cowering axe throwers stood back up and began laughing. They regrouped quickly and their chants filled the air once again. Another rock was already in the air and on its way to another spot on the protection bubble. Selini flicked her wand and shot a stream of magic directly at it. The rock grew in size much like the first one. This time, though, the axe throwers and fironi under it were much less amused or concerned as they continued to throw their projectiles at the

Govilian army. The rock smashed into the protection bubble just like the first one, and it also disintegrated on impact without making it through the surface.

Soon, several more rocks were in the air and Selini was making a great effort to keep up with the demand for her magic. As she began her third enchantment, the first hundred Frost Birds swooped out of the cavern mouth and high into the air above the protection bubble. They swirled around in the air like a hundred buzzards having found their next meal. Soon, several hundred Frost Birds were flying through the air above Shamakul's army. The fire breathing dragons inside the bubble became all aflutter as they popped up and down. It was obvious they were eager to take flight and fight the Frost Birds. But they knew they couldn't, because the harsh winter air was simply too cold for them to fight in.

Several more enchanted rocks hit the protection bubble. The loud booms from their impact and subsequent disintegration was almost all that could be heard throughout the battlefield. The fironi began to target the Frost Birds, shooting straight up into the air. It took little effort for the Frost Birds to maneuver around the oncoming fireballs, though. In the cavern, Gubuyis was helping defend the army from the steady stream of axes. He watched intently as Selini continued her enchantments. He could see that her magic was beginning to faulter as she missed a couple of the rocks. She was now unable to keep up with the flow of the catapults but was still enchanting most of them.

Zarx'l watched from way up high as several rocks never got enchanted. He knew it was time for his troops to do their part. He let out a loud roar that commanded his army to begin their assault on the weather enchantment. Without any hesitation, Zarx'l led the pack by flying directly downwards. Behind him was Vlagar. Behind Vlagar, in V-shaped formation was the rest of the Frost Bird army. The sound of rushing wind over many hundreds of wings could be heard between the booms of the rocks against the protection bubble.

Right before he would have hit the protection bubble, Zarx'l pulled up while shooting a large breath of frost directly at the weather enchantment. Each and every Frost Bird followed suit. The group's formation was broken up by several enchanted rocks breaking apart on impact. They regrouped high overhead and watched as the large amount of ice they created simply broke into chunks and slid down the weather enchantment.

"WE MUST BE PERSISTENT!" Zarx'l yelled out to Vlagar.

Once again, he began to descend upon the bubble without waiting for all the other Frost Birds to be in position. Vlagar followed and so did the others. Again, they breathed frost and ice onto the weather enchantment while dodging the enchanted rocks and fireballs from the fironi. They focused on the front part of the protection bubble where the majority of the damage had already been done, courtesy of Selini. Zarx'l hoped they could help weaken the bubble at the same time they wore down the weather enchantment.

Shamakul, who had remained calm and collected throughout the whole fight so far, called out to Gubuyis.

"We should fight," he taunted Gubuyis, "you and I! One-on-one! We must fight. If you are to truly end this debauchery, you will leave your troops to fend for themselves and take me on. Surely, you can appreciate the pleasure of such a duel! I will let you enter this shielding, and we will meet right here and test who certainly has the best of magic in them. What say you?"

Gubuyis, still casting defensive spells, replied back coolly, "I am not a fool, Shamakul. It would be exceedingly wise of you to see that now. I have little doubt that our duel would end this carnage, but that will come at the right time. Do not worry, for you will get your wish today."

Shamakul smirked at Gubuyis's response and then pointed up at the Frost Birds and smashing rocks against the protection bubble.

"Is this all you've got for me today?" Shamakul asked with a smile. He then gestured at the Govilian army, "And you brought a bunch of farmers to do the dirty work of what should have been a real army?" He paused before continuing, "Okay. How about they defend against this?"

With that, Shamakul made a downward gesture toward the ground. Suddenly, a shockwave expanded quickly throughout his army. The axe throwers began to grow in size and their eyes became wide and full of a rich, dark red color.

Not being able to fully pay attention to what Shamakul was up to, Selini asked Gubuyis, "What just happened?"

"He has just called a bloodlust chant onto his axe throwers," Gubuyis explained. "They will be much more aggressive now and less willing to reason. We must get through that protection bubble as fast as we can."

There was a scene of chaos in front of them. The Frost Birds were dodging the enchanted rocks while managing to breathe heavy amounts of ice and frost onto the weather enchantment. The catapults were releasing a steady stream of rocks. Selini was only getting a few of the rocks enchanted at any given point, as her magical abilities were beginning to dissipate. The fironi were shooting fire into the air at the Frost Birds as well as at the Govilian army. The axe throwers were riled up and throwing their axes much faster and harder than before. The Govilian army was taking damage and not being able to return any. And, Shamakul was laughing and nearly dancing, having resigned to the belief that he was winning this battle without receiving any damage.

Selini was beginning to feel discouraged that they weren't able to break through the protection bubble. To make matters worse, the shockwave sent by Shamakul into his army seemed to have encouraged his dragons to begin spitting fire at the Frost Birds along with the fironi.

Some of the fire from the dragons soon began to hit the Frost Birds, who were now in less of formation and in more of a free-for-all as they dodged both fireballs and rocks. Many of the Frost Birds were wearing special armor having specifically anticipated hits from fire. As they got hit, they were thrown off their paths. Some took minor damage and returned to their mission to destroy the weather enchantment, while others were not so lucky. The unlucky ones fell directly into the protection bubble where they disintegrated into magical sparks and smoke upon impact.

Zarx'l let out a loud roar commanding his troops to return faster and breathe harder against the weather enchantment. At his command, some of his Frost Birds returned too quickly and misjudged how close they were to the bubble. They too disintegrated on impact.

Selini fell to her knees. Gubuyis stepped forward and helped her back up.

"Father," Selini said exasperated, "I do not know if I can do this."

Her eyes filled with tears as she began to question her abilities.

Softly and calmly, Gubuyis spoke to her, "My dearest! I know you can. You are strong. You must persevere. Show your strength! Show them what you can do!"

She was becoming exhausted. Gasping for air, she stood up as straight as she could and raised her wand once again. Pointing it directly at the next flying rock, she released another magical stream of energy. The rock instantly grew in size to more than a hundred feet across and smashed against the protection bubble like all the rocks before it. It too exploded into sparks and molten rock and melted away.

Hoping to clear the air for a moment, Gubuyis turned slightly and shot a wave of purple magic directly across the frontline of his army. All the axes and fireballs in its path were pushed away, far out of sight. For a brief moment, the Govilian army experienced a reprieve from the constant onslaught. Many soldiers lay injured on the ground, being tended to as best as possible by too few medics. One soldier's shield crumbled apart in the brief silence and exposed him. He quickly switched with a soldier behind him who had a badly damaged but usable shield. Gubuyis quickly looked around and he could see the despair in his army as they had taken so much damage already, and as far as they were concerned, they hadn't even started fighting yet, only defending.

His attention was quickly drawn to the remaining Govilian Beasts as numerous battle horns sounded. A shockwave of protection shields filled the air throughout the army. Gubuyis turned around and saw that another wave of axes and fire was already on its way. He quickly raised his wand and attempted to break the ground beneath the feet of the fironi and the axe throwers. The ground shook hard and the protection bubble rippled like water, but it would not give while it was being protected.

The next wave of axes made their way to the Govilian army's frontline. There were many clanks and thunks as the axes hit shield after shield. Gubuyis could hear the painful call of injuries as many axes hit their targets. He waved his wand at the steady stream of axes and fireballs once again. This time his magic extinguished many of the fireballs almost instantly and many axes melted and disappeared in their flight.

"We must get that protection bubble down!" Gubuyis called back to Selini.

He turned and looked forward. For a brief moment, he assessed the integrity of the protection bubble not far in front of him. Another rock smashed into it and the bubble shook but remained resolute. He made a quick gesture with his hands and waved his wand directly toward the bubble. A large, purple stream of magical energy released from his hands and made its way to the protection bubble right in front of a group of trolls. The energy smashed into the surface and spread across a span of two hundred feet. Axes and fireballs alike disintegrated on their exit from the bubble. There was a loud roar of explosions and what sounded like the cracking of ice on a lake. The protection bubble held strong, though, and Gubuyis had to turn his efforts back to helping his army in any way he could.

"I won't let them down!" Selini whispered to herself as she let out a strong enchantment toward yet another rock.

Rock after rock split against the bubble's surface. The axe throwing trolls, the fironi, and all the other creatures inside the bubble had grown accustomed to nothing happening from the smashing rocks and were chanting and calling out in praise to Shamakul.

Breathing heavily now and weak in the knees, Selini let go her best efforts as more rocks were catapulted above her. She cast as fast as she could, hitting several of them in immediate succession. Three of them smashed rapidly in nearly the same spot, but all became demolished as fast as any before. The mess of molten rock and sparks blinded both sides for a moment before clearing once again.

As Selini struggled to stay upright, she began to realize she was about out of magic. Her hands shook and her head swirled in a dizzying mess as the fear of failure came over her.

"LOOK!" someone from the army's frontline shouted.

A growing wave of cheers began to fill the cavern. The drums of the Govilian Beasts sounded almost in unison as did their battle horns. Selini and Gubuyis both looked ahead and saw a large, orange crack had formed on the surface of the protection bubble. It was shifting around like a drifting lightning bolt.

Seeing the large crack forming in the protection bubble, Zarx'l commanded his army to get back into formation high above the bubble. Within just a moment, several hundred Frost Birds were amassed and ready for commands to attack once again.

Calling out to his troops, Zarx'l shouted, "We must break the weather enchantment now! We have no more options, no more choices! There is no room for failure! GIVE IT YOUR ALL TO THE LAST BREATH!"

With that, Zarx'l led the way back down toward the weather enchantment. Shamakul's dragons took notice of the renewed sense of urgency from the Frost Birds and every one of them took aim at them. As the Frost Birds approached the weather enchantment, the dragons shot heavy fire at as many targets as they could. Shamakul watched wide-eyed as the crack in the protection bubble grew while Selini enchanted yet another rock. He did not move from his position, though.

"KILL THEM!" Shamakul yelled at his troops as he pointed to the fast-approaching Frost Birds. "KILL THEM ALL!"

Shamakul looked less composed than before. He was yelling out commands in anger. He swirled his hands around and pushed them forward toward the direction of the front of his protection bubble. Fire erupted away from his entire body in a massive ball, heading straight towards Selini. It was approaching her at a great speed and quickly exited the bubble.

In the cavern, Gubuyis was busy issuing defense spells to assist the Govilian army in any way he could. The axes were coming at a quicker pace than ever before as the bloodlust spell had fully set in with the trolls. The fironi were further energized by Shamakul's anger and fire. Their fireballs had doubled in size. Gubuyis lifted the water from the stone floor of the cavern once again and made a long wall of rushing water fly into the air.

As Gubuyis helped the army, Selini's eyes grew heavy. She once again fell to her knees, unable to get back up. Her energy was expended. She leaned forward on the ground, holding herself up with one hand while trying to cast a spell with her other hand. She watched as the fireball from Shamakul came racing towards her. She clumsily raised her wand up to cast a shield, but it was no use. She was magically depleted. She took a large breath in and closed her eyes as the fireball came at her with great intensity. She knew this was it for her.

Even with his back turned away, Gubuyis knew the fireball had almost reached his daughter. He lifted his foot and slammed it against the ground. A shockwave of dirt and rock immediately escaped from under him and headed directly toward the protection bubble. It shook even the air above it, causing axes to fall from their flight. As the shockwave hit the protection bubble, it cracked even larger with speckles of it breaking apart and falling down to the ground. He swiveled immediately around and cast a protection shield in front of Selini just as the fire hit her.

Fire, wind, and heavy smoke swirled around Selini in explosive ways. Gubuyis watched as the air cleared around where his daughter had been kneeling. The fire was relentless and continued to swirl for several moments until finally, he could see her laying on the ground.

He held his breath as he watched her. It seemed as if the entire battle had stopped abruptly in order to see if she had indeed been hit.

The Frost Birds were almost to the bubble. They had started from higher than before and were coming at great speeds. Many of them were nearly exhausted from all the frost breathing they had been doing. Zarx'l knew that the high-speed descent would be too much for many of his Frost Birds to pull up from in time. They were on a trajectory to hit the protection bubble head on if it did not get destroyed. In just a few minutes from that point, he knew he would have led his troops to their death. It was too late to stop, so he let out a loud roar, to fire up his troops in their flight. Then, he took a deep breath and closed his eyes, ready for a quick death.

As Gubuyis watched Selini, a tear rolled down his face. He heard the roar of Zarx'l and knew there was no time to mourn the death of his beautiful daughter who lay motionless in front of him. The battle horns of the Govilian Beasts were sounding loudly and in perfect presentation. Gubuyis turned quickly and faced Shamakul's army. He raised his wand and pointed it directly at the cracked protection bubble. He released an intense stream of purple energy from his wand and it hit the surface. Gubuyis's hands clenched as he gave the most intense stream of magic he could muster.

Just as Zarx'l breathed out his last breath of frost and ice as strongly as he could, he opened his eyes so that he could see his last seconds. But that moment never came. Zarx'l knew the protection bubble must have been destroyed so he immediately pulled up, swooping low over Shamakul's army. He flew directly over Shamakul, who was still ablaze, as he made his way back up into the air. Hundreds of Frost Birds did the same. Many of them had relented to the fact that they were doomed to death on their approach, but then gained a renewed sense of purpose as they witnessed the protection bubble coming down.

"TAKE OUT THE WEATHER ENCHANTMENT!" Zarx'l commanded his troops.

The Frost Birds acted in unison as they worked in waves to destroy the weather enchantment with their frost. Many Frost Birds were already depleted, though, and Shamakul's dragons were now taking flight low into the air to fight off as many Frost Birds as they could. The Frost Birds that could no longer breathe frost began to defend their brethren that were not quite depleted. The Frost Birds were much larger than the dragons and it was exceedingly easy for a Frost Bird to pummel one, simply by flying hard and fast directly at it.

Shamakul watched as the Frost Birds battled with the dragons. One Frost Bird flew close to him as it wrestled in the air with a dragon. Shamakul rolled his eyes and flicked his hand in the general direction of the Frost Bird. It disintegrated into thin air as its ashes fell to the ground.

Within a few moments, Zarx'l and his remaining troops had destroyed the weather enchantment as well. Zarx'l could hardly breathe as he struggled on his last breath of frost. He knew his Frost Birds were in for the battle of their lives without the ability to breath frost as a weapon or shield. Taking to a high position, he looked down to assess the battlefield. Far beneath him was a messy looking battleground. The air was full of dragons and Frost Birds, fire was flying in all directions, and Shamakul's troops were beginning to scatter in a forward direction as they sought the warmth of the cavern. Without the weather enchantment or the protection bubble, Zarx'l knew the real battle was just beginning.

In the cavern, Gubuyis was issuing many defensive spells as the axe throwers, soldier creatures, and fironi were now advancing aggressively towards the Govilian army. The sound of drums filled the air as the Govilian Beasts moved forward. The catapults were still lobbing rocks into Shamakul's army, and they were taking some hits from them but there were just too many of them to stop.

The Govilian army recollected itself. However, many of the frontline no longer had shields. The archers were now kneeling between groups of foot soldiers and were ready to fire on command. The Govilian Beasts were issuing magical commands to energize the troops. They also issued temporary protection bubbles around nearby soldiers and archers. Gubuyis looked ahead at the oncoming army of axe throwers acting in bloodlust, fironi, and other creatures. He felt a small sense of relief that the Frost Birds were keeping the attention of the dragons for the time being. Then, Gubuyis trained his eyes on Shamakul, who was casting spells against Frost Birds as they came near him.

Knowing the only way for the least number of casualties was by stopping Shamakul himself, Gubuyis took a breath in and nodded his head. He took a step forward but was stopped by the sound of a small voice from behind him.

"Father?" Selini called out from where she lay on the ground. "Wait!"

Gubuyis turned immediately and saw his daughter struggling to get back up. He went to her side and gave her his hand. Tears rolled down his cheeks in awe and joy. She pulled herself up, looking weak and frail.

"I need to be by your side," she spoke with a weakness in her voice.

Gubuyis looked at her with a smile and spoke softly, "My dearest, you have done enough here today. I will be in good company without you. For now, please rest. You have made victory a possibility this day."

Selini knew she was unable to fight. She could hardly stand. But she struggled in her mind to let her father go against Shamakul without being by his side. She knew she would be the best defense he could have. The weakness in her, though, spoke loudly to her heart. She knew she couldn't help him and would only be a hinderance. Selini's eyes watered as she nodded her head in agreement with her father.

Gubuyis stood up straight and let go of his daughter's hand. He then moved forward and began to walk toward Shamakul. Within just seconds, a hundred swordsmen from the Govilian army had surrounded Gubuyis and joined him in his walk to Shamakul. There were very few shields left in the group, but all of them were prepared to fight to their deaths.

Shamakul saw the newly formed posse heading in his direction. He had been focused on destroying as many Frost Birds as he could while directing his army toward the Govilians. He turned and faced the large group of swordsmen with Gubuyis at its center. He then issued a large shockwave from his hands that collapsed the ground under it as it moved toward the large group. Shamakul did not seem to care that many of his own troops were being sucked into the ever-growing hole on its path to kill Gubuyis.

Gubuyis's posse remained on its path to Shamakul, fighting through his army as they progressed. The shockwave that was destroying the ground was quickly approaching and Gubuyis had to act fast in order to protect the group. Just as he lifted his wand to issue a counter spell, there was a bright white flash that filled the air before the entire group.

Chapter 19: Daggers and Magic

The hundred swordsmen and Gubuyis suddenly found themselves at the heart of the fight, right next to Shamakul himself. Confusion beset the group. Even Gubuyis was taken aback by what had just transpired. There was too little time to think, though, as the battle ensued fully before their very eyes. They were quickly being surrounded by Shamakul's troops.

Gubuyis turned in all directions to reassess his situation and immediately saw the smiling face of his son, Geller. Standing behind him was Jack, Anna, Gink, Fink, and Valkog. It became obvious to Gubuyis that Valkog had just used a portal to move the whole group in a closer position to Shamakul. Geller's smile quickly dissipated as Gubuyis was about to greet him.

"Behind you!" Anna shouted out to Gubuyis.

Gubuyis swirled around and cast a quick defensive spell that undid a spell that was headed directly toward him. Shamakul had already begun his attack despite the sudden change of their position. All around the group, the Govilian fighters were engaged in battle with axe throwers, soldier creatures, and fironi. The fight was intense and without shields to protect them from the sudden blasts of heat and the sharp edges of the axes, the soldiers were taking heavy hits.

Overhead, Gubuyis saw numerous Frost Birds in desperate attacks against the fire breathing dragons. The Frost Birds fought by body slamming the dragons or by biting. Blood, armor, and scales rained from the sky above him. He could see they were in the heaviest fight of the battle. The Frost Birds seemed to be doing a good job of fighting without their frost, but they were outnumbered by the dragons. Just then, Zarx'l could be seen flying overhead using his tail to slice into a dragon that was entangled on another Frost Bird.

By the time Gubuyis looked back down to the group, he saw Valkog, Anna, and Jack already fighting. Valkog was using quick and small portals to redirect axes back at their throwers. Several axe throwers were already laying on the ground in pain and agony from their wounds. He swirled around quickly but gracefully as he cast portal after portal.

Several trolls were approaching Jack and had him in their sights. They began throwing axes at him as fast as they could. The attack was so close to Shamakul, his troops worked even harder to compromise the Govilian group's abilities to fight. Jack quickly combined his daggers together and aimed the ensuing stream of fire and lightning at the oncoming trolls. The blast hit the front one, immediately knocking it down to the ground. Jack held his daggers together longer and the stream continued to blast each of the other trolls as well. They all fell to the ground, burning and writhing in pain.

As the group continued to advance, they stepped over injured and dead troops from both armies. Anna leaned over and picked up an axe from a heavily injured troll.

"This is mine now," she said menacingly to the troll as he feebly tried to grab it back.

Without hesitation, Anna was quickly in the fight as well. She was soon throwing the axe toward the trolls and fironi. Her aim was right on as she began disabling her targets by causing them serious injuries.

From behind Geller came a loud boom followed by several more. Jack glanced back to make sure it wasn't anything bad coming their way. It turned out to be Gink and Fink throwing different potions at various targets around them. None of the explosions seemed to be too big, but they were definitely stopping their attackers. One potion set an attacker on fire for a brief moment, while another potion turned a troll's arms into strange looking rodent legs.

Gubuyis knew they were only just holding off the attack from around them. Jack watched him face Shamakul and begin to walk forward once again. The foot soldiers, Jack, and the rest of the group all moved in the same direction in unison with Gubuyis. They were not far from Shamakul. So close, in fact, that Jack could feel the heat coming from his blaze. While they walked, Gubuyis cast several spells to counteract spells issued by Shamakul intending on doing certain damage.

Soon, the entire group was only a few feet away from Shamakul. Having stopped for a few moments, Shamakul stood quietly where he had been standing the entire time. He hadn't moved from his spot in what used to be the center of his army. No longer was it the center, as many of the troops were fighting towards the front of the cavern now.

Shamakul had not even spoken or moved when Gubuyis suddenly cast a water spell that shot a heavy stream of water, much like a bursting dam, directly at him. Before Shamakul could react to what was happening, his blazing body was extinguished. Shamakul stumbled back under the force of the oncoming water, but he remained standing. Once the water stopped, he stood up straight and wide-eyed. He was furious and his anger soon turned to laughter.

"I may have underestimated you some," Shamakul shouted out, "but you can never beat me!"

With a quick motion of his hands, Shamakul cast a protection bubble around him and his group.

"No silly portals will save you now," Shamakul spoke with an evil grimace on his face.

From behind Jack, they heard a yell from a soldier, "Watch out!"

"It's closing in on us," Geller explained. "Don't touch the bubble!" He shouted to several foot soldiers near the edge as it moved inwards.

There was a shout of pain. They all looked over to see a soldier instantly disintegrate as the edge touched him. All the soldiers quickly began to make their way to the center of the bubble where Gubuyis and the others stood.

"I believe we are to move closer to Shamakul himself," Gubuyis explained to those around him.

Valkog swirled his hands around to make a portal. Sparks flew from his talons, but no portal materialized.

Laughing, Shamakul happily stated, "Those fancy tricks won't work here."

Valkog smiled and drew a sword he had grabbed from one of Shamakul's soldiers.

"Portals aren't the only way to win this!" Valkog exclaimed as he wielded the sword around in a trained maneuver.

"Don't you think it's getting cold out here?" Geller asked Shamakul. "Maybe being on fire caused you to be incapable of noticing that, but I'd say it's definitely getting a little 'chilly' out here. What about you?"

Geller had looked at Jack who simply nodded. Jack wasn't sure it was a good time to be teasing Shamakul but figured Geller could certainly do his own thing. He knew Geller well enough at this point that he was confident there must be some kind of strategy in play.

Shamakul looked around. It was beginning to appear that the Frost Birds were winning against his dragons. The dragons were starting to freeze and fall to the ground. He then looked over to the cavern mouth and saw his troops struggling to fight, as they battled the extreme cold. The Govilian army wasn't allowing Shamakul's army to advance into the cavern, so they remained exposed to the outside winter elements. His weather enchantment had spoiled the troops. They were in no condition to fight in such a frigid, cold environment.

Anger overcame his face as Shamakul spoke, "All I am here for is Gubuyis and the boy, and it would appear that I have my prizes! It is I who have won here today. I do not need to trek an army back with me when I return to see Karakaziem. She will be pleased to have the two of you in her possession."

Immediately, Shamakul cast a spell at his own feet that burst into a green smoke which began to fill the shrinking protection bubble. Several of the swordsmen closest to Shamakul started choking and fell to their feet.

"What are we going to do?" asked Anna.

Geller stated, "We need to get out of the protection bubble fast, but we won't have time to destroy it."

From all around them, the soldiers began to attack the bubble with their swords. The protection bubble sustained no damage, there were only lots of sparks and melted sword edges. Furthermore, the protection bubble continued to move inward. The entire group shuffled forward toward Shamakul as the bubble got smaller. Shamakul smiled big.

Gubuyis cast several spells directed at Shamakul, but they were easily deflected. He tried to counteract the green smoke as well, but Shamakul again resisted his efforts with much ease. Soon, the green smoke filled the entire area in front of the group. They could no longer see Shamakul, who was last seen smiling, as if he knew he had already won. It was just a matter of time before the rest of the bubble was filled with smoke.

Geller and Valkog, who had been standing in front of Gubuyis, looked at each other as the smoke crept up to them. It appeared as though they had an idea. They gave a slight nod to each other before taking a deep breath and then ran directly into the smoke ahead of them. Within seconds, the clanking of swords could be heard, but nothing could be seen.

"Stay behind me," Gubuyis said to Anna and Jack.

Anna ran to the bubble's edge and began trying to attack it with her axe. Nothing happened other than sparks flying which they had already witnessed from the previous failed attempts. Gink threw a potion at the bubble's edge and it exploded, causing a loud reverberating boom inside the bubble, but it did not appear to do any damage to the bubble itself. Jack remembered his weapons and how magical they were. He quickly ran to Anna's side, which was already getting cramped as the soldiers moved closer and closer to each other. He combined his weapons and aimed them at the bubble. Immediately, a thick beam of lightning surrounded by fire shot from his daggers. The stream of magic shot straight at the bubble's edge and pulled his daggers upward. The stream of energy spread all across the inside of the bubble making it appear like cracked glass. The inward movement of the protection bubble suddenly stopped, and all of the soldiers looked in awe at the spectacular light show.

"Come! Come!" Gubuyis motioned for Jack. "Come over here by me."

Jack quickly made his way back through the soldiers and stood by Gubuyis.

"Hold your weapons in front of you," Gubuyis instructed Jack. "Right out in front of you and point them there."

Gubuyis was pointing directly in the middle of the smoke ahead, mere feet from their position. It was quickly filling the small space and there was virtually nowhere for any of the soldiers to go. The bubble was packed with no space to move.

Jack held his two daggers in front of him in a crisscross fashion as Gubuyis directed him. Sparks flew out of the edges and short streams of magic exited their tips. Jack didn't know what Gubuyis wanted him to do, but the actions he was taking didn't seem right in order to get a full blast of the blades' magic.

Gubuyis aimed his wand directly at Jack's blades and a forceful stream of magical energy blasted forward into the smoke ahead of them. All Jack could see was green smoke at this point. He took a deep breath in as the smoke filled the air in front of him. His daggers' energy combined with Gubuyis's spell was pushing Jack backwards. He remained standing as best as he could, but he struggled with holding his daggers in one direction. Small offshoots of magic shot out everywhere, hitting swords, shields and the protection bubble. The inside of the bubble was lit up like a lightning storm!

After a few moments, as Jack struggled to hold his breath, the green smoke filled the rest of the area. The bubble began to vibrate and ripple. Suddenly, the protection bubble burst apart in a massive explosion much like a bursting soap bubble. The outside air quickly absorbed the green smoke and cleared the area. Gubuyis lowered his wand and Jack followed suit with his daggers. Many gasps could be heard all around them as the soldiers had also been holding their breaths. Gubuyis remained still, looking forward at the point where they had aimed the daggers' energy.

Within a moment, the outside wind had cleared away all the smoke. Geller and Valkog could be seen slowly standing up. The smoke had knocked them out at some point. In front of their position was a large mass of black char.

"Did we get him?" Anna asked.

Jack was wondering the same thing. He wondered if the black mass was Shamakul's remains.

"Indeed," Gubuyis said without moving, "we got him! With the force of your daggers' magic, Jack, I combined a very strong, stunning spell. He will no longer be a threat to us!"

Fink shouted out from behind them, "A stunning spell?! What'd ya do that for?"

Jack was confused. He glanced back at the black char that was once Shamakul. It looked like there was nothing left of him as far as he could tell.

"Yes," Gubuyis replied, "a stunning spell. It would be wise to hold onto him."

Jack asked, "Is he not dead?"

"I would say not," Gubuyis answered.

"Um, did we win or not?" Anna asked, confused.

Suddenly from far behind them came loud cheers of rejoice. Jack looked back at the mouth of the cavern and saw that the Govilian army had held its position. The remnants of Shamakul's army were running away.

"Ha," Jack said to Anna, "I think we just won!"

"If we do not want to end up like them," Gubuyis pointed toward several axe throwers as he spoke, "we will want to be inside ourselves."

"Ah," Valkog stated, "I can help with that!"

Valkog cast a portal in front of the group and gestured for the soldiers to go through. After a few moments, all that remained were Valkog, Geller, Gink, Fink, Anna, Gubuyis and Jack. Jack smiled as he looked at the portal in front of him. He knew they had just achieved victory that seemed so hard to get. He felt stronger than he had ever felt in the past, even though the danger seemed so much more intense than before.

"After you, Captain," Gubuyis motioned for Jack to walk through the portal.

Jack nodded and walked forward into the portal with everyone but Gubuyis and Valkog. It took them into the cavern a small distance ahead of the regrouping Govilian army. There were cheers and battle horns sounding throughout the cavern opening as the army celebrated its victory.

All around him, Jack saw that many of the Govilian ranks had taken serious damage. There were medics working fast and furious to stop the bleeding. Many of their fellow soldiers were also doing what they could to help their brethren. The battle horns soon died down. There was still a sense of general content at the victory, but it was obvious that too many of the soldiers had been badly injured in the fight.

The portal had closed behind Jack after he came through. He wondered if Gubuyis was sticking around on the battlefield for something. As far as he was concerned, they were now out of danger and the cold would soon be a distant memory. He looked forward to celebrating back at the house in Gargantulua over a piping hot Prunklesnider. It would be so nice, he thought, if Gubuyis could join them in celebration, but he knew that there were many things Gubuyis probably needed to attend to.

"Geller!" Selini called out to her brother as she clumsily ran up to meet him.

Selini looked weak but in otherwise good health. Jack saw that her armor and clothing were badly charred as if she had walked through a lake of fire. She tossed down her helmet just as she got to Geller. Wrapping her arms around him, she smiled the biggest smile Jack had ever seen.

"I knew you were okay!" Selini exclaimed as she hugged Geller, who was still trying to discern what had happened to her. "I just knew it all along."

Jack and Anna walked over to the pair joining them in celebration. Jack just stood there smiling, but Anna gleefully joined in on the hugs. Fink hobbled over to the hugging trio, still carrying Gink on his back quite securely despite the recent events. He pulled out a small horn and gave it a blow. It sounded like a goose that had been badly injured, and was rather unpleasant to Jack's ears. Jack wondered what Fink was attempting to do with the horn, other than maybe annoy everyone! Fink put the horn away as he smiled. The group was now looking at him.

"What a wonderous occasion," Fink stated. "We have a fun story to tell ya, Selini. And ya will not be disappointed in the least."

Selini looked over each member of the group. She looked at Jack and smiled as she came to him and gave him a big hug as well. Jack crouched down some to meet her hug.

"We missed having all of you with us," Jack said to her as they embraced. "Maybe you could have kept Fink and Gink in line much better than we did."

Both Selini and Jack chuckled.

Anna finally shouted out what they were all wondering, "What happened to you?" She was gesturing to Selini's burned armor.

"It seems that we all have some stories to tell," Selini replied. "I did it, though, Geller. I used my enchantment abilities to damage the protection bubble. Shamakul underestimated us entirely."

"How do you feel?" Geller looked concerned.

Jack remembered how opposed Geller was to Selini becoming magically exhausted. At that moment, Geller seemed much more interested in her well-being than how she got to the condition she was in. Jack watched Selini's facial expression go from smiling to an almost sad look. He could tell she was thinking about how best to respond.

Finally, Selini replied, "I feel fine."

"Oh c'mon!" Geller looked a little upset. "You just ran through what looks to me like fire and you're magically exhausted. There's no way you can feel fine."

"Well," she replied back slowly, "I guess I feel pretty tired. The kind of tired where you feel like you could sleep for a month!"

Unfortunately, Selini's words were not at all comforting or reassuring in any way. She looked terrible and very weak. Her posture indicated that she was struggling just to keep standing.

"We've got to get you back home," Geller suggested. "You need to rest and rejuvenate."

Jack looked all around the cavern. There were torchlights everywhere, and the dancing flames glistened off armor and shields throughout the army. Many of the troops were helping the wounded as best as they could. Several catapults were burning uncontrollably. He could see that a couple Govilian Beasts had been killed; their bodies lay in the middle of the army.

Many fast-moving shadows danced across the cavern floor. Jack looked behind him and saw that the Frost Birds were making their way back into the cavern, flying up to the ceiling high above them. It was quite the sight for Jack to see. All the Frost Birds appeared to have taken some damage. Many were injured, and most of them showed signs of a serious battle. Zarx'l was the last to fly in. He flew down to meet Selini and the group.

"I have had the honor of fighting with you this day," Zarx'l spoke directly to Selini. "You are truly a powerful being, not to be trifled with. Your actions and perseverance today saved my troops from certain demise, and you have earned victory for the whole of the Govilian Alliance!"

Selini, looking ever more tired, responded, "This was a victory won by the best of the best. We all stayed true to our mission and for that we won the battle."

Zarx'l bowed his head in front of her and said, "You have earned the respect of the Frost Bird nation for your strength and valor."

Selini walked forward to give a small bow back to Zarx'l. He lifted his head back up and looked at her once again.

"Now, you need your rest," Zarx'l stated. "I will be bringing my troops back to Wyvergia before night fall. We have much healing to do ourselves."

Zarx'l backed up; he gave a smile and nod to the group as he jumped into the air and flew away. Once he was almost to the ceiling, he let out an enormous roar that was quickly followed by the remaining Frost Birds. Jack watched as they flew out of the cavern once again in formation. They circled above the battleground several times before a number of them swooped down to the ground. They were gathering up their injured and dead. The Frost Birds reformed their ranks and flew away at an amazing speed. In just a few moments, they were out of sight.

"Here," Geller said to Selini as he handed her a small piece of bread. "Have some of this, it will help."

She smiled at him and took the bread.

"I missed your cooking," she said to Geller. "I missed you so much. I missed all of you so much. We couldn't find you. Vlagar looked for weeks. I knew in my heart that you all were going to be okay, but I must admit, there were times where I faltered and felt like there was no hope left. I thought the worst."

"We're here now," Anna comforted Selini. "We found ourselves in a ... sticky situation, that's all."

Selini looked the group over and said, "I am so glad none of you are hurt. You are all in better condition than I could have imagined."

"Speaking of being hurt," Geller said as he looked over the army in front of them, "we need to get our injured back to Gargantulua where they will be better taken care of."

There was a sudden flash of bright white light from behind them. Jack and the others turned around to see that Valkog had just walked through a portal.

"Well," Fink stated gleefully, "we have somewhere ta be right now! It has been quite the journey this day, but we have ta attend ta some business."

Fink hopped forward to meet Valkog, who simply smiled and made a small portal for the pair. Fink hopped through with Gink in tow. The portal quickly closed behind them.

"Where could they possibly be going right now?" Jack asked slightly annoyed.

Laughing, Geller responded, "They likely have some plans for that root of flindishion they acquired. Those two have had a curious desire to get their hands on some since we first met Valkog."

"You'll have to tell me everything," Selini said to Geller and the others. "Don't leave out any details."

Anna nearly shouted out in excitement, "We found the roots we were looking for!"

"Yes," Geller added, "we have our own story to tell as well. For now, though, we need to focus on getting everyone home as safe as possible."

At that moment, Gubuyis stepped out of the portal Valkog had just come from. It closed upon his arrival. Contentment set in as he looked at the group in front of him. He smiled at Selini and walked up to her. He dropped his staff, freeing both his arms, and gave her a large hug. Gubuyis looked up from his hug with Selini and smiled big at Jack.

After finishing his long hug with Selini, Gubuyis held his hand over his staff. It immediately jumped off the ground and back into his hand. He faced Jack and the others.

"Without all of your efforts, we might have very well lost the battle today," Gubuyis said to the group. He looked a little confused, "It seems we are missing a couple."

Geller nodded his head and said, "It seems that Gink and Fink had a pressing matter to attend to."

"No matter," Gubuyis continued, "It was the efforts of everyone on this battlefield today that made this victory happen. Shamakul may have thought we brought farmers to fight. Maybe we did, but would not those very farmers have more to fight for and defend than any army that fights for nothing? I believe we brought our strongest out today and that every individual shined through."

"We must show our respect to our troops and bring them home as fast as possible," Geller spoke out as he pointed to the army. "We should not linger any longer."

Gubuyis nodded and looked at Valkog who took the cue. Valkog immediately walked forward and into the ranks. He came to a spot where several were being treated for serious injuries and made a portal for them to go through. Again and again, white flashes appeared throughout the ranks, as Valkog made numerous portals that helped transport the wounded and others back to Gargantulua safely and to where they would be greeted by more medics.

"I must thank you," Gubuyis said to Jack as Valkog was finishing the last of the portals. "I thank you for your help today. Without you, I believe we would have been in quite a bind."

Jack felt slightly embarrassed and replied, "It was the daggers, really. I didn't have much to do with it."

"It is the wielder of those daggers that creates the strength of the power in them," Gubuyis stated calmly. "So, you did more than you realize my dear sir."

Gubuyis turned to Anna and held out his hand for her to shake.

"And, I thank you for your fighting skills," Gubuyis stated. "What I saw was an individual that has come into her own self, strengthened by her will and abilities. You have shown much valor today."

There was a pause of silence as Anna did not know how to respond. She gave Gubuyis a handshake and a small bow as if to thank him for his kind words. The group looked around the now nearly empty cavern. There were only a few soldiers remaining and a few burning catapults.

"I would very much like to thank our potion masters," Gubuyis spoke to no one in particular, "but it would seem that business is what it is, and it calls for their attention."

Jack smiled. He felt relieved that the worst of this season was over. He had grown tired of the cold and looked forward to warmer days. The fire in the main room of the house in Gargantulua sounded wonderous to him as he thought about sitting at the table, chatting with the others, and eating Geller's food. It seemed as if things were going to be back to some sense of normalcy. All that needed to happen was for the day to end, and a new day to bring with it warmth and friendship.

"I have to inform you, father," Geller stated seriously. "We met some resistance with some fironi in Wellwood Forest. They were gathered at the boulder that contains the portal Jack and Anna came through."

A look of concern came over Gubuyis's face as he responded, "It may seem that we have underestimated the protections needed for it. I will bring this matter up immediately to the Govilian Council."

Valkog had just finished transporting the remaining troops back to Gargantulua and was now making his way back to the group. Jack was finally feeling the victory in its entirety. All the troops had gone and the evil wizard, Shamakul, had finally been destroyed.

"What do we do about Shamakul's army?" Geller asked Gubuyis. "They are in no condition to make it, out in that cold."

Gubuyis turned and looked out of the cavern. He climbed up a rock to get a better view of the outside and watched as hundreds of Shamakul's forces shivered and suffered in the cold winter air. Nearly all of them were ill-prepared to be out in any form of cold weather.

"We are to offer them a place to stay in the warmth of the cavern until the can leave for their homelands," Gubuyis instructed Geller. "They have no reason to fight now that Shamakul has no control over them. Extending our hospitality may be remembered for generations, but we do it because we are good, and we truly mean for life to be treasured."

"I will lead this charge," Geller spoke and stepped forward. "I will ensure that they are all welcome here and reassure them they are not our prisoners. They will be free to go as they please."

Gubuyis turned back around and climbed back down the rock he had ascended. He walked back to the group.

"It is time," he stated. "We must return home and help our injured. Then, we can celebrate our victory."

"Valkog?" Geller called back from his position near the opening of the cavern. "Can you send back some of our healers, please? I think they are in need of help as much as we are."

Geller was pointing to Shamakul's remaining forces. With that, Geller began to walk out into the cold winter day headed towards Shamakul's army.

Chapter 20: Portal Security

Oone night had passed since the group left the cavern. Jack had gotten a full night's sleep in a warm bed. He felt sore all over from the constant cold of the last few weeks, but he thought of how badly everything could have gone at almost any point. There was little to complain about when it came to his body feeling sore. He was glad to be back in Gargantulua, even if it wasn't his home on Pumpernickel Drive.

Jack spent a little time in Bolar's tavern and was immediately greeted with a hot quart of Prunklesnider given to him by a proud Bolar. He visited the barracks courtyard as well. There was no need to practice his dagger wielding, but he had come to miss the sounds of the Valindi skirmishes against the dummies. He sat and watched for a while in the early morning. It seemed as if most things were already back to normal throughout the streets of Gargantulua. The sounds of the blacksmith, not far outside of Jack's morning window, were the first sounds he woke up to that day, and it just seemed he couldn't have missed them more. Oddly enough, Jack did miss the drunken shouting of Gink and Fink at Bolar's. They were nowhere to be found throughout the morning.

Wandering through the streets most of the morning, Jack and Anna found peace in the hustle and bustle. There were definitely signs of a recent battle, though. Damaged swords and shields lay strewn about the floor and on the walls of the blacksmith's shop. The tailor's shop had many torn and tattered rags in huge piles inside the store as well as in the street just out front. Jack figured these must have been the clothes worn by many of the Govilian troops.

After a seemingly quiet morning, walking through the streets and finally enjoying his favorite Prunklesnider, Jack was ready to get back to the house where he could relax by the fireside. As both he and Anna walked into the main room of the house, Jack could hear Geller explaining to Selini the task of enchanting food for Gary.

"... so there I was with Jack looking at this huge mound of neatly stacked meat," Geller could be heard saying to Selini. "I knew there wouldn't be a problem once I saw how much there was. I've enchanted tons more food than that before. Really, the only thing was the number of spices and seasonings I brought along. I mean, I just grabbed a handful of my favorites and off we went. I wasn't expecting to have to enchant a room full of food when we set off, if you know what I mean."

Jack and Anna quietly proceeded into the main room and sat at the same table as the other two. Even though they were part of the story, they were still eager to hear it spoken aloud. Jack was curious as to how Geller was telling it.

"You said this Gary 'spider guy' made you enchant the food in exchange for freedom, right?' Selini asked. "Did he fulfill his promise and let you all go, or did you have to do something extra creative to get out of there?"

Geller smiled. It looked like Selini was looking for a creative escape for the remainder of the story.

"He was an araknolian of his word," Geller continued. "Once he saw and then tasted my cuisine, he looked very pleased. Once we all got back out to the cave opening where he originally kidnapped us from, Valkog began to brew his stew."

"I thought you didn't have any firewood," Selini commented. "How did Valkog brew it?"

Geller replied back, "Gary gave us some wood to burn. I started the fire easily with my wand, but unfortunately I couldn't sustain a fire with my magic."

"You'll have to have father teach you how to do that," Selini suggested. "It sounds like it would have come in handy on more than one occasion during your journey. Now, was that it? Obviously, Valkog must have had enough of the root fermented, otherwise we wouldn't be sitting here exchanging stories right now."

Geller nodded, "Yes, that is pretty much it. The roots had plenty of time to ferment during the time we were all petrified. Apparently, the extended time to ferment allowed the stew to be extra potent and it rejuvenated Valkog rapidly. From there, we took a portal here and learned almost immediately from Gryan that the battle was already underway. Then, we took another portal to a spot right behind the Govilian army and saw that father was just getting ready to begin marching towards Shamakul. We knew we needed to assist as best as we could, so Valkog quickly made another portal that transported all him, the guardsmen and the rest of us directly to Shamakul. We figured Shamakul would be caught off guard and we'd have the element of surprise! Unfortunately, he was way too quick to react. The only real advantage we had was the fact that father and the guardsmen didn't have to make the trek through all of Shamakul's forces to get to him."

"How are you feeling today?" Anna asked Selini.

Selini held out her hands which were visibly still shaking a lot, but she smiled anyway and replied back, "I am doing rather well, all things considered. I have never magically exhausted myself, so I guess I wasn't sure what to expect. I'm still a little weak, but I will be myself in no time."

"Are you able to rejuvenate easily, like Valkog?" Jack asked. "Or, does it just take time or some special, rare ingredient?"

Selini looked around the room as if looking for something or somebody. Her smile faded some, but remained, nonetheless. She took a deep breath in and closed her eyes for a moment as she collected her thoughts.

"I can rejuvenate rather quickly I would think," she answered. "But again, I have never been in this position before, and I'm not aware of the intricacies of the rejuvenation process. I do know it requires some special ingredients, but none too far off base that we wouldn't have in the storeroom."

Anna looked confused and asked Selini, "Have you not taken a rejuvenation potion or recipe or whatever yet?"

Geller decided to answer for Selini, seeming slightly irked as he responded, "Father hasn't had the chance to make a potion yet and our two potion masters have seemingly disappeared. After all the work we went through to get them their root of flindishion, one might think they would show a little more appreciation by sticking around to help iron out the details of a post battle Gargantulua."

"I am still magically exhausted," Selini stated. "But that will change as soon as father has a chance to make it himself."

"Why can't someone else in the city make it?" Jack asked.

"Father is very protective of the storeroom right now," Geller replied. "It is being managed by the Council to offer as much in healing ingredients as they can. Supplies have dwindled over the last couple of months, as winter's harshness has made it ever so difficult to acquire more ingredients. And, as I'm sure you can understand, it is hard to grow food crops in the darkness of the cavern. It's even more difficult to try and use some of the crop space to grow special, magical ingredients. Some ingredients just simply need the light of day to grow, and no amount of magic can change that. So, for now, we have to be careful to utilize the ingredients in the storeroom for the sick and injured. It may be a couple months before Selini can be rejuvenated while we wait for more ingredients."

Anna reached across the table and grabbed one of Selini's still shaking hands to comfort her as she offered her condolences, "Oh, Selini, I'm so sorry to hear that."

"That's why I'm pretty darn perturbed that neither Gink nor Fink decided to stick around and help us out," Geller said angrily. "I mean, they knew we would likely be able to use their help. Why leave us like this? Why leave Selini in this condition?"

A sound came from the hallway. It was Gryan walking slowly into the room. He was in the midst of some household chores when he felt it necessary to interrupt the group.

In his harsh voice, Gryan spoke to Geller, "It is time, Sir Geller. He is making his approach as I speak."

Jack looked at Geller inquisitively. He was about to ask what Gryan was talking about when Geller quickly pushed back his chair and stood up from the table.

"We must head outside," Geller commanded the group. "There are still things that need to be in order."

With that, Geller immediately exited the room and headed down the hallway toward the front door. Selini got up as well and began to follow him. Hesitantly, both Jack and Anna proceeded to follow.

"You'll want to see this," Selini called back to the two of them as she continued to walk down the hallway.

As they all exited the house, Jack saw Geller looking into the darkness above the city. All Jack could make out was the lightly swaying roots that lit up like stars in the night sky. It was a pleasant view, but he didn't know what Geller was looking for. Before long, though, Jack could hear the flapping of wings coming from up and behind the house. Whatever it was, it was just outside of view for the group.

"What is it?" Anna asked nobody in particular as she watched.

Before anyone could answer, a figure appeared high in the darkness. Jack squinted and realized it was Valkog flying with something large in his grip. As Valkog got closer to the city, he began to descend. That's when Jack realized what he was holding.

"Is that …?" Jack began to ask.

"Yes!" Selini replied. "It will be safer here than in Wellwood Forest."

At that point, Valkog was flying directly overhead, and both Jack and Anna could easily make out that he was carrying the boulder containing the portal Jack and Anna came through. Jack felt like crying. He was overjoyed that they wanted to protect his way home so much. He then realized there might be more to it than that. He considered that maybe the Govilian Council or Gubuyis himself did not want the Reign to acquire the portal, for fear that they may be able to use its magic to teleport to another world entirely where they would not be able to be contained or stopped.

"It is time to speak with father," Geller stated as he continued to watch the boulder being transported through the air.

In a short time, the boulder and Valkog were out of view. Valkog had descended in his approach to the Panthyun. It seemed that would be where the portal would reside.

Jack looked back down and at Geller and Selini.

"Is he expecting us right now?" Jack asked.

"Now is exactly the time he would be expecting to see us," Geller explained as he set off towards the Panthyun.

As the group came around their last corner and in full view of the Panthyun, they could see a hundred soldiers dressed in full combat gear. The boulder and Valkog were at the top of the grand staircase. All the soldiers were in formation, fifty on each side of the stairs.

"What is this?" Jack asked.

"Extra protection in case anyone or anything followed Valkog here," Selini explained.

Geller pressed forward without hesitation. He knew the group would certainly be welcome into the Panthyun, and he knew they were expected. The group stopped at the bottom of the stairs.

"Just in case this isn't a welcome," Geller stated to Jack, "I believe you should go first. I'll be at my ready."

"Wha ...?" Jack began.

"Oh, stop it," Selini gave Geller a small shove. "You may go first if you'd like, Jack, but you certainly don't have to. There is no danger here, though."

Jack hesitated but proceeded to take a step up the stairs. He was soon followed by the rest of the group. It was when Jack got to the first soldier that something caught his eye. The soldiers on both sides, all the way up, drew their swords in unison, kneeled down with their swords pointed onto the ground at their feet, and bowed their heads.

"What are they doing?" Anna asked Selini in a whisper.

"Well," she replied, "I believe they are making sure we know we are welcome here. They are showing their respects."

Jack heard Selini's response and he began to tear up. The sight was amazing to him. He tried his best not to be too fast or slow as he ascended the steps. It was hard for him to determine how to act in this situation, so he kept his focus on Valkog and the boulder still sitting at the top of the stairs.

As he got to Valkog, Jack greeted him, "Good afternoon. I had been wondering where you were at today."

"Good afternoon," Valkog responded. "I was instructed to keep this business a secret less anything go awry."

Jack smiled. He knew that it must have been hard to keep the secret from Jack and Anna. Gubuyis probably figured that Jack might want to go along.

"Will you be going to see Gubuyis with us?" Jack asked.

"I must deliver this portal to a secure location first, but yes," Valkog answered. "I will be joining you momentarily."

The group proceeded into the Panthyun and down the usual corridors that brought them to Gubuyis's favorite place, the library. Jack was always so astonished by the sheer size of the room they would enter into. Books and shelves filled the emptiness of the black spaces above their heads. Torchlights lit up the main floor and several stories of books above, but eventually they just seemed to fade into the darkness. As they were entering the room, Gubuyis turned in his chair. He was holding a book in both hands. He set it down and looked at Jack.

"I am not exactly sure what the intent of the Reign is," Gubuyis began talking to Jack directly, "but they are always looking for ways to expand their powers. They will seek out new magics and exploit them however they can if it can propel their desire to reign over all they see."

Anna spoke out and asked, "Will we ever see the boulder again?"

Gubuyis replied, "The Govilian Council at my beckoning has opted to protect the boulder portal from the Reign and to ensure its survival. It will be kept in a secret location here in the Panthyun. Once secured, you will be given some access to it. Recall, though, that it contains powers treasured by the Reign, and we must keep it as secret as possible."

The familiar sound of clanking and gears turning came from behind the group. Soon, the door to the library opened and there stood Valkog. Once he entered the room, the door promptly closed behind him.

Valkog addressed Gubuyis as he entered, "It is placed."

"Good," Gubuyis smiled as he spoke, "we will now implement measures to secure the portal as best as we can to prevent any further meddling from the Reign."

"Have you learned anything new that can get us home?" Anna inquired of Gubuyis.

Gubuyis nodded and replied, "I have learned that whatever this portal is, it is more than just a way home for the two of you. The Reign has determined it will be worth their while to investigate, and I believe that is because there is more power to it than meets the eye. I have also learned that the portal was only designed to be able to be opened by any one of the flindishk who were a part of its crafting. I also believe that somehow Jack has been imbued with the powers of one of these crafters, but how that transfer of power may have occurred is beyond my understanding at this point."

Jack and Anna must have both looked disappointed that they were nowhere closer to finding a way home than before, because Gubuyis quickly reassured them.

"With the boulder portal here in our possession, there will be several of us from the Govilian Council that will be studying it fervently," Gubuyis stated. "I will spend my time in my study researching what we learn from the portal's powers. Research is the key here, I believe."

"I have a different question for you, Gubuyis," Jack said.

Gubuyis paused and looked at Jack inquisitively.

"Why," Jack asked, "did Shamakul say his prize was not just you, but me as well? Why would he want me? How does he even know who I am?"

"I have very powerful magical abilities," Gubuyis started explaining. "The Reign would seek to take advantage of these very powerful abilities of mine in an attempt to expand their control over other magical nations."

"And Jack?" Anna asked.

"As for what they would desire of Jack was a bit of a surprise to me," Gubuyis explained further. "Taking Jack as a spoil of war seemed out of sorts except for the fact that he came from another planet."

Anna spoke out once again, "But, so did I. And he didn't seem to care at all about me."

"I may not yet know what the reasoning was for capturing Jack," Gubuyis continued, "but I do believe this offers us a glimpse into the ultimate mission of the Reign. I am sure Shamakul thought he had us and that we were not ever to have heard what we did and be free. I intend on consulting with the Govilian Council over this matter very soon."

Geller nudged Jack, "Good question."

"Do not forget, Jack, for I am here to protect you as best as I can,"

Valkog said.

Gubuyis spoke once again, "What I do know is that we will be dispatching spies whose sole mission is to obtain information regarding this matter. It is important for the Govilian Alliance to learn why Jack is so desired by the Reign. It may offer us a peek into their motives. It is also important that you remain protected as best as we can do."

"Maybe the Reign knows that Jack opened the portal," Selini stated. "Maybe they are thinking he can do it again."

"Am I even able to reopen the portal?" Jack asked both Valkog and Gubuyis. "Is there something I am supposed to do?"

Jack was hoping that Valkog, being a flindishk himself, might have some insight into this matter and that there may be a simple solution to getting Jack and Anna back home.

"I was not a part of the very selective group of flindishk that crafted the portal," Valkog said somberly. "I am sure Gubuyis has it right, though. I believe there needs to be a specific individual present, perhaps even the whole group, in order for it to be opened. I am still surprised that you were able to open it at all from your side. I cannot think of anything that would have made that a possibility for you."

Gubuyis interjected, "The Reign is definitely after something with the portal. I do not think they know what they seek yet, but their inquisitiveness is dangerous. If the Reign believes that you can open the portal, even if sacrificially, they may not stop at anything to get you in their possession."

"I'm so sorry, Jack," Anna said to him as she put her hand on his shoulder.

"Let us all take a walk outside," Gubuyis suggested. "A breath of fresh air could do us all some good."

After a short while, the group, including Gubuyis, walked down the streets toward the house. Jack felt somber. He had just learned that they still had no way of getting home and that the Reign was seeking him out for reasons he did not understand. It seemed obvious the Reign felt that Jack could open the portal somehow. He wondered if they knew how to open it and only needed Jack as their last piece of the puzzle. It made him almost want to be captured just so he could learn how to reopen the portal and get home. But he knew he would be powerless to stop the Reign if they were indeed able to open the portal to Earth.

"Fear not," Geller spoke to Jack as they walked, "for springtime is almost among us. Soon the sun will be shining, and the air will be warm once again. We will all be above ground before you know it."

Just then, skipping down the street in front of the group was Fink with Gink on his back. They looked rather delighted, having not had to be a part of the earlier conversation.

"WHERE HAVE YOU TWO BEEN?" Selini asked sternly of the two as they approached the group.

"Ah," Gink called over Fink's shoulders, "we have been workin' on somethin' special, we have!"

Gubuyis laughed and then quickly calmed down as he spoke, "I hope your special something has nothing to do with our storerooms this time around."

Fink replied hastily, "We had no need for any ingredients other than what we had in our own pockets."

Valkog laughed as the tension quickly eased, "I hope you found something to do with that root of flindishion you so desperately wanted. I sincerely hope it was of great use for you."

Fink reached into one of his pockets and pulled out a small vial of bone white liquid. He shook it around and it changed into a number of different colors before returning back to its original bone white.

"Do ya know what this is?" Fink asked the group, smiling menacingly as per usual.

"I do believe that I may know just what that is," Gubuyis

responded.

Fink's smile disappeared.

"Well don't give it away!" Fink exclaimed.

"Yes, yes!" Gink shouted, "We will tell ya!"

Selini, annoyed with the pair as usual, finally interjected and snapped, "Just tell us then! What could you have possibly been doing this whole time that required you to be absent?"

Fink's smile returned and he simply stated, "It is a growing potion."

"Oh, that's exciting!" Anna nearly shouted. "Now Gink can grow his legs back!"

Gink called out, "I plan on using it as soon as it's finished stewing for a few days. If it works, we had enough ta make several batches for resale!"

"What do you mean, 'If it works?'", Anna asked slowly.

Gubuyis stepped forward and looked over the vial that Fink was still holding.

He then asked, "Are you sure root of flindishion is an appropriate ingredient? I am unaware of a growth potion recipe that would call for such an ingredient."

"It's a substitute ingredient," Fink replied, "and it should work just fine from what we can tell."

Gink also replied, but nervously, "Yes, it should w-work just fine. Like he said."

"I would warn you that our healers can only do so much," Gubuyis said to the pair of them.

Gink seemed to ignore Gubuyis's last words and shouted out, "We should all go to Bolar's and celebrate!"

Gubuyis looked at Selini, who still looked annoyed with Gink and Fink, and he smiled at her. Jack liked Gubuyis's smile. It always felt like it was coming from the heart. Jack knew he could go for another round of Prunklesnider, and he wanted to hear stories of the battle prior to them getting there. He knew Selini had the ability to show memories and looked forward to seeing how victory came to be just the day prior.

It didn't take much for Gink and Fink to entice the group to relax together at the tavern. They all followed the skipping Fink as the two of them sang their usual songs of past happenings.

The group sat and talked and drank and ate together. They laughed at jokes and toasted to fallen comrades. Jack enjoyed times like these, but they always had a way of making him feel like it wasn't real. Everything seemed so right at times. Once in a while, he even felt like Gargantulua should be his new home. He knew, though, that he was being missed back home and that Anna was missed by her mother. He couldn't let himself become too comfortable, else he might not be ready whenever the time came to go home.

Raising her glass into the air, Selini said to the group, "Here's to defeating two of the Reign's six powerful wizards or mages or whatever they are. A feat which I have yet to fully appreciate."

They all raised their glasses and toasted with her.

"Indeed," Geller agreed with Selini, "our army, the Govilian army, has proved successful once again!"

As they were all still clinking their glasses together, Anna asked, "Do you think the Reign will leave us alone now that we have dealt them such a blow?"

Geller lowered his glass and looked at Anna sadly, "We will likely have to defeat all of the Reign in order to be free of their oppression and evil. They will stop at nothing to get what they desire and we have proven that we stand in their way."

"Already," Selini replied, "we have some of our Govilian scouts returning with information regarding the armies of Aruzial. There appears to be some stir in their ranks. We are not yet sure what is happening, but it would appear that Aruzial may be our next adversary."

"Is Aruzial another mage of the Reign?" Jack asked.

"A master of potions, he is," Fink stated.

Gink scoffed at Fink's comment. "We can do better than him."

Geller looked at both Gink and Fink and said, "There's something you're forgetting, though. Aruzial has the ability to conjure the ingredients he needs from thin air, including root of flindishion."

Fink looked envious as he looked over his pockets full of special ingredients of every kind.

"Well," Selini said as she pushed away from the table, "I believe it is time for me to turn in for the night. If you two find it within your powers to do so, I could use a rejuvenation potion in the morning. I am fully exhausted."

Fink nodded his head as he agreed that they both could do something about that.

Geller, Selini, Anna, and Jack all left the tavern together. They all laughed together at nothing in particular. For the time being, times were safe and dread was far away.

As Jack walked, he noticed a single, purple flower growing out from between the cracks of the cobblestone road. He bent over and picked it. Smiling, he looked it over while they continued to walk. Selini saw the flower in Jack's hand.

"Springtime is just around the corner," she said to him. "Hope and life are once again in the air."

www.ingramcontent.com/pod-product-compliance
Lightning Source LLC
Chambersburg PA
CBHW020803250626
47155CB00003B/1190